About the Author

Debbie Johnson is an award-winning author who lives and works in Liverpool, where she divides her time between writing, caring for a small tribe of children and animals, and not doing the housework. She writes romance, fantasy and crime – which is as confusing as it sounds!

Her best-selling books for HarperCollins include *The Birthday That Changed Everything*, *Summer at the Comfort Food Café*, *Christmas at the Comfort Food Café*, *Cold Feet at Christmas*, *Pippa's Cornish Dream* and *Never Kiss a Man in a Christmas Jumper*. Debbie's next title is *Sunshine at the Comfort Food Café*, which is coming out in March 2018.

You can find her supernatural crime thriller, *Fear No Evil*, featuring Liverpool PI Jayne McCartney, on Amazon, published by Maze/Avon Books.

Debbie also writes urban fantasy, set in modern day Liverpool. *Dark Vision* and the follow-up *Dark Touch* are published by Del Rey UK, and earned her the title 'a Liverpudlian Charlaine Harris' from the *Guardian*.

🐦 @debbiemjohnson
f www.facebook.com/debbiejohnsonauthor
www.debbiejohnsonauthor.com

Also by Debbie Johnson

Debbie Johnson

Coming Home to the Comfort Food Café

A division of HarperCollins*Publishers*
www.harpercollins.co.uk

Harper*Impulse* an imprint of
HarperCollins*Publishers*
The News Building
1 London Bridge Street
London SE1 9GF

www.harpercollins.co.uk

This paperback edition 2017

2

First published in Great Britain in ebook format by
HarperCollins*Publishers* 2017

A catalogue record for this book
is available from the British Library

ISBN: 9780008263713

Typeset in Birka by Palimpsest Book Production Ltd,
Falkirk, Stirlingshire

Printed and bound by
CPI Group (UK) Ltd, Croydon CR0 4YY

This book is for Helen Shaw – the Greatest
of all the Gingers!

PART ONE

Rebel Rebel

Chapter 1

Dear Zoe,

I don't know why I'm writing this – a sudden fit of the black dog, I suppose. It's one of the unexpected side effects of motherhood that nobody warns you about, the way your imagination can take hold of you like a Jack Russell terrier, swinging your mind about like a rag doll and leaving you in a crumpled heap of paranoia.

For some reason, tonight, I started worrying about what would happen to Martha if I wasn't around. Well, I say 'some reason' – I actually know exactly what the reason was. Princess Di. I was up late doing some marking, and got sucked into this documentary – ten years since she died and all that.

It was seeing those boys at the funeral that probably did it – little Wills and Harry, trying to be all brave and grown-up and just looking like little lost souls wondering where their mum was. All I could think about was wanting to give them a big hug. I'm not exactly a raving royalist, but this is nothing to do with money or class, is it? Losing your mum – a mum who loves you to bits, like Diana obviously did with her babies – is a terrible thing.

Between that and the wine and the lateness, I just ended up in a bit of a mess. You should have seen me, babe – I was just a great big pile of tear-stained mush, hugging the cushions and shaking with grief for a woman I never met, and her motherless little boys. Weirdo.

After that, I lay awake for hours thinking about it all – and about you, and Martha, and what songs I wanted played at my funeral. I never did decide – I know it should be something dignified, but ... well, we're not that dignified are we, you and me? Never have been. I keep imagining it being something ridiculous like the Venga Boys, and everyone dancing to *Boom Boom Boom* as the coffin is wheeled out. Or maybe a bit of Pulp, so you could do *Disco 2000* with all the actions.

Anyway. In the end, I decided to get up, and write this instead. Tomorrow, I'm going to package it up with some other paperwork, and go and see a solicitor and make a will. Not cheerful, but I think it'll put my mind at rest. It's the responsible, grown-up thing to do – not my specialist subject, but it needs to be done.

The main thing, of course, is Martha. Her dad's on the other side of the world and she's never even met him. My parents are uptight control freaks. The only person who loves her and knows her as well as I do is you, Zoe. I don't know the legalities of it all, and whether you can leave someone a child in your will, like you would an antique ring or a complete set of Charles Dickens first editions. I'll have to ask those questions, I suppose.

But whatever the answers are, I know, in my heart – my squished up, Wills-and-Harry-sodden heart – that she needs to be with you. You're her second mum. I know you'd get her through it all, just like you and me got each other through our crazy childhoods. Nothing was perfect – but because we had each other, we survived. You can do the same for her, I know you can.

Hopefully you'll never see this letter, Zoe. Hopefully, I'll be around until we're both 100, and wearing our dentures to Chippendales concerts and swigging gin in our care home. Hopefully we'll be giggling away at how much we embarrass Martha, and reminiscing about when we could remember what day of the week it was.

But … just in case … I wanted to write this. I wanted to tell you that I love you, and that you've been more like family to me than my own ever were. And that I need you to be there for Martha, if the worst comes to the worst. If I die in a car crash or fall out of a roller-coaster, or whatever. I know the thought will terrify you, and yes, I know that you even managed to kill that allegedly unkillable cactus we bought on holiday in Ibiza that time. I know you can't cook, and drive like a nutter, and wear odd socks, and lose your keys three times a day, and go so long between brushing your hair that you get dreadlocks.

I know all this, but I also know that where it counts, you have everything it takes to care for a child – because you'll love her as much as I could. You won't try and make her something she's not, or force her into a shape she doesn't fit, and you'll love her no matter how messy her room is. That's far more important than matching socks, honestly – so believe me when I say I know you can do this.

Anyway, I'm pretty knackered now, so I'm going to take some Night Nurse, pretending it's absinthe, and go back to bed and hope for the best. It's Martha's class assembly tomorrow, and she's playing a Ninja Fish. Don't ask. I need to be bright eyed and bushy tailed and pretend that I enjoyed all the other kids' performances as much as hers (which is a lie all parents have to tell – in reality you're just waiting for your own magical superstar to appear).

Now, I know this is random, but a few things to mention. Her favourite food is fish finger sandwiches, squashed onto soft white bread and butter. You have to really squish the bread together, so hard you leave thumb prints.

Her favourite TV show is still *Spongebob*, but she secretly also loves *In The Night Garden*, even though she thinks it's a bit babyish. She likes dressing up as Stephanie out of *Lazy Town*, and will try and wear the pink wig to bed if you let her. Don't – it leaves her real hair in terrible tangles, and then you have to use the No More Tears, which in my experience isn't that accurate a name.

If she can't sleep, she likes to listen to a CD of those stories about talking hamsters while she drifts off. Her favourite outfit is currently her Shaun the Sheep pyjamas, which she even likes wearing in the day. I don't have a problem with that and I know you won't.

If she's upset about anything at all, try singing the theme tune to Postman Pat out loud. You have to do it with gusto, or she's not convinced. If you do that, even when she's angry she can't help joining in at some point, and before you know it she'll be more interested in words that rhyme with 'black and white cat' than whatever's bothering her. Even though she doesn't watch the programme any more, it's like there's a folk memory in her brain that makes it soothing, no matter what else is going on.

And on that helpful note, I shall bid you farewell. Yeah, I know, I'm being nuts – but then again I always was, wasn't I? Poor Princess Di.

Don't forget – Postman Pat theme tune. Out loud, and with gusto. It cures all ills.

Love you loads,

Kate xxx

I read the letter through for what feels like the millionth time, and fold it back up into familiar squares. It's starting to tatter and fray, and I really need to do something about that. Like get it laminated maybe; anything to preserve the precious words, the precious hand-writing, the precious connection between me and my now-dead friend.

The main connection between us is just as precious. Well, more so, obviously, as she's a human being and not a piece of paper – but she's nowhere near as easy to protect. I glance at Martha, who is lying in a heap on the living room floor, covered in vomit, and wonder if I can possibly get her laminated as well. It would definitely cut down on the amount of washing I have to do.

That letter was written years ago. What feels like millennia ago, now. Back in the days when Martha was a happy-go-lucky, ultra-lovable little girl. She used to dress up in her Stephanie wig and I used to pretend to be Sportacus, and we'd eat satsumas together and lick the juice from our fingers like we were sampling the nectar of the gods.

Now, Martha is 16, and I could marinate her in a whole bathtub of No More Tears and it wouldn't help. In fact, she'd probably just drink it, in an attempt to find a new high. Martha lives in a whole different type of Crazy Town now.

So do I. I live in a Crazy Town without Kate. Without my best friend. Without the person who kept me sane for so many years. My shoulder to cry on, my confidante, my other half. Neither of us ever got married, or even had a serious relationship – and I think that's partly because nobody could ever live up to what we had. Friends since we were six, through the good times and the bad. Joined at the hip, no matter what her parents did to try and discourage their golden child's unhealthy attachment to the scruffy-haired foster kid from the council estate they viewed as one step down from hell.

Martha groans, and I kneel by her side. I have become adept at making sure her airways are clear, and putting her in the recovery position, just in case she does a Janis Joplin on me and chokes on her own sick.

Her dyed black hair is crusted to her pale cheeks, her skin splashed with purple that probably came from some kind of blackcurrant mixer. Her nose is pierced through with a ring, several more in her ears. Winged eyeliner that looked cool in a Tim Burton Batgirl kind of way hours earlier is now smeared beneath her eyes, and she looks like a corpse. She's wearing deliberately laddered black fishnet tights, a black denim mini-skirt now hoisted up to her bum, and a Nirvana T-shirt. There's a smiley face on the front, and on the back it says 'flower sniffin kitty pettin baby kissin corporate rock whores.'

I can see words inked on one of her arms, and squint my eyes to read them: Fuk You. I hope it's just magic marker and not a tattoo, especially as it isn't even spelled right.

Her skinny legs are still on the sofa, one of her Doc Marten boots still on, one of them half off. I'm guessing she came in, tried to sit on the couch and get ready for bed, and became overwhelmed by the industrial amounts of alcohol she probably consumed tonight. Possibly by some drugs as well – in my day it would have been ecstasy or speed. In her day, they have all kinds of fancy names that makes them sound like cute school-girls from Japanese anime books.

I reach out and stroke a long strand of sticky hair away from her face. Her eyes pop open, staring up at me like some-thing from a Hammer Horror film – bright, rich brown. Not so long ago, they'd have been sparkling with humour and the sheer irrepressible joy of life. Now, they simply register that it's me hovering over her – not the person she wants it to be – and cloud with disappointment.

She closes her eyes again, and I see fat tears start to seep out of the sides, mixing in with the eyeliner, painting a dark, dirty streak as they roll sideways.

I murmur what I hope are comforting sounds, not sure if I even believe them myself.

I think about that letter again. About those words of advice from Kate, the woman we both loved so much. Written oh-so-long ago, and now seeming oh-so-wrong. I can't do this. Martha is sinking, disappearing beneath an avalanche of grief and poor life choices, and I don't know how to save her. I don't know how to save myself.

I sit back on my heels, and start to hum the theme tune from *Postman Pat*. I don't sing it with gusto, I don't have any of that left. And besides, if there was a black and white cat in the room these days, I suspect Martha would sacrifice it to Satan.

Something needs to change. Something needs to give, before all is lost. Before I let my best friend down in a way that I will never be able to forgive myself for.

Chapter 2

I wake up the next morning with two things: a headache, and a plan. A plan to change our lives.

The headache is predictable and understandable. I'd been in bed when Martha fell through the door in the early hours of the morning. In bed, but not really asleep.

I used to be a championship level sleeper. I had an undemanding job managing a book shop, lived in a tiny studio flat across the road from Kate and Martha, earned enough money to pay my mortgage, keep me in Ben and Jerry's and set a bit aside. I avoided all stress, emotional, physical, or otherwise.

I'd cut off ties with my toxic past, and led a quiet life. Other people might have found it unambitious and boring – but not me. I'd had a lot of excitement in my early years, and was happier without it.

I thought I'd been so clever – constructing this little life for myself. Vicarious motherhood through Kate. No commitments I couldn't handle. It was very pure and simple, as All

Saints might have said, and I liked it that way. I liked the fact that the most stressful thing that had happened to me for years had been my Pot Noodle container splitting and making a chicken and mushroomy mess over the kitchen counters. At 38, I'd achieved my own personal nirvana: steadiness.

As a result, me and sleep were best friends. I used to wake up every morning feeling refreshed and with a smile on my face, looking forward to cycling to work and doing nothing more challenging than ordering in some extra paperback copies of the latest Dan Brown novel, and persuading my three customers a day to buy something by a local author.

These days, it's all changed. I've become an accidental mother, and I suck at it. I miss Kate, and I'm crap at looking after Martha. I spend most of my waking moments wishing I was asleep, and most of my sleeping moments half awake. I always have one ear open, listening for the sounds of her either coming home, or sneaking out, or setting the kitchen on fire.

It's been over six months since Kate died. Ten months since she first found the lump. I moved in part-time when Kate started chemo, full-time after she died.

Martha might think being 16 makes her an adult, and that's definitely how I felt at her age, but she's lumbered with me whether she likes it or not. And I'm lumbered with struggling through each day like a sleep-deprived zombie.

Martha is a 16-year-old girl with very definite ideas about how she wants to live her life. She'd always been what you could diplomatically call 'strong-minded', a description we saw as a positive but Kate's mum, Barbara, thought was the personality equivalent of leprosy.

But Barbara, in all honesty, has lived her entire life with a whacking great stick shoved up her arse. She was always so worried about what everyone would 'think': the neighbours, the vicar, the headmaster, passing strangers, random people who saw us on Google earth ... everyone's opinion mattered to her, apart from ours. Apart from Kate's. What she saw as a despicable streak of evil in Martha, we saw as a good thing.

We were proud of our little rebel. 'You need a bit of attitude when you're a woman in this world,' Kate used to say, and I'd agree. We'd clink our glasses, and laugh at Martha's antics.

These days, Martha's less 'strong-minded' and more 'absolute bloody nightmare.' She's punishing herself, and punishing me, and punishing the whole damn world – and doing it mainly by the light of the silvery moon. Martha's a night owl – so these days, so am I.

She was supposed to be in by eleven last night. By midnight, I'd started the ring-round. Friends, places I thought she might be. The police woman who'd brought her home one night a month ago, and who I'd stayed in touch with. I'd even texted some of her friend's parents.

She'll be fine, I'd told myself, eyes sore and brain swollen with the familiar cocktail of anxiety and anger. No she won't, I replied, sitting up on the edge of the bed and getting that letter out again. The letter from Kate, that told me I could do this.

I'd just reached the part about not forcing her into a shape she doesn't fit when I finally heard the door open, and slam shut behind her. I heard the stomping of the boots, and the running of a tap in the kitchen, and a few F-bombs being dropped as she banged into the furniture. It's only when it went quiet that I emerged to check on her, creeping down the stairs in my ancient Crocs and a ratty old dressing gown, still clutching Kate's letter.

She had, of course, ultimately been fine. Teenagers are both scarily fragile and amazingly resilient. I'd got her into bed, made her drink some water, and left her with a can of Diet Coke and a packet of paracetamol on the bedside table. Not the kind of mothering you read about in magazines, but the best I had to give right then.

I should have done the same for myself, I thought, as I staggered into the kitchen that morning, so tired and with such a thumping headache that I regretted the fact that I'd not been drinking vodka myself. At least then I'd have deserved to feel like shit.

The headache is normal for me now. It's my faithful companion to the dawning of each wonderful new day. The plan, though – the Plan to Change Our Lives – is new. New and drastic and, I think, completely necessary if I'm going to save Martha from herself.

It started with a dream. I must have had some residual

memory of an episode of *Countryfile* or something, but in my dream, I was walking along endless coastal paths over endless cliffs. Looking out at endless sea. And feeling endlessly peaceful. That was what tipped me off that it was a dream – I've not felt that kind of peace for a very long time.

For a few moments, after I woke up, I tried to hold onto it. That way you do with nice dreams: like when you've been getting intimate with Daniel Craig and a can of squirty cream and don't want it to end before the good bit, or when you've been flying like a bird.

This was one of those. I wanted to carry that feeling of peace into the real world. Into my day. Into my whole life, and into Martha's life. More than anything, we both needed some peace – and in her case, possibly a stint in a drying-out tank.

Things were bad, and getting worse. Worse than they'd ever been, and I have a lot of bad to compare it to. I didn't have the most idyllic of childhoods. I grew up in and out of foster homes, with parents in and out of jail, and my sanity in and out of sight. I'd been wild. I'd been crazy. I'd done a lot of the things that I now saw Martha starting to do – and for similar reasons. Because of pain, and loneliness, and anger. Because of feeling that the world doesn't give a shit about you, so why should you give a shit about it?

But when I was Martha's age, I'd had Kate. That had made all the difference. It's not an exaggeration to say that our friendship saved me. When others judged me – the shabby, smart-mouthed kid with the tough exterior, rejecting everyone she met as a pre-emptive measure to save them the bother – she didn't. I wasn't easy to like, I see that now – I was prickly and hard and wore my 'screw you' attitude with pride. Kate saw through that; she had x-ray vision. She was magic.

Now, I didn't have Kate – and neither did Martha. It was no wonder we were both flying off the rails, plunging into the abyss, and basically making a great big mess of things. We'd both depended on Kate for so much – which was fair enough in Martha's case; slightly less so in mine.

Kate had trusted me to care for her daughter – and much as I occasionally wanted to dunk Martha's head down the toilet, could I honestly say that I would have been any different, without Kate? No, I didn't think I could.

I had to take control, and find us both that peace we needed, and do it soon. Before one of us cracked – and frankly, it could go either way. She might be the one getting the piercings and listening to the death metal, but I'm just as close to the edge. If it was just me, that wouldn't matter – but this isn't about me. It's about that precious little girl who loved Spongebob, and wore a Stephanie wig, and brought so much joy into our lives. It's about saving her.

And now, after it came to me in a dream, I think I know how I am going to at least try: we will move. We'll pack up, and leave. We'll find a place to rest and heal. A place that isn't surrounded by memories of what we've lost, or filled with ghosts, or littered with nightclubs who don't care if teenagers have fake IDs or not. A place with endless cliffs and endless sea and endless peace. A place that brings us the comfort we need, as we don't seem capable of giving it to each other.

She won't like it, I think, downing some ibuprofen and walking towards my laptop. Of course she won't. But then again, she doesn't like anything – so I have nothing to lose.

Chapter 3

I grab a bottle of water from the fridge, and as the door closes I see – for the millionth time – the photo that's stuck up on there with a gaudy 'I Heart Bristol' magnet.

It's a photo of me, and Kate, and Martha. Taken on holiday in Dorset, maybe three years before – only three years, but an alternate reality. Most of my face is covered in a giant cloud of curly red hair, as usual; Kate is in the middle, blonde and pretty and full of life, Martha snuggling into her side.

She's using her fingers to make the classic Black Sabbath-style rock sign, but it doesn't look rebellious – just funny. Her hair was still its natural colour – dark blonde – and her eyes sparkled with happiness. We were a strangely-shaped family, but we were a family – and now it's my job to keep us like that. I want to feel that again: that simple sense of freedom, for Martha to rediscover the innocence and security that her mother's death stole from her.

Dorset. It could be perfect. Not too far away in miles, but

a different universe. I stagger over to the laptop, and start to investigate.

Within a few minutes, fate – or Google, as some people insist on calling it – has intervened. I search for property to let, and am immediately attracted to one result in particular. 'Stay with us in sunny Dorset,' it says, 'where life is simple and you can leave your cares behind.'

Wow. That would be good. I click through, and see a pretty holiday cottage complex called The Rockery near the village of Budbury. It looks idyllic, and within minutes I'm lost in the fantasy, imagining us both there – without our cares. I'm so lost in imagining this new life that I don't even notice Martha coming into the room.

"Where the fuck is that dump?" she says, so suddenly that I jump, and knock a glass of water all over the table. I swear back, in a very mature fashion, and leap around like a loon holding the laptop in the air so it doesn't get wet.

Martha leans back against the kitchen sink, smirking, as I create a glove made of paper towels and try to mop up the mess. I briefly consider punching her in the face, as I do most mornings, but talk myself out of it.

She peels a banana and starts to eat it, looking on at my efforts like I'm some kind of performance art installation.

"Thanks for your help," I say, once I've finally cleared the table, my fingers now coated in soggy, mushed up kitchen towel.

"You're welcome," she replies casually, throwing the banana

skin at the bin and missing. It splats onto the floor, where, given her teenaged angst and my superlative housekeeping skills, it might stay forever.

I sit back down, and squint through the sunshine at her face. It's the third week in August, and the weather is still bright and gorgeous. The kitchen faces out onto our small patio garden, and the light streams through the window in vivid golden streaks, striping Martha like a tiger. I see that she's at least managed a shower; her face is free of last night's zombie movie make-up and her hair is hanging wet and clean over her shoulders. She's wearing an old Glastonbury hoodie that I recognise as Kate's, and that immediately softens my attitude.

I remind myself, as I seem to need to do several times a day, that she's just a child. A child missing her mother. A child I love. I was there when she was born, screaming and bloody, and I was there when her mother died; and I'm still here now – right where I need to be.

"This," I say, pointing at the screen, "is a place called Budbury. It's in Dorset. And I thought we might ... go there."

I let the words float out casually, but hold my breath as I wait for her to respond. There's a battle royale coming, and it's one I intend to win.

"What, like, for a holiday or something?" she asks, screwing up her face in disgust as she looks at the photos. Budbury is on the Jurassic Coast, near to the border with Devon, and is absolutely picture perfect. There's a small village with a hall and shops and even a pet cemetery; there's a few pubs and a gorgeous-looking café perched on the side of the clifftops, and there's a college just a few miles away. That was an important factor, the college.

We'd both received a letter the day before from her old school, 'regretfully' informing us that the sixth form courses she wanted to do were now full. I suspect that isn't true – they just don't want her back. I'm angry on her behalf, but kind of get it – she's been a great big handful of trouble this year, and I've spent what feels like hours sitting across the desk from the head teacher, squirming on the naughty chair, listening to her witter on about Martha's problems.

I'm not at all surprised that they've declined to have her back. Martha's pretending not to be bothered by it, but I suspect the letter inspired last night's binge. It was proof that everything has changed – and not for the better.

She's staring at my screen now, frowning. The scenery around the village is astounding – a million light years from our admittedly cosy little corner of Bristol. Even looking at the beaches and the tiny little coves and the pathways clinging to the sides of the cliffs makes me feel better – makes me yearn to be there, in the fresh air, walking and breathing and just ... being. Maybe I'd get a dog, and learn to surf, and write beautiful poetry and drink scrumpy.

I'm guessing, from the look on Martha's face as she flicks through the slideshow, that she doesn't exactly feel the same.

"Looks like something from a horror film," she says,

dismissively. "Like the Village of the Damned. I bet it's stuck in a time warp as well – they probably don't even allow gingers in because they think they have no soul. Which might be a valid point."

I self-consciously tuck a tangled strand of red curls behind my ear, and bite the inside of my lip. Here we go...

"I'm not suggesting we go there for a holiday," I say, getting up and depositing the banana skin into the bin. I'm that nervous. "We're going there ... for a while."

It's now almost midday, and I've been up for hours, planning our new lives. Lives full of happiness and laughter and recovery – building up, moving on, going forward instead of backward. For some reason – possibly desperation – it's become a symbol of everything I think we need. This major life change is, though, news to poor Martha.

"No way. No *way!* I wouldn't even go there for the weekend, Zoe, never mind to live. And you can't make me. I'm 16, and you can't make me."

I fill the kettle. I need another coffee – I've only had seventeen so far today. I stay silent, gathering my thoughts, listening to Martha fizz and pop in the background. She's so loud I fear for the safety of my eardrums. For a moment, I fear for the safety of my laptop as well, but I realise she's just closed the lid, with a thud. Like that's the end of it, and Budbury will now fall into the sea and float out into oblivion.

She is 16. And I can't make her. This is a replay of a conversation we've had many times. It is her ultimate weapon – and one I need to let her keep, because she really doesn't have many left. If I take away her ability to harm me, she will revert fully to harming herself.

I remember myself at 16: sofa surfing at friend's houses, hiding in Kate's garage with a sleeping bag until her parents found me and kicked me out, no money, no job, no home. All I had was my spirit – and the determination that I would escape the world I'd grown up in, and find my own way in life. If someone had taken that away from me, that hope, that belief in my own independence, I'd have been left with nothing.

Martha isn't me. She still needs me, no matter how much she refuses to acknowledge that. Inside, beneath the make-up and the piercings and the attitude, she's still a baby – still bloody and screaming – and I have to remember that.

"I know I can't make you," I reply, my face clouded in steam from the kettle, "but I can at least talk to you about it, can't I?"

"You can talk about it, but don't expect me to listen!" she yells, arms crossed over her chest in what she thinks is defiance but actually just makes her look scared and defensive. "My home is here. My friends are here. My life is here – and you're not dragging me away from it all just because you're having some kind of mid-life crisis, all right?"

I pour the water onto the coffee, splashing my hands with scalding liquid. She may have a point there. I think I'm doing this for her – but is it actually me who needs to get away? To escape from the pressures of this place, and all its memories; from a past that makes me cry and a future that makes me panic?

"Look, Martha," I say, in as quiet a voice as I can manage, "I know I can't make you do anything. And I know you don't even want to listen to me. But your mum asked me to look after you, and that's what I'm going to do."

I know immediately from the look on her face that I've said the wrong thing. It has always made her angry, and probably sad: being left to me in a will. Being trapped here with me, without access to any of the life assurance money or the profits selling the house would bring, without the independence she thinks she wants.

"And anyway. That's not why I'm here," I add quickly, before she can start a rant. "I'm here because I love you. Feel free to mock, or spit in my eye, but it's true – I love you. I've known you since you were a baby, and I will always love you. I know I'm not your mum, and never will be, but please don't ever think I'm only here because a lawyer asked me to be. I'd be here anyway."

I see tears spring into her eyes, and she angrily swipes them away. Crying is a sign of weakness to Martha, and seeing her fight against it fills me with emotion. I want to take her in my arms, and stroke her wet hair, and tell her that everything will be all right. But I know she won't let me do that. It would push her over the edge, and she wouldn't forgive me.

"Okay, I know that. I know you would ..." she mutters, her fingers screwing up into tight fists in front of her, as though she's trying to keep herself calm, desperately trying to avoid using the L-word. "I know that, but I still don't want to move away. I'll be better. I won't go out as much. I'll … I don't know, I'll stop puking on the living room floor. I'll work harder. I'll start smoking menthol … whatever you like. But not that – I won't go and live in the 1950s, all right?"

I bite back a bout of inappropriate laughter at that little speech. She'll start smoking *menthol*? To hijack a phrase I'm told is popular with the kids these days, WTF? Or even WTF-ing-F? How bad have things become, that Martha sees swapping one cancer stick for another as a sign of commitment to a new lifestyle?

I suppose it is, at least, a step in the right direction. The only problem is, I'm determined that we'll be taking a lot more steps in another direction – all the way to Dorset. I've been pondering it all morning, and it's doable. Kate, straight after her diagnosis – well, straight after the bit that involved us and a bottle of Grey Goose – had gone in to see her bank manager and her solicitor.

She wasn't by any means wealthy, but she had a proper job – head of English at a high school – which came with a pension, and when she'd bought the house she'd done uncharacteristically grown-up stuff like take out shedloads of life assurance. Money, for the time being, wasn't an issue. The mortgage was sorted, there was a lump sum for Martha when she was older, and there was a chunk set aside for the next two years while Martha was still living at home with me.

After taking advice from the legal people, she'd structured things so that I managed the cash until Martha was either 18 or 21, at my discretion.

That in itself had made us both laugh, unlikely as it seems. We'd sat on the sofa, telling each other it wouldn't come to that, that the treatment would work, that she'd carry on as a boob-less wonder and we'd all be together until we were ancient, smelly old crones.

But if it didn't … then Martha's financial future was going to depend on 'my discretion.'

"I know it's just a legal phrase," Kate had said, grinning at me despite the grimness of the situation, "but really? You're an absolute nutter, Zoe. Remember that time you spent a whole week's worth of wages on tickets to see Fun Lovin' Criminals? Or the time you got a taxi all the way back from London because the woman sitting next to you on the train was eating a pickled egg?"

"Well, you must admit that Scooby Snacks was a classic of our time … and I swear to God, if you'd smelled those pickled eggs, you'd have done the same …"

"Okay. But what about when you were 19, and you decided you were going to hitch-hike round the UK trying out all the Little Chefs because you liked those cherry pancakes so much?"

"That one was a bit weird. I think I only made it as far as Bath. But … yeah. I am a nutter, you're right. Are you sure about this? About me, and Martha, and … my discretion?"

She'd reached out and held my hand, squeezing my fingers as though I was the one who needed reassuring, and said: "100%. I'd trust you with my life – and I trust you with Martha's."

Remembering that now, as I look at Martha – the child who has selflessly just offered to start smoking menthol to placate me – I wonder if Kate hadn't been a bit of a nutter herself. Or whether she saw something in me that I couldn't quite see in myself.

"I think," I say to Martha, who'd helpfully taken the first mug of coffee out of my hands and started drinking it herself, "that you need to stop smoking completely. You're 16. You probably don't have a raging case of the black lung just yet, so quit while you're ahead. And as to Dorset ... well, don't throw one of your diva fits, sweetie, but you're not doing so well, are you?"

Martha opens her mouth to argue with me – in fact it's usually the only thing she open her mouth for these days, other than to insert a menthol, presumably – but I hold up one hand to stop her.

"Nope! Not listening! I'm not having an argument with someone whose face I pulled out of their own vomit last night, all right? You're not doing so well, and that's that. Neither am I. I think we need to make some changes. We need a new world order, because this one sucks."

I'm saved from the oncoming tirade by a knock on the door. We both stare at each other, momentarily taken aback, before we hear a familiar voice: "Coo-ee! It's only me!"

For once in complete agreement, Martha and I do a neatly choreographed eye-roll, and sigh in mutual exasperation.

"It's Sunday, isn't it?" I say, glancing at my watch and seeing that it is dead on noon. Our common nemesis is nothing if not punctual.

"Yeah. Shit. We forgot. How does Sunday keep happening so often?" she replies, looking genuinely confused.

"I don't know ... it's like we're trapped in some kind of hell dimension, doomed to eternal knocks on the door and 'coo-ees', and ..."

"And the next line – any minute now ..."

We both pause, our heads on one side like curious budgerigars, and grin as we wait for the inevitable.

"It's only me!" shouts Barbara again, and I can just picture her on the doorstep, faffing with her scarf and checking her cameo brooch and sniffing the air like she's a bloodhound on the track of moral iniquity. "Don't like to intrude," she trills, "but I'll just use my key ..."

Martha stares at me. I stare back.

"She's lying," says Martha, swigging down the last of the coffee. "She loves intruding. You should get the locks changed."

She strides off to go and get properly dressed, and I attempt to smooth my crazy curls down into something less likely to make Barbara make the sign of the cross when she sees me.

It's Sunday. Again. Which means that Martha gets the unrivalled joy of lunch with her grandparents – and I get a few more hours to plan our escape to the West Country.

Chapter 4

By the time Martha comes home, I have e-mailed the landlady of The Rockery, checked out the courses at the college,
and looked for dogs at the nearest rescue centre. I've made
notes, and looked at our finances, and pondered the idea of
renting out my flat to make it all stretch a little further.

I mean, it's not like I need my flat any more. It's across the
road, the bottom half of a sandstone terrace, and is now more
of a museum to my previous existence than a functioning
residence. It's full of books and clothes I'll never wear again
and cheap hippy jewellery I used to think made me look
super-cool at festivals. I don't need it any more – technically
at least.

And yet for some reason, I've kept it – probably because
in the same way that Martha needs that 'I'm 16, you can't
make me' reassurance, I also need my 'I can run away if it all
gets too much' reassurance.

It has happened a few times – I've made the desperate dash
over there, winding my way through the recycling bins and

neighbourhood cats to let myself in. To lie on my own bed, in my own territory. In the end, I decide against it – I'll keep the flat, and instead I'll use my life savings. I've got an ISA – which Kate made me take out – that contains the less than impressive lump sum of just under £5,000. But I don't need much, and that'll keep me going for a few months at least, allow me to pay my way instead of just using Kate's money.

There's a lot to sort out, and I'll have to think about it later – because right now, I can hear the strained chatter of Barbara and her husband Ron in the hallway.

I close the lid of my laptop, and hide the papers beneath it. Barbara has a keen eye for detail – especially any detail that backs up her belief that I am a terrible human being incapable of caring for her precious grandchild.

Martha slopes into the room looking sheepish and border-line embarrassed. I suspect this is because her grandparents have spent the last few hours telling her how wonderful she is, and she played along. I don't blame her – it's definitely the path of least resistance.

She left her nose and ear piercings out, and tied her hair up into a ponytail. To the casual observer, she could pass for a normal teenaged girl. 'Normal' in the sense that Barbara and Ron would use the word, anyway. I know that every time she does that, Martha hates herself a little. Tempestuous as our relationship can be, she can at least behave like herself when she's at home – not the Stepford Teen version of herself that she presents to her grandparents.

Barbara is wearing a smart tweed suit that makes her look like one of the presenters on the Antiques Roadshow. Her hair is perfectly bouffed and frosted with spray, and her make-up is suitably age-appropriate for a respectable woman in her early 60s. Her smile, as she stares at me with laser eyes, is almost as frosted as her hair.

I suppose, if I were to look at myself from her perspective, I might feel a little frosty too. She's never liked me. I was the bad influence, the wayward gypsy, the blemish in Kate's otherwise perfectly managed childhood.

Barbara was always convinced that every wild thing Kate ever did – the travelling after she got her degree, the crappy jobs she started off with, the boyfriends with names like Chili Pepper, the fact that she became a single mum – was because of me.

It wasn't true of course. There was a reason Kate and I clicked the minute we met.

A reason that Kate – clever, pretty, popular, from a stable home – immediately took me under her wing, despite the fact that I was none of those things. The reality was different. Kate had a wild streak all of her own – sometimes it even put mine to shame. She was daring and bold and yearned to break free of the constrictions of her cloying home life. The travelling – where she met Martha's father (a polite word for 'had a one-night-stand-with-while-under-the-influence-of-weed-and-booze') – was nothing to do with me. I wasn't even there.

The crappy jobs were just her way of finding out what she

really wanted to do, before she settled on teaching. The boyfriends with names like Chili Pepper ... well, to be fair, at least a few of those were down to me, and my borderline crusty pals with dogs on strings and only a passing acquaintance with personal hygiene.

Barbara either doesn't know any of that, or wilfully ignores it. It's easier to have a scapegoat. A scapegoat who is now sitting at the kitchen table still in her dressing gown, rocking electric-shock-chic hair and wired on coffee.

"Zoe!" she says, taking it all in. "How nice of you to make the effort! Late night, was it?"

Yes, I think. A late night spent looking after your butter-wouldn't-melt grandchild. I don't say this of course – especially as Martha is shooting me imploring looks over her shoulder. I take a deep breath, and remind myself that Barbara is Kate's mother. That she is a woman who has lost her only child, and will probably never recover. She covers it as well as her make-up covers her wrinkles, but it is still there – the pain, and the anguish. The loss.

"Did you have a nice lunch?" I ask innocently, refusing to rise to the bait. I have mastered the art of war when it comes to Barbara – and I win my battles by being relentlessly civil in the face of her poking and prodding. Frankly, it drives her nuts. When I was younger, I used to lock horns with her all the time – with the whole world in fact – but these days? Zen master in a dressing gown.

"Lovely, thanks, Zoe," says Ron, who is hovering in the

background in his chinos and perfectly pressed polo shirt, his threadbare hair carefully arranged over his scalp. He's not so bad, Ron. I once spent an impromptu night down the pub with him and he was a laugh. Sadly he's one of those men doomed to be forever overshadowed by a far stronger wife.

"Yeah," chips in Martha, keen to avert the conversation from my late night and her shenanigans. "We went to that place outside town that has the really good onion rings."

"I know the one," I reply, smiling. Smiling, and now conscious of the fact that I've not eaten all day. My stomach lets out a huge grumble in response, and Barbara wrinkles her nose at me like I've just soiled myself in public.

"Right, Ron," she announces. "We better go. And Zoe? You might want to consider buying some bleach for this kitchen, you know. Cleanliness is next to Godliness and all that."

I nod enthusiastically, as though this is the best suggestion I have ever heard, and wait while Martha sees them to the door.

When she comes back, she is quiet. Pensive. Thoughtful. None of which are words I usually associate with Hurricane Martha.

"Are you okay?" I ask, reaching out to briefly touch her fingers. Predictably enough she snatches her hand away, but she does sit down opposite me at the kitchen table. She points at the laptop and the papers peeking out beneath it.

"Are you still planning the great escape?" she asks, sounding hollow. Her face is paler than usual, and her dark brown eyes are pools of liquid sorrow. It's not the way I want her to look, or feel, and I am overwhelmed with sadness at the shitty situation we've all found ourselves in.

"Yes," I say, firmly. "I know you're not keen, Martha, and I understand why. But perhaps you have to trust me on this one. Or at least try to."

She is silent for a few moments, chewing the inside of her cheek so hard I know she must be drawing blood. Eventually she nods, abruptly.

"I'll try. Gran was ... well, she was full on today, you know?"

"In what way?" I ask, frowning. Barbara was, as you can imagine, deeply unhappy when Kate told her that Martha would be staying with me if the unthinkable happened. And I know that when it did, she considered some kind of legal action to get her away from me. It was only a letter left by Kate, as well as Martha saying she wanted to stay in her own home, that stopped her.

She's never stopped trying to persuade Martha, though. She lavishes her with gifts and cash and adoration, all in an attempt to convince her to go and live with her and Ron instead of the red-haired she-devil.

"In a 'we-only-want-what's-best-for-you' way," replies Martha. "You know. The way where I live with them, and wear a lot of pink leisure wear, and learn to bake, and watch My Little Pony videos as a special treat at the weekend ..."

I burst out laughing. One of those unattractive snorty laughs, where you almost choke. Somehow the image of

Martha dressed in a candyfloss velour tracksuit watching cartoons strikes me as so funny, I have to let it out. Almost against her will, I see a slight upward curl on her lips. For Martha these days, that passes as an uncontrollable belly laugh.

"It's not funny," she says, not sounding convinced.

"It is though," I reply, still giggling. "Just a little bit. But … look, I know it's hard. Your gran is … a strong character. But she loves you, you know that. And she loved your mum."

"I *know* she loves us! But she really doesn't understand us, does she?"

"Not even close. She never has. It doesn't make her evil. But … it doesn't make her someone you'd want to live with either. This is where we are, now, Martha. We all want it to be different. We all want your mum to still be here. I lost my best friend. Your gran lost her daughter. You lost your mother. None of us will ever be the same again – but we have to go on living. I'm worried about you. About school. About your social life. About the fact that you can't spell 'fuck.' I'm worried about everything – and that's why I think we need a change."

She nods again, and stands up. She's not that tall, but she's really slim and willowy and always reminds me a bit of Bambi, not quite knowing what to do with her legs.

"Okay," she says, turning to leave. "I'll think about it. And don't worry about me being able to spell 'fuck' – I can still say it properly, and that's what counts."

Chapter 5

The next few days come and go with relatively little drama. Martha is on her best behaviour, which is verging on the terrifying.

She's not mentioned the move again, and neither have I – I suspect she is trying to placate me, trying to prove that she can be a good girl after all, hoping I've miraculously forgotten all about it.

I haven't, of course. I've done nothing but think about it. Thinking that seems to involve chewing the ends of a lot of pencils, drinking a lot more coffee, and doodling pictures of rose-trellised cottages on the back of receipts from Bargain Booze.

I carry on my email conversation with the amusing Cherie Moon, landlady at The Rockery holiday cottages; I contact the college in Budbury, and I send a very immature message to Martha's former head teacher saying we're both happy to never be returning.

Soon, I've made progress. Cherie Moon – my new best

friend – has confirmed that we can take one of her two-bedroomed cottages on a six-month let for what seems to be a very excellent price. She's asked all kinds of questions I didn't expect, and seems a lot more interested in why we're moving to Dorset than my credit rating, which is unusual in a landlady.

I'm not sure why, but I told Cherie about Kate, and Martha, and the fact that we are looking for a fresh start. She'd made lots of sympathetic comments, and expressed views that Budbury, and the cafe she ran on the coast, 'specialised in fresh starts.'

I do have brief and fleeting concerns that maybe she's some kind of cult leader – she has the right name for it – trying to lure us into a quasi-religious community where we'd be expected to tithe our earnings and sleep with the high priest and make jam out of tea leaves and rat entrails. But then again, I always did have an over-active imagination.

I reward myself for all this progress with a couple of episodes of *Game of Thrones* – it could be worse, I think, Martha could be in Sansa Stark's shoes – and a glass of wine. I may or may not have drifted off to sleep. Something definitely happened, because the next time I was aware of my surroundings, I had a red stain on my jeans, slobber on my chin, and it had gone dark outside. Classy.

Edging back into hazy consciousness, I wipe my face clean, retrieve the empty wine glass from the side of the sofa, and hide my eyes while I switch the TV off. I'd left *Game of Thrones* running and the episodes had been on auto-play – the very worst kind of spoiler.

I glance at my watch, and see that it is after eleven pm. I've actually been out for a few hours, in one of those deep and dreamless sleeps you have when you're completely exhausted.

I can still hear the sound of a bass-line thudding through the floor of Martha's room, like a sonic boom. It must be bone-rattlingly loud in there. She may have to face life without ear-drums if she carries on like this.

I do a bit of housework – and by that I mean cramming even more plates into the dishwasher and hoping for the best – and decide to try and turn in for the night. Or at least lie in bed with a good book. I sleep in what used to be the spare room of the house, which is quite small and looks out over the garden. I've never been able to bring myself to sleep in Kate's room, even though it is by far the biggest. It's still too much ... hers. The whole house, to some extent, is a bit like a constant reminder of the life we used to have; the woman we loved, who filled it with energy and warmth and security. The woman we lost.

But we live in the rest of the house. We use it; we make meals, and mess things up, and wash clothes, and leave books lying around, and dump our bags in the hallway. The rest of the house has moved on a little – it's evolving with us, around us.

Kate's room, though? That's still haunted. Still a no-go zone. Like there's some kind of emotional cordon around it; crime scene tape for the mind. The door stays shut, although I do occasionally find myself standing outside, touching the handle, imagining she's still in there. Getting ready for work, or a night out, faffing around with hair straighteners or using one of the seventeen different types of perfume on her cluttered dressing table, sniffing them all and usually deciding on the Burberry.

Sometimes I even go so far as to open the door, and the disappointment of seeing that neatly made bed; seeing the wires of the hair straighteners tangled in an unused heap like coiled snakes; smelling the seventeen different types of perfume ... well, it's a killer, I can tell you. Some doors are simply better off left closed – at least for the time being.

I amble up the stairs, feeling croaky and stiff, like an 80-year-old version of myself. I pause outside Martha's room, lingering there as I debate whether to knock or not.

I don't want to push her, or intrude ... or, if I'm entirely honest, interact with her at all. I'm tired too, and we both need a bit of space. But I also really don't want to be listening to death metal all night, while I try to concentrate on reading the latest Kate Atkinson book. Jackson Brodie deserves my full attention.

So I knock, practicing my super-friendly, no-conflict-here smile, and wait for her to answer. She doesn't – possibly because of the ear-splitting level of the music. I knock again, my super-friendly, no-conflict-here smile possibly fading a little. I wait some more. Still nothing.

After that, I bang on the door double-fisted, yelling 'Martha! Turn that racket down!' at the top of my voice. God, the neighbours must absolutely love us.

The super-friendly, no-conflict-here smile has by this time well and truly done a runner. It has been replaced by its angry relative: the super-unfriendly I'm-going-to-kill-you face.

Annoyed, tired, and already feeling tomorrow's headache coming on, I decide that her privacy is an over-rated commodity, and push the door open. I usually avoid doing such things – you never know what you're going to find in an angry teenaged girl's bedroom – but I've had enough.

The door slams backwards, and I storm into the room. I intend to rip the plug to the stereo out of the wall, and entirely possibly throw her awesomely cool record player (the kind we all got rid of in the 90s) out of the window. I might, depending on how that goes, snap her entire vinyl collection into tiny black smithereens.

Of course, I don't do any of this. Not because I am cool and calm and restrained. But because I realise that there is a bigger issue to deal with than the music.

The room – smelling suspiciously ripe and herbal – is empty. Martha, adorable child that she is, has snuck out.

Chapter 6

It's my own fault, I think, as I make my way towards town. If I hadn't passed out in front of the goggle box, she wouldn't have been able to sneak past me and into the night. I'd known she was more upset than she'd been letting on – about the letter from college, about life in general, the potential move to Dorset– but I'd let her escape to her room and fester in it.

I didn't even bother doing the usual ring-round of her friends. She'd moved on from them. I did, however, ring Steph – the police lady who had become half a friend. After bringing Martha home that night, we'd bumped into each other a few times in town, and she'd always been kind, not only asking how Martha was, but asking how I was as well. So few people ever asked that, and I was pathetically grateful. Funny how you can present a tough front to the world, but a random act of kindness from a virtual stranger can bring on the water-works.

So tonight, I took a chance, and called her, trying to sound light-hearted but feeling the weight of the world bearing down on my shoulders. The rational part of me knew Martha would be all right – but the part of me that read a lot of books was extremely concerned with serial killers, rohypnol in drinks, and strange European men who kept girls in sound-proofed cellars for years on end.

"Yep, I've just seen her," Steph confirmed. "She was with the same people as before – that gang that hangs round the bus station – and it looked like they might have been heading for The Dump."

The Dump is a local nightclub, on the edge of Bristol city centre, and it's about as lovely as the name implies. The Dump isn't its real name, of course – but it's how it's known to locals. It's had about five different names since I've been old enough to pay attention, and seems to change it all the time in an attempt to revamp its slightly dodgy image.

It's a squat 1970s building on the edge of a small strip of kebab shops and tanning salons, and it's been there forever. Me and Kate used to go there, and it's never once gone out of fashion. Probably because it was never even in fashion – it's not a cool club.

Its floors are sticky with decades of sweat and spilled beer; it always smells of smoke despite the ban, and the fire exits are rickety old metal steps corroded by rust. I'd had many very fine nights there myself, in a different lifetime.

After I finish talking to Steph, I decide that I will simply go and find Martha, and bring her home. I don't know why I'm freaking out so much – but some kind of instinct is telling me that this is important. That if I let this one slide, it will be followed by an avalanche. That I'll never get her back again. I'm sure I'm over-reacting, but trust that instinct anyway.

Wearing flannel pyjama trousers, Kate's Glastonbury hoodie and my Crocs, I march all the way to the club. I'm slightly out of puff as I arrive, and definitely out of patience. By the time I bump into Steph, I probably resemble a furious gnome who buys her clothes in a charity shop.

"Did you see her go in?" I ask, after we've said hello. "Because you know she's only 16 … they shouldn't be letting her in at all …"

"I know, I know," she replies, placatingly. "And this place is overdue a raid. But I didn't actually see her go in, no, so there's nothing I could do. You know how it is."

I nod. I do know how it is. When I was younger, I adored the fact that the doormen at The Dump didn't pay too much attention to how old you were. I was coming here from the age of 15 onwards and nobody ever batted an eyelid. All it took was seventeen layers of foundation, a push-up bra, and a lot of attitude.

"Wish me luck," I say, trying for a smile, "I'm going in."

I stamp over to the doorway, and see a large, beer-bellied man with a shaven head, smoking a cigarette and looking at a video on his phone. I try to walk past him, through into the dingy entrance I know so well, but he holds out a hand and stops me.

"Do you have ID, love?" he asks, with half a smile. He

probably thinks he's being funny. On a normal night, I might think it was funny too.

"I'm 38," I snap back, glaring at him. I'm feeling angry now – angry at the whole world. Me and Martha have more in common than she'll ever understand. "And I'm looking for my … my daughter. She's only 16, and I think she's in there. Bet you didn't ask *her* for ID, did you?"

The bouncer takes a smart step back, and I realise I've been right up in his face. Or his chest at least, which I've also been poking with my finger as I spoke. I'm not a tall woman, or a big one – truth be told I could fit into Martha's clothes if I was so inclined – but in my experience, most people are a little bit afraid of an angry ginger. Especially an angry ginger who looks like she's just got out of bed, and could explode like a nuclear missile at any moment.

This man is almost a foot taller than me, and probably weighs in at twice the amount. But I am not in the slightest bit concerned – I have the eye of the tiger, and he's going to hear me roar. It's funny how easily I slip back into this: the tough girl; the angry girl; the girl who takes no shit and is always ready to rumble. The old me, in other words.

"Okay, okay, calm down …" he says, now completely backed up into a corner, holding his ham-sized fists up in a gesture of surrender. "Go in and look for her. I won't even charge you. And if she is 16, I'm sorry – I do check IDs, honest, but the quality of the fakes these days is unbelievable …"

I back away, and clench my fists at my side. His co-operation has taken the wind out of my sails, and I realise that I'm more angry with myself than him. It's not his job to keep Martha safe – it's mine. And I'm not doing it very well.

I walk in, and despite its many revamps, it still somehow smells and feels the same. I know where Martha will be – the freak show dancefloor. The place for the indie crowd, the rock crowd, the retro crowd.

I clomp down the narrow stairs, passing clubbers wearing Vans and DMs rather than Crocs, all of them sporting very fine eyeliner, even the boys. There's a lot of black, and facial furniture that makes Martha's few piercings look tame. They stare at me with a mix of confusion and hostility, and I realise that I must look insane: my age marks me out as someone's mum, but my random clothes and crazy lady hair mark me out as someone who needs a crisis intervention team. I smile and wave just to scare them more. Young people, eh? They always think they invented weird.

As I descend, I hear the music change from the thumping rhythms of hip-hop to the thrumming guitars of a Muse track. I recognise it immediately: Uprising. An absolute killer of a song, all that clapping and beeping and 'screw you world' chorus-ing.

The room is dark, and only half full. It's a Wednesday night, after all. Most Goths and emo kids are safely tucked up in bed. The ones that are there, though, are going wild – the dancefloor is throbbing with shuffling bodies, dark hair being swirled around, arms waving in the air, a steady stomp of feet on wood beating in time with the song. A strobe light plays over them, picking the dancers out in individual flashes: a pair of excited eyes beneath black eyebrows; a grinning face singing along; a dark fringe swinging from side to side; fists pumping the air in communal rebellion as the chorus grinds on: we will be victorious...

I have a moment of pure excitement: some kind of emotional muscle memory, or maybe a flashback to simpler times. Times when this was my tribe, too – when I would be out there stomping and swirling and bursting with the thrill of it all. With the music and the dancing and the sheer amazing possibility of what the night might hold. Of knowing that no matter how bad it all was in the outside world, here, with my people and my songs, it could still all be okay. Better than okay. It could be amazing.

The song draws to a triumphant close, and I scan the crowd as it does that weird between-tracks pause, where everyone waits for a second to see what the next choice is going to be, and whether they want to dance to it or not.

I spot her, standing in a small circle of shadows, arms thrown over each other's shoulders. The strobe passes, and for a split second it focuses on Martha's face: glistening with sweat, grinning, eyes ecstatic. 16 years old, and drunk. High on life, and God knows what else. 16 years old, dyed hair, piercings, surrounded by older kids who are more extreme versions of her. 16 years old, but to me, forever a little girl.

I want to rush over, and wrap my arms around her, and

sing the Postman Pat theme tune with gusto. I want to take her home and feed her fish finger sandwiches, and let her sleep in her Stephanie wig and her Shaun the Sheep pyjamas. I want to tell her I love her, that I will always love her, that she is my whole world. That I would die for her. That I would do anything to protect her and keep her safe.

As I stare at her across the room, I feel the tears rolling down my cheeks. Here, in this place, where Kate and I used to dance and sing and laugh and drink, always believing that we were somehow immortal, it feels okay to cry. It feels right and proper, like some kind of tribute to be paid to the memory of my dead best friend, and everything we meant to each other.

Kate is gone. I am alone. And Martha needs me.

All of this happens in a split second, the tears and the sadness, so sudden I almost fall to the ground. But I can't do that. I need to get my girl, and get us both home.

A Foo Fighters song has come on, and the crowd is dancing again. I walk across the dancefloor, beer-sodden toes slipping around in my plastic shoes, shouldering people out of the way, weaving through the gyrating bodies. I walk towards her, and her friends, and they all turn to look at me.

Martha's face falls into a place somewhere between anger and embarrassment, and the tribe tries to close in around her. I'm guessing they know who I am. I'm sure she's told them stories about her control-freak fake-mother, and I'm sure they're sympathetic. Somewhere, somehow, I've become The Man – how ironic.

One of them, a tall, skinny guy with a spider web tattooed around his neck, stands between us. He probably thinks he's cool. He probably thinks he's tough. He probably thinks I'm scared of him.

He's probably wrong.

I gesture for him to come closer, so I can make myself heard over the sound of Dave Grohl, and whisper into his ear: "I need to talk to Martha. So back off, don't try and stop me, and I won't pull that nose ring right out of your nostrils, okay?"

He rears up, trying to look unimpressed but not entirely pulling it off. I meet his eyes, and he seems to realise that I'm being serious. He doesn't back off – that would be too big a bravado fail – but he doesn't resist when I slide past him, either.

For a moment, I feel bad – he can't be more than 19 himself. Still a kid, despite the tats and the attitude. What right do I have to judge him, or threaten him? None at all – apart from the right that being Martha's fake-mother gives me. Still, I glance over my shoulder at him, and mouth the words: 'Thank you.' He frowns – for some reason that seems to scare him even more.

Martha stands frozen, completely still, her arms folded across her chest. Her eyes don't look quite right – they're trying to focus on me, but keep sliding around. She's clearly drunk, at the very least. I meet her gaze, and the world fades around us. I try to ignore the music and her friends and the strobe light and the jostling of young bodies dancing away their anger.

I close the gap between us, and lean close so she can hear me.

"Martha, it's time to come home," I say, simply.

"Why?" she replies, her expression torn between a sneer and sadness. "It doesn't even feel like home any more. She's not there. You hate me. Even that crappy bloody college doesn't want me. There's just ... no point."

Part of me – a part I bury very quickly – actually agrees with her. It does all feel pointless. Like an endless battle, a constant round of pain and recovery and more pain. And the house – that lovely little house in a nice part of Bristol – doesn't feel like home any more. It feels like a prison, for both of us, with Kate's ghost wandering the halls and whispering into our ears at lights out. I want to curl up in a ball and go to sleep, for the next two decades at least. But I can't. Because of her. Because of Kate. Because they both need me to be the best person I can be.

"I don't hate you," I say, keeping my voice steady. "I love you. And I know these are your friends, and that you think they're looking after you, but it's time to come home."

"They are looking after me! More than anyone else does!" she shrieks, stamping her foot onto the dancefloor. I cast a quick glance at the friends in question, and understand the power that they hold over her. Despite their challenging appearance, I'm sure they're not bad people. I'm sure they are, in their own way, looking after her. And I completely understand the lure of that – of rebellion, of escape, of finding a crowd of like-minded rejects to make you feel less rejected yourself.

But I also understand how dangerous it could be for her. She's new to this battlefield, and she doesn't have the armour she needs yet. She doesn't have the shell I had by her age, layered on over years of instability and neglect.

"I know you think that. And we can talk about it all later. But now, I need you to come home. Please."

I'm amazed at how calm I'm sounding, when inside I just want to yell and scream and possibly pull her out of that place by her hair if I need to. Maybe this is one of the secrets of parenthood: resisting those urges, and walking the better path.

"Look," I continue, watching as she chews on her lip, tearing the flesh away with her teeth, "I get it, all right? It feels like the whole world's got it in for you. You've lost the best mum in the world, and now everything's gone to shit. It doesn't feel fair, or right, or like the pain will ever end. And losing yourself in moments like these is the only way you manage to stay sane. I get it. I understand. I don't have any answers, Martha – but I do know I want you to come home with me. I love you, and I want to help you."

I can see tears shining in her eyes, and a debate raging across her face. There's a battle going on inside her: the tough Martha who wants to tell me to eff off and run away to live in a squat, and the good Martha – the one who knows, deep down, that what I'm saying is right. I stay silent, and let her think it through, spending several surreal moments surrounded by dancing kids and feeling the strobe light flash over my disastrous hair.

Eventually, after more chewing, and the angry swiping away of those annoying tears, she says: "Can I finish my drink first?"

I am instantly submerged with relief. The good Martha has won out – and letting her finish her drink seems like a small price to pay for what feels like a huge victory. In fact, I feel like a drink myself.

She wanders off to the side of the dancefloor, where empty glasses and beer bottles are lying on a shelf. She picks up a green bottle, and swigs from it. Her protector from earlier – Spider Man – hovers behind us, and I wonder momentarily if he's going to cause trouble. If he's going to try and persuade her to stay.

Instead, he gives me half a smile, and offers me a bottle too. Peroni, which is classier than I expected. I nod gratefully, and take the drink from him. I kind of want to hug him for that small gesture, but think it might terrify him. I take a gulp, and realise that I've been running on adrenaline for a while now. Knowing that Martha is safe, here with me, and not locked up in a cellar with a creepy old dude, releases some of it. Enough for me to actually enjoy a quick drink of lager, and enough for me to respond when the first notes of the next song kick in.

It's instantly recognisable, and impossible to mistake for anything else. The strutting guitar riffs of David Bowie's *Rebel Rebel* blast out into the room, and a collective whoop of joy goes up from the crowd. I look at them flocking to dance, David still issuing the rallying cry of freaks the world over. I feel the beat, deep in my soul, and my toes start to tap. This was one of our songs – mine and Kate's. We danced to it at home, in her garage, and here. On this very dancefloor, so many times – pouting and prancing and spinning and doing silly actions, feeling the music and the lyrics lift us higher than any drug ever could.

I take a long, deep chug on the beer, and place it down on the shelf. I look at Martha, and raise one eyebrow. She used to dance to it with us as well – bopping around the living room in her pink ballet tutu when she was four; jumping off the sofa to it and into our arms. When she was older, we'd go giddy with it, all pretending to sing into hairbrushes or wine bottles, sticking our chests out and mincing all over the room.

She gives me half a smile, showing me that she remembers – and then we're off. Both of us, winding our way into the crush of bodies, the black-clad teens and the tattooed wonders and the pierced babies of the world. We are in the very middle of the dance floor, where the action is – and we go for it.

We strut and we jump and we wave our arms and we spin each other round and we laugh and we pull faces. We pose and we pause and we leap – we shine in the strobe lights, hair cascading around our sweating faces. We jig and we stretch and we point at each other as we sing that magical, wonderful line – hot tramp, I love you so. We are brilliant. We are awesome. We are the bloody Diamond Dogs, and we are howling at the moon.

When the song fades to its close, we wrap our arms around each other, and we weep. We weep for Kate. For poor David Bowie. For ourselves. We weep for all we have lost, for all that we had, for all that we will never have again.

PART TWO

Changes

Chapter 7

We pull away from the kerb, waving at Barbara and Ron as we go. The car – Kate's Nissan, which I've hardly used in recent months – is packed to the rafters. I've insisted that Martha sits in the front with me, so I don't feel like a taxi driver all the way to Dorset.

Ron puts his arm around his wife as we turn the corner, and the whole basis of my belief system crashes in when I see her wiping tears from her eyes. Why did she have to choose now to suddenly become human?

I grit my teeth, beep the horn, and drive on.

I think Martha's still in a state of shock, silent and pale beside me. After our impromptu night out at The Dump, she seemed to have some weird idea that dancing to one David Bowie song was enough to make me want to stay – perhaps she thought we'd become buddies, and go out boozing together, maybe do the festival season or something.

Instead, it just made me realise that I was in as much danger of spiralling out of control as she was. This was for my sanity as well as hers, which might be selfish, but there you go – don't they always tell you to put the oxygen masks on yourself before you try to help others?

Part of me feels sorry for her. I had to watch as she wrestled with her own lack of power, her own inability to come up with an alternative. She had three choices: live with her grandparents, run away, or stick with the crazy red-head. I genuinely thought option two might be a goer, so I'd kept a close eye on her in the intervening time, checking for escape tunnels and the sudden disappearance of essentials like her phone charger or her eye-liner.

Instead, she seemed to grudgingly accept it – which made me nervous. Was she lulling me into a false sense of security? Did she have an evil masterplan? Would a group of teenaged ninjas land on the car roof from a helicopter, hooking her up to ropes and winching her away to safety? Would Peter Parker – my secret code name for the guy with the spider tattoos – emerge from the shadows and whisk her away to a life on the fringes of society?

I glance over at her as we pull out onto the main road. She is staring straight ahead, and I know she's also worried about her grandparents.

Barbara had blustered and flounced once I told her our plans. Blustered, flounced, and ultimately had to accept it – because Martha didn't want to come and live with them instead. That, I know, must have hurt. She'd lost her daughter, and now she must feel like she was losing Martha as well.

I feel for her, I really do – but my priority has to be Martha, and at least giving her the chance to move on with the rest of her life.

The cottage is booked; the college has confirmed that they can take Martha, and my boss at the book shop had barely disguised her relief when I said I was leaving – not because I'm crap at my job or anything, but because times had been hard there, and she didn't really need an extra pair of hands.

I'd said my farewells to the friends I have; bought Steph the police lady a bunch of flowers, cancelled the milkman, and sorted our finances. I'd spoken to Cal, Martha's dad, on the phone, and explained what was happening – he seemed concerned but laid-back, in that Aussie way I'd come to expect from him.

He's not a big part of Martha's life in the real world. Theirs was a chance encounter, and he lives thousands of miles away. Kate had always been happy with that, and as a result, so had Martha. He'd wanted to come over for the funeral, but in the end we all decided it would be too much of a head-fuck for Martha – your mum's dead, but here's your dad.

Now, we were finally on the road. Leaving the house wasn't as hard as I'd expected. It makes me feel guilty to say it, but in some ways, it's a relief.

A relief to get a bit of a break from all the casual heart-break that living there sprinkled over every day: coming across one of Kate's hair bobbles down the side of the sofa, strands still entangled in the metal bit; dealing with the junk mail that still arrived in her name; finding that TV shows she'd set to be recorded still popped up on the box.

I didn't want to forget Kate – neither of us did – but I think we both needed a calmer time to at least try and heal. This was what I thought, anyway – Martha was staying quiet on the subject.

I glance over at her, her black hair tucked behind her ears, Doc Marten-clad feet propped up on the dashboard, phone in front of her, thumbs flying.

"Who are you texting?" I ask, still slightly concerned about the invasion of the teenaged ninjas.

"Donald Trump," she replies, deadpan.

"Oh. What's he saying?"

"He says you're a loser. And that you have worse hair than him."

I glance into the rear-view mirror.

Donald may have a point on both counts.

Chapter 8

I've been in this part of the world before, but today it feels like I am seeing it with fresh eyes. Today, I am not visiting for a holiday, or here for a day trip. Today, I am arriving at my new home.

Maybe for that reason, everything feels especially vivid and bright.

It's the beginning of September, and though the sun is still shining, the temperature is lower; as though Mother Earth is trying to prepare us for the change in season. As we leave the sprawl of modern life behind us and disentangle ourselves from the congested snake of the roads around Bristol, everything seems to slow down.

The roads themselves become smaller, less busy. The cars slowly change character: less nippy city-mobiles and more tractors. Fewer flashy number plates and more function. We see less signs for McDonalds and services and more for country pubs with quaint names: The Thatched Cottage, The Jolly Sailor, The Fisherman's Rest.

The surroundings grow more green, the fields stretching out endlessly around us, the hills and valleys curve and undulate like verdant streamers. The sides of the roads are edged by hedges and gnarled trees and wildflowers in their final bloom; by old-fashioned red post boxes and cattle grids and turn-offs into distant farms.

We stop seeing places that sell Krispy Kremes and pizza, and start seeing small stands at the side of the fields, solitary ladies reading books by tables of fruit and fresh bread; a booth of free range eggs and an honesty box next to them; we see unfamiliar place names and men perched on combine harvesters and sunlight dappling through the arched boughs of the trees stretching overhead. We see a whole different world starting to unfold.

Martha pretends not to be interested, but I can tell she's noticing everything. Taking it all in, digesting it. Whether it makes her want to vomit or rejoice is impossible to figure out, her face is completely dead and still, carefully schooled not to show any emotions at all.

I try not to dwell on this, to worry if I've broken her. If I've dampened down her resistance to the point where she has nothing left. If I've done exactly what Kate didn't want me to do, and forced her into a shape she doesn't fit.

We came to Dorset and Devon and Cornwall a lot when she was little. When she thought that hunting for crabs in rock pools was the height of excitement.

Days of endless sunshine and sometimes endless rain but

always endless fun. Me, her and Kate, free-wheeling around the countryside, traipsing along the coastal paths, singing in the car and dancing on the beach. I suppose we'd taken that for granted – everyone does. We all notice the disasters, and never make time to appreciate the small acts of happiness. Of companionship and laughter and ease.

Now, I'm making this drive in what feels like solitude. Martha has spoken little other than to tell me when she needed to stop for the loo, and has remained glued to her phone. I ponder throwing the phone through the window, hoping it might land in a field and get pecked to death by a flock of confused crows, but know that a digital detox would be pushing things too far. Depriving a teenager of Wi-Fi these days is cause for a call to Social Services.

I'm using the sat nav, and wish I could reprogramme the voice. If it's going to be the only voice I hear, it'd be nice if it sounded a bit more friendly. Sat navs always seem very judgemental to me. Also, a bit rubbish – it completely misses the turn-off to The Rockery, the cottage complex we'll be staying at, and I have to do a 78-point turn in a narrow country lane to retrace our route.

Martha, despite her silence, has clearly been paying attention.

"We're nearly there," she says, sounding full of joy and hope and optimism. Not.

"Yes, we are," I reply, wrestling the steering wheel around and hoping for the best.

"You know it's going to be really boring, don't you?" she asks, finally deciding to look me in the face.

"I don't know that, no. In fact it might be great. You'll have a new college, and make new friends, and I'm sure there'll be a lot to do."

"Like what?" she asks, glumly, gesturing out at the beautiful countryside that surrounds us. "Go bird-spotting? Identify rare and unusual types of mushroom? And I don't imagine I'll be making many friends. People round here aren't going to be like people in the city."

That, I think, as I get us back on track and head down the same road again, is exactly the point – but I don't actually say it. I pretend I'm concentrating on driving, and try not to imagine how many rare types of mushroom she could actually find if she put some effort into it. And whether any of them could be brewed up into a mind-expanding cup of tea.

"People here will be just as interesting as people in the city, so don't judge until you've met them," I eventually say, risking a sideways glance at her. Her nose ring is glinting in the sunlight, which weirds me out a bit.

"Well, I bet there aren't any black people, for a start!" she snaps back.

I ponder this, and decide that she has a point. Bristol is big and bustling and cosmopolitan; all forms of human life exist there. It's where she's grown up, and what she's used to. This ... isn't. She'd have probably loved living in the countryside when she was a little kid – but right now, she's 16, and I've dragged her away from an exciting fleshpot of earthly delights and different cultures to what she clearly sees as some kind of hell dimension.

"Probably not," I admit, squinting my eyes as I look for the turn-off again. It seems like someone's moved it. "As this is a small rural village in the West Country. But that doesn't mean the people here won't be fun, or interesting, or have their own stories to tell."

I finally spot the turning, and do a sudden heave to the right, forgetting to change down to second gear and giving us both a scare as we wobble. There is a pause, and a mutually agreed silence, while we both thank the God of Crap Driving for letting us get away with that one.

I look around, driving at one mile an hour now, tires crunching slowly on the gravel path as we head for a small carpark. I see one of those wooden summer houses, which seems to be a games room, with a ping pong table and air hockey and stacks of board games. I see a playground, with swings and a slide and a small climbing frame with rope netting hanging from it. And I see a path through two stone walls, leading us into the main cottage complex.

It all looks pretty, and well-kept, and welcoming. The 'welcoming' part may, of course, be down to the fact that there is a giant hand-painted banner attached to the wall, saying, in rainbow and glitter lettering, 'Welcome to Budbury Martha and Zoe!' It's flapping in the gentle breeze, and each time it does, a small flurry of glitter flies off and floats away in a bright cloud, like Tinkerbell's exhaust fumes.

I stop the car, and turn off the engine. It hums and buzzes for a few seconds, then goes quiet. This is it, I think. We're here. We made it in one piece, just about.

Martha doesn't seem quite as relieved, predictably enough. She is staring at the pretty banner as though it is the most disgusting and repulsive thing she's ever seen. As though it's releasing the Ebola virus into the sky, not multi-coloured glitter.

"I think you're wrong," she says, horrified. "I don't think they'll be interesting, or fun. I think ..."

She pauses at this point, as I have ignored her and got out of the car. I straighten my arms into the sky, and stretch my legs, and breathe in the clear air. It's late afternoon, still bright, but with a cooler edge that makes me wish I had a cardigan on. I can hear laughter and chatter from the other side of the wall, and feel suddenly nervous.

I wasn't expecting a welcoming committee – or people at all, truth be told. I'd hoped to slink in, unpack, lock Martha in her dungeon, and maybe sleep for an hour. I'm not the world's most skilled in social situations – not beyond one to one anyway. I tend to clam up a little; retreat into a self-protective shell. 'Turtle Up', as Kate used to call it.

So, I'm nervous – about meeting these people, and, more honestly, about these people meeting me. Kate was the only person who ever really understood me – she never judged, and she always got it. She always knew why I sometimes did the things I did or behaved in certain ways; she just instinctively figured it all out, even quicker than I did. Now I find myself out of my comfort zone, without Kate, and in charge of a teenager who probably wants to stab me in the back as I walk towards the path.

"I *think*," she says, continuing her one-sided conversation, "that they are going to be dull. And boring. And completely and utterly ... normal."

Her voice falters on that last word, trailing off into a stunned silence. I can't say that I blame her.

It's hard to maintain use of the word 'normal' when you're looking at Dracula, Frankenstein and The Mummy engaging in a hula-hoop competition.

Chapter 9

As we emerge onto the path, we see a green space, lawned over apart from a central bedded area with a water feature, draped with flowers. The cottages are arranged around the green, in pairs and terraces and one big house on its own, all built with pretty pale stone. So far, so normal.

It's the people on the green that change it into something weird. The people who are all, so far as I can see, dressed in various types of horror outfits. There are a couple of vampires with cloaks and teeth and blood down their faces; a fully wrapped and humungous Mummy; a hairy-headed werewolf, and a steampunk-type Victorian who may or may not be Dr Jekyll or Mr Hyde. There is a small pack of young zombies, and a boy with fake bolts through his head and green face paint. It feels a bit like we've walked into an impromptu meeting of the Hammer House of Horror fan club.

Steampunk Dr Jekyll is a strikingly tall young woman with flaming pink hair, the Werewolf is handing out bottles of cider, and there's a tiny raisin of an ancient old lady rocking a Catwoman suit. Not usually a horror character, but pretty scary given her age. Running around her feet is a leggy black Labrador, complete with devil horns. Even the dog is evil.

I take a couple of hesitant steps forward, Martha now lagging behind in understandable confusion. Possibly fear as well. It's not too late, I tell myself; we could jump back in the car and be home by tea-time...

Before I have the chance to act on that impulse, we are spotted. One of the monsters – a full on Bride of Dracula, around six-foot-tall and frankly terrifying – sees us, and waves.

"Hello!" she bellows, the word slightly distorted by her fake fangs. At least I assume they are fake. "Come on over – we don't bite!"

That line gets a laugh from the rest of them, and I take tiny steps in their direction. I tell myself it's to give Martha time to recover from the shock, but that would be fibbing – I'm feeling a bit discombobulated myself.

The Bride of Dracula strides over towards us, and up close she is even more imposing. A big, powerful older woman, built as though she could carry the world on her back, grey-streaked brown hair flowing over wide shoulders. She is bare-foot, and wearing a torn old wedding dress that shows off an impressive cleavage. She looks like Wonder Woman's gothic grandma.

Her face is wrinkled and tanned, creased into a welcoming smile as she pulls out her plastic teeth.

"Bloody things ..." she mutters, "Honestly, I couldn't eat a soggy parsnip with those things in, never mind a vestal virgin! You must be Zoe!"

I nod, and before I get the chance to speak, she has me wrapped in her arms, crushed to her bosom, and is almost bouncing me up and down in her enthusiasm. I'm a lot shorter than her, and I get a bit of an eyeful – in fact I've not been that close to another woman's boobs since I went through my brief and failed experimental phase many years ago.

At first, I panic, and have the urge to punch her in the ribs and run away – I'm not big on hugs. But she seems so genuinely delighted to see us, and her hugging is so utterly heartfelt, that after that initial moment of freak-out, I just give in, and let myself be smothered for a few seconds. Lord knows I need a hug. By the time she releases me, blinking into the sunlight, I'd quite like to burrow back in there and let all my cares get squashed away.

She holds me by the shoulders so she can inspect me, and I see her frown, then shake her head so all that long hair swishes around.

"Good job you're a red-head," she says, poking at my curls, "I think I might have just rubbed fake blood in your hair ... I'm Cherie, by the way. Cherie Moon."

Before I have the chance to respond, she's moving on to Martha, and giving her the hug treatment as well. Uh-oh, I think, as I see Martha try and shrivel away from her, this won't end well: Martha might not be in fancy dress, but she has plenty of horrible behaviour up her sleeve. I look on, my fingers screwed up into fists with the tension, expecting screams and yells and possibly karate kicks.

Instead, Martha does the same as me – she simply gives in to it. After one touch, she seems to collapse into Cherie's arms, and even endures it when she strokes her hair and mutters soothing noises into her ear. I even think – though I might be wrong here – that I see the glint of tears in Martha's eyes when she is finally released.

Good lord, I think to myself – what's going on here? Does this woman have supernatural powers after all? Maybe it's like it happens in a film or one of those teen TV shows I'm technically too old for but secretly love, and she is a real-life vampire with the power to magic us all into submission...

Cherie spoils this potential illusion by letting out an enormous belch, giggling, and apologising.

"Sorry about that, ladies – there've been a few ciders too many, it seems! Anyway, come on, come on, I want you to meet everyone ..."

I look at Martha and raise my eyebrows as Cherie walks towards the others.

"Normal enough for you?" I ask. She just shrugs, and looks as confused as I feel.

As we approach the rest of the horror movie cast, I notice a few more details about the hula-hoopers. The Monster is a tall man, bright blue eyes glinting in his painted face, his hair blonde and surfer-long. He's bare-chested, and although the chest in question is green, it's also totally ripped. Kind of Young Matthew McConaughey does Frankenstein.

He's doing a mean hip swivel, keeping the bright orange hoop flying, even though he is creased up with laughter. Next to him is Count Dracula, dressed in a smart black suit complete with waistcoat and cloak, and I notice that he's a lot older than he looked at a distance – 70s at least – but with a healthy, weather-beaten face that shines through even the white make-up. He's also doing all right with the hoop.

The Mummy, however … well, she never stood a chance, as she's approximately three years pregnant, and the size of a hippo. She's pulled the bandages off her face, and they droop around her shoulders with her long dark hair. The hula hoop is, tragically, completely still – she's looped it over her head, and it's simply got stuck around her body, perched solidly on the top of her baby bump. She's looking at it morosely, as though wondering how all of this ever happened to her.

Frankenstein stops swivelling, drops his hoop to the ground, and steps out of it. He lifts hers back over her head – there's no way it's ever going to go in the other direction - and gently kisses her on the lips. Ah, I think. That's how it happened.

At this point, the devil dog spots us, and runs immediately over to investigate. He sniffs my Converse, and I give him a quick tickle behind his velvety ears. Martha, who isn't that keen on people but adores dogs, drops straight to the ground to let him lick her face. He does so enthusiastically, his tail wagging at the speed of light, as a lady dressed as some kind of evil nurse walks over to us. She's wearing a slightly slutty, blood-spattered outfit, but offsets the short skirt with a pair of leggings underneath – like she's not quite confident enough to go full slutty.

She's not tall, and she's curvy, and pretty, and has exactly the same kind of crazy hair as me, except hers is brown. Mainly brown – there is one green streak in the mass of locks, curling at the side of her face, half grown-out.

She holds out her hand for me to shake, and smiles at me with such warmth and kindness that I immediately want to adopt her as my big sister.

"Hi – I'm Laura, and this," she says, pointing at the dog, "is Midgebo. He has no manners at all, I'm sorry. Welcome to Budbury."

I nod, and smile, and try to look less bewildered than I actually feel.

"Erm ... nice to meet you, and thank you. And don't worry about the dog – Martha has no manners either."

There's a brief 'humph' noise from beneath the tangle of teenager and Labrador which lets me know she heard that, which is fine. I intended her to hear it.

"Laura ... why is everyone dressed like this?" I ask, gesturing at the party with my fingers. I notice a table set off to one side, laden down with bottles of cider and cupcakes with tiny icing skulls on top and bowls of gooey jelly with what look like eyeballs floating in them.

"Oh! Well, we always dress like this on a Sunday ..." she

says, grinning. "Right before we sacrifice a goat to the Sacred Lord of Darkness."

Martha's face emerges from the flurry of Labrador, and she looks interested. Laura notices, and quickly shakes her head.

"No, sorry – I was kidding! No goat sacrifices here, I'm afraid. At least not as far as I know. It was Frank's birthday party last night. That's Frank, over there, the hula-hooping Count Dracula. It was his 81st. We always have a big fancy dress bash for him. Last year was the Wild West, this year was horror legends. We had all these outfits left over, and the food, and it was pretty much the last day of the holiday season, and we knew you guys were coming, and ... well, any excuse for a party, in all honesty."

I nod, as though that makes sense, while I hold out one hand to help Martha back up to her feet. Predictably enough, she completely ignores it and struggles up alone, leaving my hand hanging. I feel a mild flush flow over my cheeks – one of the many curses of The Ginger Brethren – and take a deep breath. What did I really expect? That we'd move to Dorset and Martha would suddenly turn into a model teen? She hadn't told anyone to fuck off yet – I had to accept the small mercies and move on.

Laura also notices that, of course, and gives me a sympathetic smile. She points at the zombie pack, who I now see, closer up, are all teenagers – Martha's age, maybe 14 through to 18 or thereabouts.

"The blonde zombie over there," she says, gesturing at a

petite girl with a long ponytail, "is my daughter, Lizzie. She's almost 16. Next to her – the zombie in the beanie hat - is her boyfriend Josh, he's 17, and a couple of their mates from the village."

"Wow," I say, gazing at them. "It's impressive – the way she's managed to incorporate black eyeliner into her zombie outfit."

"Oh yes," replies Laura, looking on proudly, "she wouldn't be caught dead without her eyeliner – or even undead! And over there is my son Nate, he's 13. He's the junior Frankenstein. The pregnant Mummy is my sister Becca, and the cutie with her is Sam. Or Surfer Sam, as he's known for obvious reasons. Frank is married to Cherie, in case you were wondering. And the girl with the pink hair is Willow, and Catwoman is Edie May. She's 91, but don't let that fool you – she actually won the hula hoop challenge, the others were just playing for the losers' spots ..."

It's a lot to take in. A lot of names, and information, and stuff to remember. Details to file away. None of which seems to be easy at the moment, as all I can see in my mind's eye is a 91-year-old Catwoman hip-swivelling her way to victory.

This place isn't just weird – it's super weird.

The thought must have come across on my face, because Laura is laughing at me, and Martha is edging away from me. For a change.

"Don't worry, I know it seems a lot. And it's all pretty strange – I only moved down here myself last summer, and it took me weeks to remember everyone's names. I'll be around to help you settle in, as much or as little as you like. I live here at the Rockery, and so does Matt. That's Matt, over there – the scary doctor."

She goes a little dreamy-eyed as she says this, and I can't pretend I don't see why. Matt is sitting off to the side, an elderly Border Terrier at his feet, strumming away on the guitar.

He's big and beefy and even dressed in a white coat covered in blood, looks like the kind of doctor who would immediately raise your blood pressure. In a good way. Floppy chestnut brown hair, hazel eyes, all-round handsome. As though he senses us watching, he looks over, and waves at Laura. She waves back, and they give each other a smile that makes me feel like I don't exist. That nobody else in the world exists. It's sweet and lovely and intimate, and it straight away makes me feel lonely. I don't think any man has ever smiled at me like that – certainly not while sober.

I drag my mind away from that thought, as it is bordering on self-pity, and instead look around to see how Martha is reacting to all of this insanity.

She is standing behind me, hands shoved in her pockets, and studiously ignoring the nearby zombie teenagers. My heart falls a little, and maybe breaks a little as well. I had hoped, as soon as I saw them, that it might make the difference – seeing people of the same age, of the same eye-liner inclination, of the same footwear tribe (most of the zombies are wearing Doc Martens, which never go out of fashion, even after the apocalypse). I suppose I'd hoped that she would see them as potential friends – but instead, she's pretending not to see them at all.

I am gazing at Martha, and feeling sad, when Laura slips her arm into mine and links me.

"Don't worry," she says, quietly, following my gaze. "It just takes time. Give her a chance to get used to it all, to us. To the fact that you've dragged her kicking and screaming away from her friends."

I tear my eyes away from Martha, and back to Laura. It sounds so simple when she says it, but I'm not so sure.

"Maybe," I reply. "I hope, anyway. She's ... well, she's been through a lot."

"I know," Laura answers, simply. "Cherie told me. And you might not know it to look at her now, but Lizzie was the same. She lost her dad. I lost my husband. We were broken when we arrived here, and she hated me for making her come. These days, she's ... well, she's still a pain in the arse some-times; she's impossible to get out of bed, she's addicted to her phone, she swears too much, and she punches Nate in the kidneys most days, but ... well, that's all normal pain-in-the-arse stuff, isn't it? Nothing we can't cope with."

Wow, I think, looking at Laura through fresh eyes. I'd been standing here, feeling jealous of her and Matt, and assuming that I was looking at one of those perfect families. Mum, dad, two kids. Lashings of love all around.

And while I was right about the love – that much is obvious

– I'd been wrong about the circumstances. Laura is a widow, and Lizzie and Nate have suffered the same kind of loss as Martha, and nothing is as simple as it seemed on the surface. Maybe, just maybe, this place will do the same for us – sprinkle some fairy dust on our lives until we reach the point where all I have to worry about with Martha is her lazing around in bed. Not, you know, overdosing in a nightclub toilet.

Martha herself has taken a walk, obviously not into the whole meet-and-greet party vibe, and is starting her new life in Dorset the way she probably intends to carry on: alone. I watch as she mooches from cottage to cottage, pausing to look at the names they all have engraved on slate plaques outside them, frowning as she does. She looks forlorn, and isolated, and very, very young. It's like a kick in the teeth, and I suddenly wish we hadn't come. Somehow, being surrounded by everyone else's happiness – even if there is sadness just a layer beneath – feels like too much.

I have an urge to change my mind right then. To scoop Martha back up, and load her in the car, and drive us to the nearest pub, where I will happily let her use her fake ID and allow us both to get absolutely shitfaced.

Before I can give in and act on the impulse, Martha turns back, and joins us. Her face is slightly more animated than it has been all day, and she's pulled her bobble out so her black hair is flowing over her shoulders.

"What's the name of our cottage?" she asks, abruptly.

"Erm ... Lilac Wine, I think?" I reply, frowning in confusion.

She nods, as though she's just figured something out.

"Right. Jeff Buckley. And there's Cactus Tree, which is Joni Mitchell, and Poison Ivy, which is the Rolling Stones, and Mad About Saffron, which is that hippy dude Donovan. Plus over there there's one called Black Rose."

She raises her eyebrows at me expectantly, and I answer: "Thin Lizzy?"

All of the cottages at the Rockery – a name which now makes much more sense – are named after songs. Quite cool songs as well, in a retro kind of way.

"Wow," says Laura, shaking her head in awe. "I can't believe you figured it out that quickly, and you know all the songs as well ... you two are way cooler than us!"

Martha glances at her, glances at me, and replies: "Well, one of us is at least."

It's cheeky, and could have been nasty, if it wasn't for the fact that she's almost smiling. Not full on – not grinning or anything crazy like that – but definitely almost.

"We're in Hyacinth House, behind the others and next to the pool," says Laura, and waits a beat for us to figure that one out.

"The Doors," I say, at exactly the same time as Martha. I resist the urge to offer her a high-five – I think we all know how that would end – and instead satisfy myself with a small, internal whoop of joy. Perhaps this will all be okay, after all. The healing power of rock music might at the very least have given us a chance.

Cherie wanders back over to us – I've seen her watching me and Laura, as though she's giving us the chance to get acquainted before she butts back in. She's perched her plastic fangs in her hair, and they look a bit like they might come back to life at any moment and start gnashing down on her head.

"Martha figured out all the cottage names straight away," says Laura, eyes wide as though Martha has performed some kind of miracle.

"I'm not surprised," replies Cherie, reaching out to smooth Martha's hair behind her ears and somehow, amazingly, managing to keep her hand. "I could tell right away that this was the right place for these two."

Chapter 10

Our first night in Lilac Wine is neither a roaring success or a complete disaster. On a scale of 1-10 – with 1 being 'please pass me the Valium' and 10 being 'zippety-doo-dah' – it's probably about a 6.

The cottage itself is lovely; all exposed beams and chintzy furniture and comfy cushions. There's a gorgeous old fireplace that I can imagine lying in front of on colder nights, accompanied by a bottle of gin, and a battered pine dining table laden down with gifts of wildflowers and home-baked bread and cupcakes and organic wine. These people are definitely feeders.

There are two bedrooms, both of which are en-suite, which is excellent news as it means Martha and I can avoid seeing each other naked by accident. There's also, bizarrely, a TV in my bathroom – which, I don't know, might be a good thing? Maybe I can watch Antiques Roadshow while I'm having a poo. Take that, Fiona Bruce.

Most of the other cottages are now empty after the end

of the main summer season, although there are some holiday lets coming up – I expect to be seeing strangers wandering around at some point or another, and vow to try not to scare any of them with my feral appearance. I mean, I'm hardly the epitome of groomed style and sophistication when I'm at work – it can only get worse now I'm a country bumpkin.

Lilac Wine looks out onto the main green area, and at the moment, the only people living at the Rockery are us, Laura and her kids, and Matt, who it turns out is the village vet and lives in the big house called Black Rose. They seem to share custody of Midgebo, the dog, which I suppose is a good a way as any of taking baby steps towards something more official.

Cherie and Frank live at his farm, and the others at various places in the village itself – which I presume is where they all take themselves off to by the time their welcome party dies down.

I unpack my things, allowing myself a small surge of optimism as I do so, hoping that I've made the right call. That Martha will ever forgive me.

She is quiet and moody as we mooch around the grounds and the cottage, taking it all in with sad, dark eyes, as though all of it has nothing to do with her at all. But ... well, she isn't actively hostile, and I have to take that as a positive. There are no tears, no tantrums, no self-harm or Zoe-harm, all of which I possibly expected. I tell myself that it will be fine –

but somehow a disconnected Martha feels almost worse than an explosive Martha.

After a night of watching crap telly and drinking most of the wine that was left for me, all alone on the sofa, I finally give in and go to bed. I've been putting it off for some reason. Maybe part of me was hoping that Martha would emerge, and we could talk. Or listen to music. Or anything at all. I suppose I'd forgotten, though, exactly how good teenagers can be at sulking – especially ones like Martha, who have plenty of reason to.

As I sip the wine, and watch the crap telly, and ponder everything that's happened to us both, I feel like sulking myself. I miss Kate so much it feels like a throbbing pain in my chest.

Eventually, when I recognise the signs of a morbid drunk coming on, I make my way up the stairs, learning the new creaks and groans and noises that all older houses come with. I pause outside her room. The door is open, just a tiny crack, and I push it a little.

I see her, bundled up in the covers, black hair splayed across her forehead, a ghostly light cast over her face by the phone that sits next to her on the cabinet, plugged in to charge. She's frowning even in her sleep, her legs occasionally jerking like a dog having a bad dream. I love her so much, and I'm so desperate to reach out, to help her. To get her through this.

I glance around the room, the moon shining in through the still-open floral curtains, and see her suitcase abandoned in a corner. Still zipped up and bulging, as though she hopes she won't be staying.

Quietly, sadly, I tip-toe across the carpeted hallway to my own room. I fall onto the bed, fully clothed, and pray to a God I'm not sure I even believe in.

Chapter 11

Martha's first day at college rolls round quickly, and I cling to it like it's a lifeboat all made of hope. Perhaps, I think, this will change everything. Perhaps she will be inspired by her new teachers; enthused by her A-levels; won over by new friends. Perhaps she will finally decide to give this place a chance, and stop acting as though she's been sentenced to death by Dorset.

The first dent in those rather pathetic hopes comes when she gets on the bus in the village. I drive her there, park up, and offer to wait with her.

"Worried I'll do a runner?" she says, staring at me from the passenger seat.

"It wouldn't be the first time. You did a runner from Miss Clarke's class that time because you didn't want to sing in the assembly."

"I was eight!" she replies, sounding exasperated. "And you and mum were the ones who always told me to follow my instinct, that if something felt wrong, it probably was ..."

"Oh. So it's our fault it is?"

"Yes," she snaps back, staring out of the car window at the centre of Budbury, "everything is."

I follow her gaze to the bus stop. It wasn't hard to find – there is in fact only one. In high season, tourist buses run through as they trek up and down the Jurassic Coast, but from this time of year onwards, there's only two buses a day in both directions. Plus this one – the bus that takes local kids a few miles down the road to the high school and its college.

There is a small gang of young people hanging round the bus stop, as of course is usually the case in small towns. I've never figured out why the bus stop becomes the hub of under-age social activity, but it always seems to.

The weather feels cooler, with a brisk breeze blowing up from the coast, and the kids are wearing a lot of check flannel and beanie hats and chunky jumpers. The younger ones – including Nate and Lizzie, who's in her last year at school – are in a hideous purple uniform, the older ones in jeans and boots.

"It could be worse," I say, looking from them to Martha, who is dressed head to toe in black, nose stud in, dyed hair back-combed in a tribute to Amy Winehouse kind of way.

"Yeah? How?" she asks, looking genuinely confused.

"You could be a year younger, and have to wear that purple uniform."

She snorts, but doesn't respond. She's too busy watching

the school bus roll along the one narrow road that threads through the village. Her eyes squint at it, and her fingers clench into a fist around the backpack on her lap. I realise how nervous she is, beneath the anger and the tough veneer, and reach out to give her hand a very quick pat.

"Go on. You'll be fine, you know – just give it a chance."

She shoots me a look that might mean 'go and drown yourself in the nearest toilet', but I choose to interpret as 'thank you, I will', and climbs out of the car, slamming the door behind her. She strides over to the bus stop, head held high, strutting along as though she hasn't got a care in the world. Attagirl, I think, smiling as she goes.

Lizzie and Josh and her gang have already boarded the bus, and I see Lizzie waving frantically at her through the window, banging on the glass to get her attention. She's on the top deck – as the cool kids always are – and is making 'come and sit with us' gestures through the pane. Aaah, I think. What a sweetie.

Martha looks up at her, gives no response at all, and gets onto the bus. She's the last one on, and I see her take a seat on her own, on the lower level. I cringe a little inside as I see her snub Lizzie, but know there isn't much I can do about it.

Instead, I blow out a big breath as I watch the bus pull away, and feel ... well, in all honesty, I feel relieved. This in turn makes me feel guilty, so I decide to get out of the car, and go for a walk. Isn't this one of the reasons I wanted to come here, anyway? The endless paths and the endless cliffs and the endless space? Never mind that I'm so tired and ragged and borderline weepy that I could quite happily fall asleep in the car, and stay there until it's time to collect Martha at the end of the day. No, that won't do. I will go for a walk.

The village is small but perfectly formed, I see, as I amble along the narrow pavement. Small terraced houses line the road, along with a handful of shops – a pharmacy, a gift shop that has a 20% sale on conch shells, a butcher, some tea rooms. No book shop, which isn't surprising but does make me sad. The world needs more book shops. I pass a small bakery, and the Community Hall advertising 'zumablates' for the over 60s, and navigate the flower-filled buckets outside the florists. I see a sign for the pet cemetery, which I vow to visit some time when I'm feeling less fragile, like in 2021.

I nod to people as I pass, a bit freaked out by all the 'good mornings' and smiles, and follow my nose down towards the coast. I see a hand-painted wooden sign for the Comfort Food Café, and decide that that's probably where I'd been heading all along. It's Cherie's cafe, and Laura manages it, and Willow works there, and basically from what I heard on the day we arrived, it's the absolute centre of the Budbury universe.

After about ten minutes of walking, I reach a small carpark, next to the bay. The bay is a perfect horse-shoe shape, the September sunlight streaking down onto waves that are racing in to foam over the sand. There are a few holiday-makers left, some with toddlers, some with dogs, all enjoying the last few days of what we could loosely call summer. There's an ice cream van parked up, a bored-looking lad reading a collection of poetry by Yeats inside the cab. I silently applaud his taste, and start the trek up to the cafe itself.

The path is long but not steep, with low-level steps cut into it and a handrail to hold onto when it starts to feel so high it's vertigo-inducing. I pause every now and then, and let myself soak up the view. The higher you get, the more the colours change: sea that looked grey and white from land level now looks iridescent, merged shades of blue and green and turquoise, rippling and rolling on its way into the bay.

The clifftops stretch off into the horizon on either side, yellow and red, rock meeting sand, jaggedly rising and falling as they disappear into the distance. I can see people walking along the paths, doing exactly the same as me, and pausing to enjoy the spectacle of the morning sunshine on the water. It's so quiet as well – it may be the seaside, but it's not the kind of place you find banana boats or fairground rides; all you can hear is the sound of the seagulls shrieking as they dive, the waves fizzing inland, and the occasional bark of a stick-chasing pooch.

It's so different from home – it even smells different. It smells of salt and brine and wilderness, the clear air sharp and refreshing as I gulp it in. And I do gulp – I realise that as I stand there, perched on a path at the edge of the world, I am starting to feel some of that freedom I've been yearning for. I'm not sure if it's the thought of my fresh start that is making me feel so liberated, or the stunning views, or simply knowing that I can spend the whole day without feeling Martha's resentful glare boring into my back, but I am feeling it. It's though inch by tiny inch, something in my chest is unclenching.

Or maybe, I decide, as I resume my climb, I'm just having a heart attack.

When I reach the top of the path, I walk beneath a gorgeous wrought-iron arch, decorated with beautiful metallic roses painted in red and green. At the top of the arch, in curved iron letters, I see the words: Welcome to the Comfort Food Café. They lift my spirits as I walk beneath, and out into a sloping garden.

There are wooden benches and chairs, the surfaces at slightly alarming angles, and a make-shift stage that looks as though it was used for the birthday party. The ground is grassy, and scattered with intermittent remnants: plastic fangs, a crucifix, a discarded plastic clown mask blowing around in the breeze. Jeepers.

To my left is the coast, stripes of colour as the sky plunges to the land and the land is lapped by the sea, and over in the far corner I see a paddock that is currently empty, but contains a small roofed shelter and several dog bowls. Doggie crèche for customers, I presume, which is a brilliant idea.

In front of me is the cafe itself. It's mainly made of windows, and those French doors that are basically also windows, all set in a long, ramshackle structure that seems to have expanded organically as it's been needed. It's one-storey, but windows in the eaves tell me there is probably either a flat or some kind of storage room up in the attic. One customer is sitting outside, sipping a cup of tea and reading a paper that keeps flapping and folding in the wind. He nods at me as I pass, and pull open the door.

Inside, there aren't any clown masks blowing around, but it's still pretty weird – just weird in a good way. There are about four people inside, including a frazzled-looking blonde lady with a toddler who is currently eating a red crayon, and a fit-looking middle-aged couple dressed in full-on walker gear, stacks of maps on the table in front of them with their toast.

There are long tables, and tiny tables, tables for one and benches for eight, each one bearing a small vase filled with wildflowers. There's a serving counter laden with cakes and sandwiches and biscuits, and an ice-cream freezer full of delicious sounding substances like Honeycomb Whip and Blackberry Bash and Peachy Cream Dream. An upright fridge is full of cloudy lemonade and ginger beer and dandelion and burdock and cola, and in the background I can hear one of my favourite sounds in the whole world: the sound of an industrial-sized coffee machine.

All of these things are fairly standard for a cafe – but the decor sets it apart. Having now met Cherie Moon, I'm less surprised – but it is, to say the least, eccentric.

I wander around for a few moments, looking at the oddments and found objects on display – some hanging from the ceiling, some mounted on the walls, some on shelves. Fossils, a red kayak, bongo drums, a huge boomerang, framed photos of the coast, an old-fashioned black-and-gold Singer sewing machine, a mobile made of 7-inch vinyl singles.

Narrowly missing banging my head on a dangling oar, I make my way to the back of the room, where an entire wall of bookshelves is bathed in sunshine, tiny dust particles floating in the yellow stripes falling in from the windows.

There are piles of boxed board games – old ones like Ker Plunk and Buckaroo, as well as chess and draughts and Chinese checkers. A few jigsaws, and an ancient set of dominos in a box. A load of colouring-in books, and some word puzzle collections, and several old tomato tins crammed full of coloured pencils – a lot of which need sharpening. A particular vice of mine, pencil sharpening.

Beneath the games, the magic starts to happen – at least for me. There are rows and rows of paperbacks – Danielle Steel, Jilly Cooper, Thomas Hardy, Len Deighton, Stephen King, Daphne du Maurier, Nora Roberts, George RR Martin, Shakespeare's sonnets, Spike Milligan, and everything in between. Hardbacks, too: Churchill's biography, heavy books about Dorset's history and geology, the story of the Beatles and Roxy Music and Led Zeppelin all in print.

There's a section for kids as well, full of battered and tattered and much-used copies of *The Gruffalo* and *James and the Giant Peach* and *Dr Seuss* and the Potters, both Harry and Beatrix. For a boring old book-end like myself, it's blissful.

Everything's ramshackle and higgledy-piggledy, and although that fits in perfectly with the whole vibe of the cafe, I still have a professional urge to alphabetise them and put them in subject order. Oddly, although I am a proud slacker on the household chores front, I do like a nicely kept book shelf.

For a single moment, I miss my job: the enormity of the change, of what I've given up, comes rushing in and swamps me. I was never a career woman, but I liked my job. I loved being around books, and talking to people about books, and that new-book smell when we got a delivery in and I first opened the box with the Stanley knife.

Now, I'm just an unemployed teenager-wrangler.

Before the sour mood can get a hold of me, a giant slab of sponge cake appears in front of my face. The cake is on a plate, which is attached to a hand, which, I see when I turn round, startled, is attached to Laura.

She grins at me, and wafts the cake under my nose. It's still warm, little wisps of steam wafting up from it, and it smells … delicious. Almost as good as new books.

"Apple?" I say, frowning as I try and identify the aromas. "Cinnamon? And … something else. What is it?"

"Pumpkin!" she says, delighted that she's foxed me. I don't have the heart to break it to her that my culinary skills are about on a par with Noddy's, so it's not that much of a victory.

"It gets quiet from this point in the year," she explains, leading me over to a small table in the corner, where she sits me down and puts the cake in front of me, along with a fork and spoon and a small pot of fresh pouring cream. "So when it gets quiet, I get inventive. Last winter it was all about the hot chocolates – chili hot chocolate, orange hot chocolate, mint hot chocolate, rum hot chocolate ... well, you get the picture.

"Last summer, I introduced a load of chocolate bar milk-shakes, and this summer I experimented with ice cream. There's not too much left now, but you can see them in the freezer over there. Now I'm getting ready for autumn and winter – and that means spices, and orchard fruits, and lashings of everything warm and comforting."

As I'm listening to her, practically salivating, she's making 'eat up' gestures with her fingers, miming the spoon-to-mouth action.

"Bet you haven't had breakfast, have you?" she asks, raising one eyebrow at me. Her face is smeared with flour, and there are equally floury handprints on her stripey apron. She smells of sugar and spice and all things nice, and is basically a kind of gingerbread woman come to life.

I think about it, and realise that no, I haven't had any breakfast. I made sure Martha did, surreptitiously looking on as she managed a bowl of granola and strawberries, but completely forgot my own.

"No," I reply, pausing only to shovel a spoonful of sponge and cream into my mouth. My taste buds almost explode, and I decide that if I choke to death now, I will at least die happy. Laura sees my orgasmic expression, and it clearly thrills her.

"No," I say again, once I've swallowed the best cake ever baked in the entire known history of cakes, "but it was worth the wait for that. You're a very talented woman."

"Why, thank you," she says, nodding her head in a mock bow. Her curls have started to frizz from the heat of the kitchen, and I feel a moment of barnet-based solidarity.

"Did Martha get off to college okay?" she asks, using another spoon to steal a mouthful of cake for herself.

I nod, and she sees my hesitation. Possibly my embarrassment.

"What is it? What's wrong?" she asks, frowning.

"Nothing really ... it's just ... well, Martha, right now, isn't an easy girl to like. I feel terrible saying that, but it's true. Lizzie tried to get her to sit with them this morning, but she blanked her. I can only apologise in advance if Lizzie's upset by that."

"She might be," replies Laura, shrugging, "who knows? She's hard to predict. But there's no need for you to apologise. Teenagers aren't always easy to like. I mean, you love your kids, always, but you don't always like them. They're two different emotions."

"I'm starting to realise that," I answer, chasing the last chunk of sponge around the plate. "I mean, I love her to bits, and my heart breaks for her, it really does. But this morning, when I watched the school bus trundle off down the street,

I felt ... God may well strike me down for this, but I felt relieved to see the back of her! Tell me honestly – does that make me evil?"

Laura laughs, and tucks a stray curl – the green one – behind her ear.

"And why do you have one strand of green hair?" I add, as I don't think she'll mind.

"Oh! Well, the hair thing was to go with the bridesmaid's dress I wore for Cherie's wedding on Christmas Eve. That was quite the party, I can tell you – the whole of Budbury was there, as well as some visitors from Scotland and Australia, all over. Frank's first wife, Bessy, died a few years ago, and she always used to cook him burnt bacon butties and thick tea for his breakfast – so after she'd gone, he started coming here for brekkie, and Cherie started making it for him. Then me.

"It's a bit like that, here – everyone has their comfort foods, at least the locals do, and we make sure we supply it ... Sam likes Pot Noodles because it reminds him of his home in Ireland; Scrumpy Joe – the werewolf – likes almond biscotti because it reminds him of his Italian grandmother ... and Edie May ... well, that's a long story.

"So, I did have some pink hair – the result of a close encounter between me, a bottle of wine, and Willow's hair dye – and then it was green for the wedding. Who knows what could happen next?"

I nod, taking all of this in, and wondering what my comfort food would be ... there wasn't much from my childhood, that's for sure. Bizarrely, my fondest memories are probably from Barbara's kitchen – much as she disliked my friendship with her precious Kate, she did occasionally feed me, and did a mean Shepherd's Pie. I make a mental note to give her a call later – or, as I'm not that self-sacrificing, maybe just send her a text.

"And as for your other question ..." she says, confusing me – I've already forgotten asking it – "the one about you being evil for feeling relieved to see the back of Martha? Well, no, Zoe – it just makes you human. It's one of those closely-guarded secrets of motherhood – we all feel it sometimes, but none of us let on in case it makes us look like terrible parents. Even when they're little and cute – like Saul over there, with his mum Katie – you need time away. A break, where you can just breath and try and remember who you were before kids arrived on the scene. And when they're teenagers, it's even harder – they can be so bloody ..."

She struggles to find a word, so I step in: "Annoying?"

"Yes!" she says, banging her hand on the table in agreement. "And irritating."

"And contrary."

"And exhausting ... keeping up with a teenaged girl, all the stresses and dramas and mind-games, is like running seven marathons in a row, while wearing a Chewbacca outfit. It's no wonder we all need a drink at the end of the night! And that's just a normal teenager – never mind the ones who've gone through the mill. The ones like Lizzie, and Martha, who have every reason to lash out sometimes."

I'm looking at Saul and Katie as we talk. He is cute – chubby and blonde – but he is also now repeatedly hitting his poor mother on the side of the head with a wooden spoon. I'm not sure how cute he is once I notice that.

"Martha," I say, wishing I had some coffee, "is lashing out a lot. At me, at school, at the whole world really. One of the main reasons I made the move here was to give her a chance to slow down. She was racing off at 100 miles per hour all over the place. There was a lot of alcohol, definitely smoking, undoubtedly some drug use – hopefully low level, please don't worry that she'll be dealing smack at the school car park! – and a lot of sneaking out and hanging round with older kids, going to places she shouldn't be. She even got brought home by the police one night."

"Ah! Sounds familiar – hang on, I'll be right back," Laura replies, getting to her feet as though she's read my mind, and fetching over a coffee pot and two mugs. On the way, she tops up Katie's cup, gently taking the wooden spoon out of Saul's hand as she leaves, and offers more to the walkers.

When she's settled back down, and I am nose-deep in caffeine, she continues: "Sounds familiar because my sister Becca was exactly like that when she was a kid. The local police and A&E triage nurse were on first-name terms with my parents for a while. It was all sex, drugs and rock and roll with her."

"Becca?" I say, recalling an enormously fat Mummy with a hula-hoop lodged on her stomach. "The pregnant one?"

"Yep – but she's not like that now, obviously! These days her idea of a wild night in is watching Poldark while she drops some Rennies ..."

"That sounds pretty good actually ..."

"I know, right? He can scythe my garden any time! Anyway, she's all cleaned up these days. She was before she met Sam, and before they made Binky. Turns out she had her reasons to lash out as well, we just didn't know it at the time."

"Right," I say, knowing it's nosy but unable to stop myself. "And how long did that take? For Becca to clean up her act, I mean?"

"Oh ... well ... you shouldn't judge Martha by Becca's past, I'm sure Martha will be an entirely different kettle of cod ..."

"How long?"

"Um ... about 14 years or so? But hey! Becca never does anything by halves – even visiting me, here. She couldn't just visit ... she had to go and fall in love and get up the duff, didn't she? It's just the way she's made, and I wouldn't change her for the world. I'm sure one day, you'll be able to look at Martha and say that, too."

Oh Lord, I think, clasping my hands around the hot mug of coffee and considering drowning myself in it. If it's going to take Martha 14 years to clean up her act, I might as well. I don't have the stamina to last that long.

Chapter 12

The next few days stretch into a week, and that week stretches into two. The weather is changing, the sky often patterned with dark grey cloud among the blue, the wind whistling up from the bay, the summer-dry grass soaking up the frequent showers. The wildflowers have faded, and already the trees around the Rockery are starting to shed, their leaves crinkling into flyaway gold and bronze shards.

I'm changing, too, I think. I've spent a lot of time walking, and thinking, and reading. Along the cliffs, on the beach, miles along to the old boat shed that nobody seems to use any more. My fitness levels are definitely on the up, and I've found myself pondering things my busy brain usually chooses to avoid.

Pondering Kate, and the hole she's left in our lives – how much she'd love it here, and how much I'd love to be sharing it with her. Pondering Barbara, and her spiky texts and cold veneer, and how much pain she must be hiding beneath it. Pondering my own parents, who I've not seen for so long and have no desire to see.

My father was a petty criminal and drug user, and he wasn't especially good at either. This resulted in him repeatedly getting caught in possession of stolen goods, getting caught with a handbag he'd just liberated from an old lady leaving church, getting caught with enough marijuana to keep the Grateful Dead tour bus happy stuffed into his socks, and getting caught with his ankle in a Rottweiler's mouth during an attempted burglary. Honestly, he was so inept, he might as well have walked round wearing a stripey shirt, an eye mask, and carrying a bag marked 'swag.'

My mother was only 16 when she had me, and already on a downward spiral. Her specialty was forging cheques, which seems a quaint crime these days. Martha probably doesn't even know what a cheque is. My mother, who blessed me with my red hair, was also good at getting caught – for the forgeries, for benefit fraud, and on one glorious occasion for relieving my primary school of its Guide Dogs for the Blind collection box.

The whole of my childhood was chaos. Either chaos at home, or chaos in foster care. I'm not sure which was worse – but I do know that I would probably have been better off if I'd simply been given away at birth. Now, with the adult wisdom I was working hard to attain, I see the tragedy of it all wasn't just mine – it was theirs as well. Their wasted lives, and lost potential, and constant circling pattern of self-destruction. Self-destruction that almost took me down with them.

When I was old enough, I cut myself off from them. It wasn't even hard – because they barely noticed me anyway. I sometimes wonder what happened to them, and occasionally have the urge to reach out. Someone – a mutual friend I bumped into in town – told me years ago that my mother had 'cleaned up her act.' That she was in counselling, and had a new flat, and would probably love to hear from me.

I'd nodded, and smiled, and got away as fast as I could, taking the long way home to Kate in my paranoia – concerned that someone would be following me, and my escape plan would be foiled. Yeah, I know – it's all those books I read.

Now, here, in this beautiful place, I have decided that one day, perhaps, I will reach out. That one day, I might actually be grown up enough to put the past behind me, and go and find her. Not, though, today – today I was dealing with my usual problem.

Martha.

Because while the weather was changing, and I was changing, she ... wasn't. Or maybe she was. I just didn't know – because she barely ever spoke to me. Don't get me wrong, she wasn't being aggressive, or wild, or even defiant. She's not once smelled of booze, and I haven't even caught her having a fag in the woods behind the cottage.

Every day, she's got up on time, and gone to college. Every day, she's come home, eaten dinner, done homework, and gone to her room to listen to music. Music she doesn't even play too loud. It's been a rinse-and-repeat cycle of this since she started college, and bizarrely this behaviour has me almost as worried as when she was swigging vodka from her water bottle and sneaking out to go to The Dump.

I've tried to communicate, to cajole, to joke. To get her to go on walks with me, or come for a swim, or out for a pub lunch. Each time, I've been closed down. Shut out, with a level of cold politeness that freezes my blood. I'm not used to politeness from Martha. I'm used to screaming and swearing and the ever-present threat that we may end up rolling round on the floor pulling each other's hair.

This morning, I told her to come straight to the Café after college, instead of home, as we'd been invited to dinner there. The people I'd started to get to know, and who I was thinking of as friends, would all be there – and, well, free food.

She pulled a face at me, then seemed to remind herself that even doing that was giving too much away.

"Come on, it'll be fun," I'd said, trying to budge her from her indifference.

"If you say I have to come, then I will," she replied, clutching her backpack and staring at a fascinating spot over my shoulder. "I don't have any choice, do I?"

"Martha, please don't be like that!" I'd squeaked.

"Like what? Obedient? I thought that's what you wanted. I'm here, aren't I? I'm going to college. I'm getting on with my work. I'm being a good little robot child, just like you asked."

"That's not what I wanted, or what I asked ... and you

know that. Come to the cafe with Lizzie and Nate and Josh, and at least give it all a chance, will you? There'll be cake!"

I don't know why I added that. Cake might be a deciding factor in many things, but changing a surly, grief-stricken teenager's mind isn't one of them. She didn't reply – she was too busy slamming the door behind her and leaving the cottage.

So now, as I sit in Paperback Corner in the cafe, I feel nervous. I'm not entirely sure if she's going to turn up, or if she does, if she'll speak to me. She's never rude to the others – in particular, she seems to respond well to Cherie's particular brand of care – but she doesn't really interact either. I caught her staring at Surfer Sam's backside a few days ago, but she's only human – and he is an especially fine specimen of manhood. When I'd tried to catch her eye and laugh about it afterwards, she gave me the reptile gaze and turned away.

Lizzie and Josh seem to have given up trying to make friends with her, and I can't say that I blame them. They're still polite around each other, but there's no warmth. I know from Laura that Lizzie feels bad for Martha, and wants to help her, but like myself she's being frozen out. They don't chat on the bus, and Martha's ignored her friend request on Facebook – the ultimate teenaged knock-back.

I am flicking through a battered copy of Jamaica Inn as I wait, with 91-year-old Edie May sitting next to me. She is engrossed in the latest Jack Reacher novel, bless her. Edie, I have been discovering, is wonderful company. She was a librarian for years, and has an endless knowledge of books and poetry. Her enthusiasm for literature only seems to be rivalled by her enthusiasm for *Strictly Come Dancing*, which she is bubbling with excitement about as the latest series is imminent.

Like bookish people the world over, we are happy to sit and read and occasionally chat, not seeing it as a snub if the other person disappears off into another world for a while mid-sentence.

Laura is in the kitchen with Cherie, whisking up something that smells delightful. She's trying out parts of her autumn and winter menu on us, and I'm happy to be the guinea pig. Becca is here, slumped on a bean bag that she actually brought with her, saying the wooden chairs were 'some kind of torture device.'

She's slouched in a corner, Sam next to her, holding her hand and saying something that makes her laugh. She's due this week, but has convinced herself that 'Binky' will be late. It doesn't seem to be filling her with joy, and I can't say that I blame her – she's endured a long, hot summer while the size of a house, and now has some screaming agony to look forward to.

Matt is outside with Frank, doing something rugged and masculine with fence posts and a hammer, and Willow is at home with her mum. Willow's mum, Lynnie, suffers from early-onset Alzheimer's, so she can't always get out. I can only imagine how hard that must be, but it never seems to affect the pink-haired wonder's mood. She's always upbeat and cheerful and cracking some weird joke or another.

Scrumpy Joe, who runs a local 'cider cave', has come bearing gifts, which are clinking away in a carrier bag as he walks through the door. Midgebo immediately runs over to investigate, clearly disappointed when his frantic sniffing only turns up some large brown bottles.

I glance at my watch, and see that it's almost half four. That means the college bus should be reaching the village, and the young people should be making their trudge to the cafe.

"Don't worry, dear," says Edie, without even appearing to glance up at me, "she'll be fine. This is the best place for her. Stroppy teenagers are our specialist subject."

"Really? There aren't that many of them ..."

"Well, when I say teenagers, I mean people who act like them. And that's including Cherie over yonder, in her time, as well as my beautiful Becca. Stroppy, I tell you. But there's only so long you can stay angry, or sad, when you live in a place like this, with people like this. You'll see, you will."

She's still not taken her eyes from Jack Reacher, but I try and believe her. Even if she sounds a bit like some kind of West Country Yoda, with her curvy accent and near-mystical pronouncements.

I give up on Jamaica Inn. I've read it thirty times already, and I'm too distracted watching the door. As soon as I put it back on the shelf, they arrive – or at least Nate and Lizzie and Josh do.

They pile into the café, an explosion of colour (mainly purple), and chatter, and laughter. Josh is nudging Lizzie, who is giggling, and Nate drops his bag to the floor before bellowing: "Mother! Mother, where art thou? Your only son has returned and he needs *cake!*"

I have to smile at that one. He's a 13-year-old-boy. Of course he needs cake. I glance at Lizzie, who has bounced over to say hello. She's one of those kids who has so much energy she seems to bounce everywhere, as if she's attached to an invisible pogo stick. I know she's 16 very soon, and has all the sarcasm to go with that age, but she also seems to be living in a very different world to the other 16 year old I know.

I say hi, and don't even ask. It's not fair to ask – to put Lizzie in a position where she feels like she has to be Martha's watchdog.

"Don't worry, she's just behind us," she says anyway. "She was on the bus, but avoided us on the way back. We kept being deliberately slow to annoy her – ha ha, she should have jogged ahead! Anyway, she'll be here any minute ..."

Sure enough, the door swings open, and Martha appears. She's wrapped up in Kate's Glastonbury hoodie, which seems to do a constant jig between the two of us, and her long black hair has been whipped around her face by the wind. She nods in our direction, at least acknowledging our existence, before dropping her bag onto the pile and heading for the toilet. Teenagers. You will know them by the trail of their backpacks.

I'm relieved she's here, but also sad to see her like this.

There's just no joy left in her. No, not joy ... she hasn't had any of that since Kate got ill. There's no *anything* left in her. Not even fight – or at least that's what it feels like to me.

"You need to give her a bit of time," says Lizzie, patting my hand like she's my mum. "It's hard, what she's been through. And moving here when she didn't really want to – that takes a lot of getting used to, it makes you feel so angry. And it's harder for her – at least when my dad died, I still had my Mum. Martha, well, she's only got –"

She trails off, looking flustered, as she realises that what she was about to say might be construed as vaguely insulting. I laugh, and shake my head to show her I'm not. Insulted, that is.

"Yeah. I know. She's only got me. I'm doing my best, but ... well, you're right. I need to give her some time."

Martha emerges from the ladies with slightly more organ-ised hair, and minus the hoodie. Underneath she's wearing a David Bowie T-shirt that I think is actually mine, but now doesn't seem to be the time to cause a scene. I'll just steal it back next time it's in the wash, which may or may not be within the next year.

Predictably enough, she ignores us, and instead perches herself on a stool by the counter, where she proceeds to read a copy of King Lear. She's come to the café, straight from college, as I requested, and now she's doing school work. I can hardly complain, can I?

I try not to stare at her, and look around the room instead.

I notice that Midgebo, maybe hoping to make up for the crushing disappointment of the cider bottle stash, has headed for the pile of discarded teenagers' backpacks. He starts to rummage, burying his furry black nose into the mound of canvas, using his paws to dig as though he's looking for a bone.

Laura emerges from the kitchen, her face rosy and a three-foot halo of frizzy hair around her face, to see what's going on.

"Midge! Bad dog!" she says, her heart clearly not in it. It's almost impossible to chastise Midegbo, he's so appealing.

The dog looks at her briefly, tongue panting out from his excavations, then goes immediately back to it. Eventually, after an especially determined tunnelling, he emerges with his prize.

A now battered packet of Marlboro Lights.

He runs around the room with them in his mouth, scattering half-bitten cigs all over the place, ragging the packet back and forth like it's a chew toy. Laura grabs hold of his collar, and tells him repeatedly to drop. He repeatedly ignores her, mashing and shaking the pack until it is showering them both with tobacco and mushed up paper.

Eventually, she manages to wrangle them out of his grip, and is left with the soggy remnants held in her hands. Everyone is watching, most people trying not to laugh.

"I thought he was on the nicotine patches?" says Becca from her bean bag, which is enough to push everyone over the edge.

Everyone except me, of course. And Martha, who is looking on in absolute horror. She notices my expression, and immediately pretends to be engrossed in King Lear again. Lizzie, sitting next to me, obviously sees this silent exchange.

"They were mine!" she says, jumping up to her feet and shouting it to the rooftops. "Those cigarettes – they were mine! I only tried one, and I didn't like it, and I won't do it again, but … they were mine, honest!"

Everyone is now looking at Lizzie. Becca is smiling, in a 'yeah, right' kind of way. Cherie has emerged from the kitchen to see what the fuss is about, a tea towel slung over a shoulder and hands on her hips. Laura looks strangely proud, considering her daughter's shock announcement.

Or maybe it's not so strange, I decide. Because every single person in this room knows – with the possible exception of Nate, who is looking a bit confused – that those cigarettes do not belong to Lizzie. Every single person in this room knows that they actually belong to Martha, and Lizzie was simply engaging in some mis-guided attempt to protect her from my wrath.

Funnily enough, though, I'm not actually feeling that wrathful. I'm actually feeling ever-so-slightly hopeful. Because I am looking at Martha. Who is looking at Lizzie. And actually smiling.

Chapter 13

I fall into a rhythm over the next few days. A pleasant one. I get up with Martha, drop her in the village, and watch her get onto the bus, then go and walk, sometimes for hours. For two days in a row now, she's actually gone and sat near Lizzie and her gang – not next to them, but close enough that they can talk, and lend each other their ear-phones. Small steps, but steps in the right direction at least.

And last night, we had a minor breakthrough on the domestic front. Martha cooked dinner. Only beans on toast, admittedly, but she did it voluntarily, and joined me at the dining room table while we ate. I learned a tiny bit more about her school life, and by the end of one stilted conversation, felt on top of the world. Things have been so uncomfortable between us recently that even that small gesture was enough to lift my spirits.

I even purposely instigated a minor tussle over ownership of the David Bowie T-shirt, just for kicks. There was a flash of her old fire, I got the T-shirt thrown in my face, and I was smiling beneath it – it felt more like old times. Even she was trying to hide a grin by the time she went to bed.

After I've dropped her off, I traipse across the clifftop paths, looking down at the sea from my hillside perch, breathing in the now cool air and watching life unfold on the beach. Sam, who is a coastal ranger, has given me a little spotters' guide that details local plants and birds and wildlife, and I amuse myself by learning their weird names and figuring out the different types of gull and keeping a sharp look-out for migrating chiffchaffs and spotted flycatchers.

The weather is hovering between a few final sunny days, and full-on autumn. The sky can darken quite suddenly, and it's fascinating to watch the changing shades out over the bay, sunlight sweeping into sulky grey, the colour of the water changing with it.

Today, it looks like all hell is about to let loose. The sky is already almost black, the wind is fierce, and there's an ominous sense of pressure in the air. The rain is coming in short, vicious bursts, and the atmosphere has that pent-up feeling it gets before a humdinger of a storm. The ground is muddy, and I consider getting some proper walking boots. Maybe some of those fancy walking poles with spikes on the bottom – they'd make great murder weapons as well. Just in case.

I sit for a few moments at my favourite spot – a bench on the next bend along from the cafe – and survey my new empire. I'm genuinely excited to see the seasons unfold; to watch the colours shift and the nights close in and maybe, if we're lucky, the snow come down and turn the whole place into a winter wonderland.

We've signed up for the cottage for six months, so should be here for Christmas ... wow. Christmas. I'm actually sitting here, perched on my bench, wrapped up in three layers of fleece, imagining our first Christmas in Budbury. Not just our first Christmas in Budbury – our first Christmas without Kate.

Last Christmas had been awful. Kate had a mastectomy a week before, and as soon as she felt even marginally better after that, started chemo. Being Kate, she'd planned ahead, and there were gifts under the tree for both of us on Christmas morning. Kate herself had felt too sick to eat our festive lunch, or maybe she was just pretending – I'd cooked it, and discovered I could even ruin Marks and Sparks ready meals. What can I say? It's a gift.

Now, I need to start thinking ahead. I mean, what would I get for Martha? What do you give the girl who has nothing? I start to turn a few ideas over in my mind as I pack up my mini-binoculars – also a gift from Sam – and make my way across the coastal path towards the cafe. The storm is coming in thick and fast, and I almost expect to see a Hollywood-style twister hovering over the bay.

I visit the cafe most mornings, spending time there with Laura and whoever else is passing by. Sometimes it's tourists, or early-bird walkers. Sometimes it's locals – often Katie and her little boy Saul; often Frank and Cherie, eating breakfast together while they browse the papers.

Sometimes it's Scrumpy Joe, grabbing coffee and home-made biscotti before a busy day at work in the cider cave, and sometimes others – Ivy Wellkettle, who runs the local pharmacy, or Edie May, my book-reading buddy.

The faces change daily, but one thing always remains the same: I am welcomed there as though I am part of the family. It is taking a little getting used to – I've never been part of a real family, apart from mine and Kate's strangely-shaped version of one – and at first, I was worried. Concerned that I'd outstay my welcome, that they were just pretending to like me, that it would all fall apart.

I am at least old enough and ugly enough to recognise these paranoid thoughts for what they are: phantoms from my childhood, hangovers from years of being the odd one out. They have no place in my new reality, and I fight them off with the mental equivalent of flame throwers. Enough things can go wrong in life, I know, without creating crises of your own making.

Today, when I arrive at the cafe, soaked to the bone from the now-constant sheets of rain, I see the usual mixed bunch.

Laura waves from behind the counter, steam rising from the coffee machine and fluffing up her already enormous hair, and Edie is perched on a tall chair opposite her. She has a collection of felt tip pens and one of those adult colouring books spread out on the surface, and is concentrating hard on shading in a pattern made up entirely of Siamese cats.

Frank is at a small table alone, dressed in his usual farmer-about-town outfit of checked shirt and heavy gauge cords, his silver hair neatly trimmed and a burnt bacon buttie in front of him. He nods, and lifts one finger – the countryside equivalent of a full-on hug.

"Wicked storm on the way, mark my words," he says, shaking his head wisely. I'm not impressed with his prediction – even I could have come up with that one, I think, as I hang my dripping coat up.

Becca is there, on her bean bag, vast and swollen and miserable looking. She gives me a small wave then goes back to her book, which I see is called *Parenting for Dummies*. She's crossed out the 'Dummies' and scrawled the word 'Becca' on the cover instead, in black marker pen.

On another table, I see Willow, pink hair tied up in a short, scruffy pony, dressed in an outfit that wouldn't look out of place on the set of Star Wars, wearing silver spray-painted Doc Marten boots with untied ribbons instead of laces. She's with her mum, Lynnie, who has wild grey hair and is wrapped up in her dressing gown. I glance at her feet and see she has muddy tartan slippers on.

I feel a tug of quiet sympathy, and go over to say hello. I can guess what's happened, as Laura has already warned me about it. Lynnie, who suffers from Alzheimer's, occasionally wakes up before Willow and decides to go walkabout. Sometimes she goes to the Community Hall, where she used to hold yoga classes, and sometimes she goes to a place only known to me as the House on the Hill, which was formerly some kind of private children's home where she used to teach art and crafts and meditation. Other times, she heads straight for the cafe – as most people around here seem to.

Willow looks tired, and her eyes are red and puffy. Poor thing. She tries a smile when she sees me, and I pat her on the shoulder, nodding to Lynnie as well. I've never actually met her before, and I'm not sure what to expect.

I'm pretty sure that what I don't expect is for her to reach out and grab my hand, and I jump a little as she does, luckily damping down my natural instinct to lash out at her surprise touch.

"Auburn!" she says, sounding way more delighted to see me than most people ever do. "Come and sit with us – this lovely girl here is telling me all about her dog, Bella Swan! Apparently, she's named after some character from a movie about vampires, would you believe? And she's a border terrier, just like our Pickle!"

I glance at Willow, who nods at me, exhausted. I do as I'm told, and sit, while Laura appears behind me and places a mug of coffee and a plate of buttered toast on the table. I see the remnants of the same in front of Willow and her mum. Outside, the rain is clawing at the window pane, as though it's testing it for weaknesses and trying to find a way in. All the lights are on in the cafe now, it's so gloomy outside.

"This isn't Auburn, mum," says Willow, gently. "This is Zoe. She's just moved here, with her … step-daughter Martha."

I feel the familiar prickle of tension when she says that.

Nobody ever knows how to define my relationship with Martha, including us.

"You have a sister called Auburn?" I ask, deflecting attention from the momentary awkwardness.

"Yes," says Willow, smiling. "Mum had a tendency to name her children when they were born, depending on how they looked."

"Not just how they looked, how their spirits felt," adds Lynnie, looking confused, as though she's trying to figure out how Willow knows all of this, and whether she should be alarmed by it.

Willow nods, pats her hand, and continues: "I was long and lean, you see."

"You still are," I add, pointing at her supermodel-long legs.

"Indeed I am. So I got Willow. Auburn had hair exactly like yours, even in the baby photos she looks like her head's on fire. My brother Angel looked like a cherub, so that's fairly self-explanatory. The oldest had a weird ear, I'm told – he got a bit squashed during the delivery – so he ended up with Van, after Van Gogh."

"Right," I say, nodding as though all of that makes perfect sense – which it does, in its own way – "and where are they all now?"

"On their journeys to self-enlightenment!" pipes in Lynnie, looking proud. Willow just raises her eyebrows, and I decide that's a conversation for another day. They might be climbing Machu Pichu or finding their zen in a Tibetan monastery, or they could be working in Matalan. Who knows? Either way, poor Willow has, for some reason or another, ended up staying here, caring for her mother alone. It is a stark and painful reality, and my heart contracts for her – my mum just acted as though I didn't exist; Willow's doesn't even seem to know who she is. I don't know which is worse.

I eat my toast and drink my coffee, and we chat about the weather and plans for Halloween, and make suitably 'ooh, it'll be Christmas before we know it' noises, trying to behave normally in the most abnormal of situations.

Frank occasionally snorts about something he's read in the paper; I can hear Edie chirruping away to Laura, and Becca … well, she's pretty quiet, apart from the odd moan and groan. I glance over after one especially audible grunt, and wonder if she's all right. She's holding her sides with her hands, and her face is screwed up with pain. She's dropped the Parenting for Becca book on the floor, possibly in disgust.

I walk over and pick it up, noting that several of the pages have been scrawled over with highlighter pen and tabbed with fluorescent post-its.

I squat down next to her, and hand her back the book. She clutches it so tightly I hear a few of the pages tear.

"You all right?" I ask, gently, not wanting to draw attention to her. She's clearly trying to become invisible, which will be quite the task as she is the size of a baby elephant.

"Yep," she puffs out, as though even speaking is tricky. "Just having some of those practice contraction thingies ... Braxton-Hicks, I think they're called ..."

She bites her lip, and I see that her pale face is coated in a light sheen of sweat. Her long dark hair is tied back into a messy pony tail, loose tendrils escaping and tumbling over her shoulders.

"Okay," I reply, casting my mind back all those years ago, to the day Kate went into labour. We were only kids ourselves – 22 – and thought it was all an exciting adventure. Right up until the moment the screaming agony hit, and then it became ever-so-slightly less fun.

Becca is starting to turn slightly green now, wriggling around on the bean bag as she tries to find a comfortable spot for the bowling-ball shaped wedge in her stomach.

"Do you mind me asking, Becca," I say, reaching out to tuck damp hair behind her ear, "how often you've been having these practice contractions for?"

"Um ... I don't know. Not long. It's nothing to worry about. It'll pass."

"I'm sure it will. But when did they start?"

"About two this morning. Sam was fast asleep so I went downstairs and drank milk. Felt like punching him in the face when he got up, all bright eyed and bushy tailed and ... thin!"

"Yeah. I can imagine. You showed amazing restraint. I'd probably have decked him. So, have they carried on since then? And are they ... I don't know, getting closer in time or anything?"

I try to keep my tone even as I ask this question, but she is a sharp cookie. She glares up at me, and snaps: "I'm fine! I know what you're thinking, and I'm not in labour! I can't be – I'd know if I was! I'm ... I'm not *ready*!"

As she shrieks that last word, there is a terrific rumble of thunder as the storm finally breaks, a deep, vibrato cracking sound that is followed almost immediately by a sharp flash of lightning. It illuminates Becca's pained face, and I realise we are in the eye of the storm in more ways than one.

She grabs hold of my hand, and squeezes my fingers so tightly I know for sure I'll never play the violin again. The wave of pain whooshing through her is clearly so intense she momentarily loses control, and lets out a small howl.

Frank looks up over his paper, his bright blue eyes concerned; Edie and Laura stop their chatter and stare at us, and Willow and Lynnie turn around to get a better look.

I see Laura wipe her hands on a tea towel before she scurries over. She's wearing an apron with Superman's body on it, and a slogan that says: "Supercook."

"What's going on?" she asks, sounding understandably concerned. "Becca, are you all right?"

"No, I'm not bloody all right!" her sister screeches back at her, all pretense at quiet gone now. "I'm having these stupid Braxton Hicks things and it kills!"

I meet Laura's eyes, and shake my head.

"She's been having these Braxton Hicks things since the

early hours, and they seem to be coming every couple of minutes," I say. Laura rolls her eyes, and squats down on the floor next to Becca.

"Sweetie, you're in labour," she says calmly. "The baby is coming, and we probably need to get you to hospital."

"I don't want to go to hospital! I want to stay here. And I want Sam. And ... oh shit ... oh no ... Laura, I think I've just wet myself! What's happening to me?"

"Your waters have broken, love. It's perfectly normal, don't worry. You're going to have to take those leggings off, all right? We don't want your baby's first view of the world to be a lycra-mix gusset now, do we?"

The small crowd in the cafe draws closer, and I feel a rush of sympathy for the poor woman at the centre of it all. I know, from talking to Laura, that Becca has a chequered history with drugs and health.

Since she quit drinking, smoking and pretty much everything else a few years ago, she's instead been addicted to abstaining – refusing to even take a paracetamol for a headache, or a Strepsil for a sore throat. I can completely see why she's been ignoring the signs, and avoiding going to hospital, where she fears they will pump her full of lovely drugs and spoil her track record. As a result, she's left it too late – and we all know what is going to happen next.

Edie has been on the phone already, and jumps down from her stool in an astonishingly limber way for a woman of her age.

"There's been a pile-up near Dorchester, because of the storm," she says, frowning so hard her entire face becomes one big crease. "Tractor overturned. Ambulances might be scarce to come by, so they suggested we get her into a car and take her to the hospital as soon as we can – as long as it's safe to drive. It's not looking that safe out there ..."

We all glance at the windows, at the blackened sky, the gushing rain, and the whole world feels like it's shaking from the power of the wind. It doesn't feel safe – it feels like we might all wake up in Oz.

Becca reaches up and clasps hold of Edie's papery-thin hand. I hope she doesn't squeeze hers as hard as mine, or her bird-like bones will turn to dust.

"Edie! I can't do this!" she whispers, as though nobody else can hear. As though she's not the star attraction, surrounded by worried faces. As though tiny little Edie May is the most powerful being in the entire universe.

Edie leans down and kisses the side of Becca's sweaty face, and pats her damp hair.

"Of course you can, child," she says, reassuringly. "You're my beautiful Becca. You can do absolutely anything, can't you? Think of everything you've gone through. Everything you've survived. And think of this gorgeous new life you're bringing into the world, for you and for Sam and for all of us. And think about the next episode of Strictly – by then, this will all be done with, and we'll be watching it together, tucked up under a blanket with a nice mug of tea!"

Becca mutters something dark and threatening about Anton du Beke, and let's go of Edie's hand. The pep talk seems to have calmed her down a little, and she gulps in some fast breaths.

I'm aware of the group huddling around us now, and wonder if we should be doing something like boiling water or fetching towels, like they always seem to do in TV shows.

"Can you get to the car?" I ask, looking at Becca doubtfully. "We could probably carry you, between us ..."

"NO!!!" yells Becca, loud enough that the word probably reaches all the way to Cornwall. "No! I can't walk, and you're not carrying me, and I don't want to go to hospital! I never wanted to go to hospital ... I'll be fine ... I've read all about this ..."

Laura is shuffling around at the bottom end of things, tugging Becca's leggings off as discretely as she can.

"I know you don't want to go to hospital," she says patiently to her sister. "And I'm not bloody surprised that it's come to this. You were never going to do this the easy way, were you? Now, for God's sake, what do you expect us to do?"

"I expect you to help me have this bloody baby!" grunts Becca, rolling around, holding her stomach. "Where's Matt? He can do it!"

"Matt's in Charmouth delivering a litter of pug puppies. And even if he was here, he's a vet, not a doctor, you daft cow!"

"Ha! I wish I was a cow, this would be so much easier ... Frank! Where's Frank?

"I'm here, darling," he says, shuffling forward, looking slightly embarrassed by the whole affair. "What do you need?"

"Frank," says Becca, panting in gusts of air while she's between contractions, "you're a farmer. You have cows and sheep and stuff. You must have delivered babies before now. You can help me, right?"

He scratches his silver hair, and frowns, and gives it some thought.

"Weeeellll ... it's a fair bit different at the working end of a ewe, Becca. And I don't reckon you'd like it much if I tied a rope round it's hooves and pulled it out of you ..."

"Hooves! It won't have hooves for fuck's sake! It's a baby ... and ... oh, God ... this hurts so much!"

"Right," he says, paling slightly beneath his outdoorsman tan. "I'll go and look for Sam, then ..."

He turns and legs it, preferring the storm outside to the storm inside.

We're all frozen and useless, standing around waiting for someone to take charge. Laura, who has had two babies herself, seems to be veering between calm and supportive and completely freaking out. Edie is back on the phone to the ambulance people, who have offered to 'talk us through it', and I'm mentally preparing myself to be an impromptu midwife.

Leadership, when it finally comes, arrives in an unlikely form.

Chapter 14

Grey-haired, dressing-gown clad Lynnie moves forward, and pushes her way past us. She crouches straight down onto the floor, and without hesitation gets a full eyeful of what's going on. The rest of us have been cringing, reluctant to get too close. I for one had visions of a slippery space alien shooting out like a bullet, and me failing to catch it. I'd forever be the Woman Who Dropped The Baby.

"Okay, dear," Lynnie says, when she emerges again. "Not too long to go now. You've clearly been labouring well all day, so you're a natural at this. I can see the crown of the baby's head, and I'm going to need you to stay calm. I need you to focus on your breathing, for me – can you do that? Take a nice, long, deep breath in through your nose – count for four – and a nice long deep breath out of your mouth."

Becca clutches onto her, and nods. She starts breathing in, while Lynnie does a slow count, and I notice that we are all doing it along with them. All of us – Frank, Edie, Laura, Willow – are joining in. It probably does us all some good.

The calm is offset slightly by the fact that as we finish our count, another ominous roll of thunder crashes the room. Childbirth during the Apocalypse.

"When the waves of pain come, dear," says Lynnie, encouraging Becca up into a more comfortable position, "I want you to welcome them. Welcome them, because with each contraction, the miracle of your new baby is getting closer ... breathe, now. That's it. One, two, three, four ..."

As we all inhale, I see the door to the cafe slung open, and Sam comes running towards us, Frank on his heels. He's dressed in his usual ranger gear of khaki fleece and multi-pocketed trousers, and his blonde hair is dripping from the rain. He pauses, takes in the scene, and allows himself a moment of pure panic before he dashes into the fray.

They're followed straight into the cafe by another man – tall, blonde, wearing jeans and bizarrely some kind of cowboy hat. If he's a random passing customer looking for some carrot cake and tea, he's in for quite a surprise. His face is largely in shadow, but I look on as he assesses the situation, listens to Becca's groans, and calmly takes off his sodden hat. He lays it on a table, and strides towards us.

"Get some boiling water and some towels," he says, firmly. I'm so relieved to hear someone finally say it, I barely register the fact that he has a foreign accent. Instead, I join Willow in a mad dash to the kitchen.

He is crouching down between Becca's legs, without a shadow of embarrassment. Lynnie stays by her side, holding her hand and counting her breath in and out, keeping not just Becca but everyone else steady. Sam is on the other side, stroking her forehead and whispering encouraging words. I can't help but smile as I hear Becca unleash a striking tirade of foul language on him just after he says he loves her.

"This is all your penis' fault! I'm going to chop it off when this is all over!" she shrieks. Frank creases up at that one, and comes over to help us bring over the supplies. I've also found a packet of ibuprofen in the knife drawer, and wave them vaguely in front of Becca's face, asking if she wants any. It's not gas and air – or a lovely epidural – but maybe it's better than nothing.

She scrunches up her eyes, as though pretending the tablets aren't there, and shakes her head to say no. Crikey. She really is hardcore.

The blonde man dips his hands in the hot water, flinching as he realises that it really is boiling, but manfully resisting the urge to cry. He leans down to take another look, and then gives Becca a big, crooked grin. There's a scar down one side of his face that makes him look a bit like a pirate, especially when the lightning strikes.

"All right, beautiful – here he comes. Or she, who knows? Either way, this baby wants out ... and we're going to get the job done, okay? Next contraction, I want you to push, yeah? Hard as you can. Real hard ... and keep pushing, with each contraction, 'til I tell you to stop!"

Becca nods, and does as she's told. I've no idea who this man is, maybe the local doctor who I've not had a chance to meet, but he's definitely a godsend. The rest of us would probably still have been googling 'how to deliver a baby in a cafe' by now.

"Come on now ..." he says, patting her leg reassuringly, "You can do better than that – give it a bit of welly!"

Becca screws up her face, her cheeks puffing out and going bright red, making her head look like a giant balloon that could pop at any minute. She pushes, and I think we all push a little with her. I know Laura does, I can practically see her doing it, sitting off to the side, her nostrils white and her Supercook apron all askew.

"Head's out. That's the hardest bit, love. One more time, my beauty, and we'll have ourselves a baby ..." says the man, lying flat on the floor, and getting stuck in.

Becca gives a huge yell, and we all hear a weird squelching noise as the baby plops out. The bloke on the floor takes it into big hands, announces that it's a girl, then quickly wraps her up in a towel, rubbing her a little until she cries.

It's a loud cry, making itself heard over the thunder. Something about it – that angry, desperate yowl – breaks the tension, and the relief in the room is something you can almost touch. There's a baby. And it's alive. And it's crying.

So am I, I realise, as I watch Becca take her baby into her arms. There's still stuff going on down there – I remember this part from Kate and Martha, just when you think it's time for cigars all round, it's actually time for after-birth and stitches – but for the next few moments, we're all just thrilled.

I'm not the only one feeling tearful, I notice, as I look around the room. Laura is in pieces, openly sobbing as she scoots across the floor to get a closer look, and Frank is wiping his eyes and trying to look masculine while he does it. Sam is repeatedly kissing the baby and Becca and even Lynnie, who is looking at it all so calmly you can't imagine that just minutes ago she didn't even know her own daughter.

Edie does a little trot over to us, holding the phone in her hand, and triumphantly shouting: "They'll be here in ten minutes! I told them she was having triplets and they started getting a bit more concerned!"

We all laugh at that, and I edge forward to get my first proper look at the baby. Still wrapped in a towel and attached to the cord, I can see dark brown tufts of moist hair sticking up from her scalp. Her eyes are open, and are a dazzling shade of blue, just like her dad's. Her skin is soft and looks as though it would be furry to the touch, and one tiny hand is out in the air, clutching at nothing, perfect little fingernails on the end of perfect little fingers.

Becca is in floods of tears, with joy or the relief of the pain being over or maybe both. She's never struck me as a crier before – she's a tough old city girl like myself, except her and Laura grew up in Manchester – and it's strangely moving to see her give in to it all.

I feel privileged to be here, with these people, in this one miraculous moment. The happiness I feel all around me completely eclipses my own worries, my anxiety about Martha, the pain of missing Kate – instead, I feel wrapped up in the communal celebration, like I'm coated in a fleecy blanket made entirely of hope. The storm can just bugger off. Nothing can ruin this.

Lynnie leans over to stroke the baby's delicate face with a gentle hand, and smiles.

"She's so soft and furry. You should call her Peach," she announces to Becca and Sam.

"That's a lovely name," replies Becca, gazing into her daughter's face. "But Sam and I have already decided what she'll be called, haven't we?"

Sam nods, unable to take his eyes away from his new daughter's face.

"Yes," he replies, looking up briefly, seeking out the person he wants to tell most. "Everyone – meet our daughter. Edie Theresa."

Chapter 15

Edie is thoroughly delighted, and takes off her specs to wipe her eyes. As far as I can tell she has no children of her own, although she does have a small tribe of nieces and nephews and grand nieces and nephews. This obviously means the world to her, and she is spluttering with happiness by the time the ambulance people finally arrive, the door crashing open in the wind.

They scurry into the room, carrying bags and equipment and looking reassuringly competent while they examine both Becca and the baby.

"What's her Apgar score?" Becca asks, while one of them gently takes Little Edie from her arms to check her over. That Parenting for Becca book has clearly been doing the trick.

"It'll be great," says the paramedic, a small, round blonde woman, "I can already tell she's perfect. There only seems to be one baby, though, not triplets, unless there's something you're not telling us ..."

She looks around the room, as though searching for hidden

babies, and Edie waves her wrinkled little hand apologetically.

"Sorry! That's my fault ... I'm 91, you know, my dear ... and I do get confused!"

We all bite back a snort at that one – Edie's one of the least confused people I've ever met. The paramedic shrugs, and goes back to her work.

"Well, you've all done a great job here," she says, "but we should get mum and baby back to the hospital for a once over from the maternity team."

"I don't want to go to hospital!" wails Becca, and we all pull a communal face. I'm beginning to suspect that even if Becca lost an arm in a tragic combine harvester accident, she'd want to stay at home and superglue it back on.

"I reckon you probably need to, love," says the blonde pirate hero baby deliverer. "I'm not a craftsman when it comes to these things, and I think you need a bit of attention down below, if you get my drift."

Becca makes a long 'uggh' noise, and grits her teeth.

"Oh shit," she says, trying to crane her head so she can get a look at 'down below' – something I've been studiously avoiding doing. "Do I need stitches? Am I going to end up with a Frankenstein fanny? Sam, will you still love me if I do?"

Sam is laughing openly, and the rest of us are trying not to. He kisses her, properly, on the lips, and replies: "Course I will. Even if you end up with bolts through it."

"Hopefully it won't come to that," chips in the paramedic, preparing a stretcher to pile our new mum onto. "It'll be a work of art. Better than new."

Laura emerges from the kitchen with a set of scales. Those old-fashioned ones, with a big, enamel basin in a pretty shade of pastel green. She lays a tea towel over it so it's not cold, and raises her eyebrows at the paramedic.

She nods, smiling, and places Little Edie into the cradle, where she kicks her chubby legs and pokes her arms around. We all look on as the needle hovers and jerks and finally settles.

"9lb 2 oz!" shrieks Laura in astonishment. "She's an absolute whopper! I'm so proud of you, sis!"

We all chirp in with words of amazement and congratulations, while Becca, the baby and Sam are finally made ready to make the move to a slightly more clinical environment.

It's wild outside, but none of us care. We crowd around them, waving them off as they make their way down the hill via the longer path that is paved for wheelchairs and prams. Becca waves back, one solitary hand gesture, like she's the Queen bidding a fond farewell to her subjects. Little Edie lets out a long, powerful howl, and the sound echoes back up to the top of the cliff.

We gaze after them for a few moments, hair blowing, teeth chattering, watching as they are loaded up into the ambulance. Wow, I think, as the van doors slam shut. I'd heard that phrase about it taking a village to raise a child. Little Edie had a head

143

start – it took a village to deliver her. The ambulance engine starts, and they finally drive away. We carry on staring, long after its exhaust trail has disappeared, snatched up by the gale.

Edie finally breaks the spell, dashing back into the cafe, collecting all her pens and colouring books, stashing them in the fluorescent orange Vans backpack she takes everywhere with her. Not your typical old lady gear, but then again nothing about Edie is typical.

She hooks it onto her deceptively frail shoulders, and gives us all a dazzling grin.

"I must make a move!" she announces, heading for the doors.

"Edie, it's awful out there – wait a while!" I say, frowning in concern. She's only tiny. We may never see her again.

"Pah! I've weathered worse storms than this!" she snaps back. "And I can't wait to tell my fiancé all about this …"

As she exits, I feel the familiar confused frown forming on my forehead. I've heard Edie refer to her 'fiancé' several times now, and she always seems to take home an extra portion of cafe treats when she leaves. Laura often has it ready packed in small foil boxes, waiting to be carted home to her tiny terrace in the village.

"What's the score with Edie's fiancé?" I finally say, looking at Laura and Frank for answers. "She's always talking about him, and takes food home for him, but I've never met him. And isn't she a bit on the senior side to have a fiancé – why don't they just bite the bullet and get married?"

Laura exchanges glances with Frank, who makes a 'you tell her gesture' with his hands.

"Right," says Laura, as she bustles about clearing up towels and the kitchen scales, "well. The score with Edie's fiancé is that he died during the Second World War. He's called Bert, and he's actually dead. To everyone apart from Edie, that is."

Okay. I turn that over in my mind, while Laura waits slightly nervously for my reaction. I just nod, and try not to look at all freaked out.

Truth be told, I'm not. Edie's delusion – apparently enabled by everyone in the entire village – does no harm to anybody, and obviously keeps a wonderful old lady very happy. I'm down with that, as the kids say.

I suddenly realise, as I go to help Laura with the clean-up job, why I like it so much here. Why I seem to fit in, in a way I've never felt before.

It's because they're all as mad as I am.

Chapter 16

I'm fully expecting that to be the end of the drama for the day, as nothing could possibly top the impromptu delivery of a baby during an extinction-level storm.

Laura has produced a bottle of Bucks Fizz, and is pouring us all glasses. She's paired it with freshly baked apple and cinnamon muffins, and it's a tremendous way to celebrate.

Frank and Laura spend a few minutes informing various people – Matt, Cherie, Laura's parents – about the arrival of Little Edie, and Willow is sitting with her mum in a window seat. The storm is clearing as quickly as it started now, and streaks of pale yellow sunlight are breaking through the clouds in the baby's honour, casting glittering stripes over the waves that are rolling into the bay.

I take a muffin and a glass, and sit down with them. Lynnie is breaking small lumps of muffin away, eating with delicate precision. I don't know how she manages it – they're so delicious that I have to fight the urge to stuff the whole thing in my mouth at once.

"Of course," she says, as though she's continuing a conversation that none of us have been having, "after my children were born, I fried up their placentas, and ate them. Jam-packed with nutrients, you know, and a little like liver when you cook them with onions ..."

The muffin suddenly tastes a lot less delicious, and I take a gulp of the Buck Fizz instead. Willow grimaces, and does the same. Lynnie continues to munch away, completely unaware of the fact that she's made us both feel slightly nauseous.

"Where's the hero of the day gone?" asks Frank, standing behind us and looking out of the window.

"Well he's not out there," I reply. "Unless he can fly as well."

"I wouldn't be surprised," shouts Laura from the counter. "He definitely seemed to have superpowers. Looked a bit like Thor as well ..."

She gazes off into the distance as she says this, her hands pausing mid swipe with the tea towel, and I suspect she's gone to her happy place.

I look around the cafe, trying to locate our mystery midwife, and now also feeling very curious, as none of the locals seem to know who he is either. I'd been working on the assumption that he was from Budbury, but it appears that I was wrong.

Just as I'm starting to think we all hallucinated him, he emerges from the gents – where, understandably enough, he seems to have gone to clean up. Childbirth. It may be a miracle of nature – but it ain't pretty. That bean bag will definitely be taking a one-way trip to the rubbish dump, that's for sure.

As soon as the door to the gents' shuts behind him, Laura is out from behind the counter, and on him like cling film. She wraps him up in a huge hug, squeezing him so hard he pulls a pained face. He's quite a lot taller than her, and he rests his chin in the fuzz of her curls until she finally lets him go.

She stands back and looks up at him, blushing. Maybe it's those Thor thoughts coming back to haunt her.

"Thank you," she says, eventually. "For everything. I don't know what we'd have done without you."

"I reckon you'd have done just fine, love," he says, grinning. "I was just there to catch. Done it a couple of times before – I live in the back end of nowhere, and the odd medical emergency isn't uncommon. I'm your man for a dislocated shoulder as well."

"And where are you from? And what's your name? And why are you here?" she says, in a rush of questions. Makes her sound like a bit of a nutter, but to be fair we're all wondering the same.

"Thought you'd have recognised the accent by now ..." he replies, strolling over to recover his cowboy hat. "Although I have only lived there since I was 8. Would it help if I called you a Sheila?"

Laura laughs, the starry-eyed look going nowhere fast as she watches him. I can see where she's coming from. He's tall, is indeed built like a superhero, and has the wavy blonde hair of a surfer. His eyes are a deep shade of brown, and the scar

149

on his face does little to make him less attractive. He also, I start to realise as soon as he lays on the accent a little thicker, looks vaguely familiar.

Before I can quite put my finger on it, he strides over to our table, nodding to Lynnie and Willow, then fixing his eyes on me. I gulp slightly, and worry that I'm about to choke on my last piece of apple muffin. I might spit it all over him, then knock over my glass of Bucks Fizz – classic me stylings.

"Am I right in thinking you're Zoe?" he asks, smiling at my confusion. "I've only seen photos, and the odd glimpse of you in the background on Skype, but that hair of yours is a pretty distinctive trademark."

He holds out his hand for me to shake, and I'm now aware that absolutely everyone else in the cafe has stopped eating, drinking, and possibly breathing, while they watch this new scene unfold. I reward them by doing my very best goldfish impression.

"I'm Cal," he says, taking my hand from the table and shaking it without any participation from me. "Martha's dad."

Chapter 17

Now, of course, I understand the flip side to sharing in the joys and triumphs of the folk at the Comfort Food Café. They also get to share in my floundering.

I feel like a flaming idiot, and probably look like one, as I can feel my whole face exploding into the blush to end all blushes. Luckily I'm wearing a jumper, or the whole world would get to see the fact that when I blush, it goes all the way down my neck and blossoms in bright scarlet flashes on my chest. It's super-attractive, one of my very best features.

Cal stands before me, in all his glory, and I have the urge to slap myself on the side of the head and let out a Simpsons-style: 'Duh!'

Why hadn't I realised? Why hadn't I recognised the accent and put two and two together? Why hadn't I recognised *him*, never mind the accent? It had been pretty chaotic, and we were all concentrating more on Becca than the mystery man, but still ... I should have known.

Laura is watching with interest, frowning, obviously

confused, as though she's wondering exactly the same thing. This must all look incredibly weird from the outside looking in.

In reality, it's not that surprising – it's not like me and Cal have ever met, or been in especially close contact. Kate came home from her backpacking adventure to Thailand with a bad case of athlete's foot, some wonky carvings of elephants, and a baby in her belly. This was before the days when everything was digital, and she only had a couple of blurry photos of the man who was generous enough to give her the third item on that list. Although I use the term 'man' loosely, as he was only 19 at the time.

Kate herself had been as blurry as the photos when it came to her recollections of the encounter that would not only change her life, but create an entirely new one.

All she could really remember was that he was Aussie, blonde, drop-dead gorgeous, and a great shag. Obviously the final description has never been repeated to Martha, for fear of making her vomit.

Kate had a home address and phone number for him, but knew they weren't much use as he was continuing on his travels and wasn't sure where he was going to land next. He was following his wild streak, and we later pieced together that it led him to Vietnam, Cambodia, India and – bizarrely – Florida before it eventually took him back home to the land of Oz.

It was there – when Martha was two – that Kate finally

tracked him down. Previously, if she'd called and asked for him, she put on some phony accent and pretended she was trying to sell him double glazing. His poor parents must have wondered what the hell was going on, and started to lose their rag after the third time, when they'd already asked to be taken off the sales list twice.

After that, she was more honest – saying she was an old friend who'd lost touch with him on his travels and was wondering when he would be back. They never knew, and it was obvious that he hadn't kept them especially well-briefed on his whereabouts either. Often they weren't even sure what country he was currently in.

And, you know, she couldn't really leave a message – 'could you please tell him hi from Kate, who he met in the Rubber Pearl Bar in Bangkok, and also that he has a daughter?' It wasn't the kind of thing you could pass on third hand.

When she did finally call and find him at home, I think she was as surprised as he was. I suspect she'd always thought it would never happen, and wasn't in the slightest bit bothered – by that point, Barbara and Ron had gotten over their mass hysteria, completely won over by baby Martha's charms, and we'd all found a groove that worked for us. She didn't want anything from him – not money, or time, or for him to share the burden. She just thought he had a right to know.

He'd wanted to come to the UK straight away, once he picked himself up of the floor, but she'd persuaded him not to. He was only in his early 20s himself then, so he hadn't taken much persuading – his urge to do the right thing was tempered by his understandable terror at the thought of suddenly finding himself as a daddy, when he was barely grown-up himself.

Over the years, they'd all fallen into a rhythm that allowed everyone to function, feel appreciated, and not feel pressurised into doing anything they didn't want to.

He started his life working on farms in 'the back end of nowhere', and we'd continued on our weird but merry way, Kate buying her terraced house and me moving in across the road. There were a few phone calls a year, the odd Skype once it was invented and we'd all figured out how to use it, and he sometimes sent gifts or photos. He'd asked to come and visit more than once, but Kate had always found a reason why it wasn't a good time.

I never quite understood why that was. She certainly didn't seem to have any bad feelings towards him, and always said she was grateful for the fact that his over-exuberant bedroom performance had given her the best gift a woman could have – Martha.

Maybe she was worried that it would rock the boat, mess things up at our end. Her career started to take off, and Martha was thriving, and we were more settled than anyone could possibly have predicted, given the situation and the people involved. Martha never seemed too concerned – she was happy in her unorthodox setting, because of course it wasn't unorthodox to her, it was what she'd always known.

Whatever Kate's reasons, Cal had remained a slightly mysterious figure, on the periphery of our lives. There'd been talk of Martha going out to visit him – of us all going out to visit him – once she got older, but ... well. Events kind of overtook us on that front, and Kate would never be visiting anyone ever again. That thought drenches me with sadness, and I'm starkly aware of how unfair it is that I'm getting to meet Cal, without her at my side to laugh at it all with me.

I'm dragged out of my stupor by Willow, who helpfully throws half her apple and cinnamon muffin at my head. It bounces off the halo of my trademark hair, and crumbles onto the table in front of us. A terrible waste of a good muffin, but enough to bring me back to my senses.

I stand up, and shake his hand properly. It feels weird – I'm not often in a formal enough situation where I have to shake hands with anyone, especially the man half responsible for creating the wondrous and multi-faceted beastie that is Martha Harris.

"Um ... er ... what are you doing here?" I finally manage to articulate, aware of the fact that everyone else is still watching, still listening. I meet Laura's eyes over his shoulder, and widen them significantly. She gets the message immediately, and starts to scurry around doing tasks to mask her curiosity. I can tell she's not really concentrating on what she's doing when she puts the scales in the fridge, but at least it breaks the spell.

Frank announces in an overly loud voice that he's going to

fix the baby changer in the ladies, as it always seems to be on the fritz, and Willow engages Lynnie in a conversation about baby yoga that she cleverly knows will immediately appeal to her.

I get the feeling they're all still half listening – apart from Lynnie – but I appreciate the effort. I get up, and steer Cal over to another table. Laura makes a brief appearance, plonking down another bottle of Bucks Fizz, then whizzes of to do some more chores.

I pour Cal a glass – Lord knows he deserves it – and swig some straight from the bottle, as I've left mine on the other table. I realise this is probably not the best way to make a good impression, but, well, he's Australian. I'm sure he won't mind.

"Okay," I repeat, once my hands have stopped trembling. "Let's start again. First of all, yes, I am Zoe, and it's lovely to meet you. Secondly, thanks for what you just did – you've earned yourself a place in Budbury folk history for all of eternity. And thirdly – what are you doing here?"

He laughs, throwing his head back to reveal a strong, suntanned neck, vivid against the white of his shirt. His golden hair is wild and slightly long, curled over his collar, and his cowboy hat adds to his otherworldly appearance. He couldn't look more out of place in a small English village if he was dressed as a sumo wrestler.

"Well, Zoe – I didn't see that I had any choice other than to just head here and see what I could do to help. I knew that if I asked, we'd be in the same old position we've always been in – you'd have a good reason why I shouldn't come, and I'd let you convince me. I should've come for the funeral, but I accepted what you said – you were probably right, it would all have been too much for her. I was okay with holding on, seeing how things developed. But the last time I spoke to you, you sounded ... I'm trying to find a diplomatic way of putting this, but I've lived in the bush too long, so I'm fresh out of diplomacy ..."

"It's all right. I can take it," I say, wondering if I can.

"You sounded ... tired. Bloody exhausted, if I'm honest. Like you just didn't know what to do, and like this move down here was a last ditch attempt to sort shit out. I can only imagine how hard all of this has been for you – losing Kate, dealing with Martha ..."

"I'm not 'dealing' with Martha," I snap, sounding – and feeling – unpleasantly defensive. "I love Martha. She's not a bad case of shingles or something. I want to be here for her. I've always been here for her."

There's an unspoken addition to that sentence that doesn't go unnoticed, even if I don't actually vocalise it.

He raises one eyebrow, and his deep brown eyes go all serious on me.

"Yeah, I know. You've always been here for her, and I've always been on the other side of the world. I get it. It wasn't always my choice, but I get it. And I don't want you to think I'm expecting to waltz into her life and suddenly take over, go all Superdad on her. That's not what I meant. I just want to help, okay? I'm finally old enough and grown-up enough to be able to do that. Maybe she'll take one look at me and tell me to get on my bike, who knows? Can't say as I'd blame her. But I want to try, all right?"

I nod. I drink a bit more Bucks Fizz. I try and sound a lot more calm than I feel. He sounds as though he's trying to keep a lid on things as well, and there's nothing to be gained here by both of us going off like over-emotional rockets.

"All right," I say, after a couple of deep breaths. "Yes. I understand, and obviously, you're her father. But ... how long are you here for, anyway? Don't you have a farm to run?"

"Took some leave. Haven't had a holiday in six years, least they could do. So I can be here as long as it takes. As long as you two can put up with me, or think I'm useful, or need me. If nothing else, I'm good at delivering babies, changing light bulbs, and barbecuing. Plus, I'm handy in any crisis that involves killer snakes or spiders roaming round the tall grass."

He's smiling, and leaning back in his chair so he doesn't appear too threatening or invasive, and I like the fact that he's doing that. He's giving me the space and time he thinks I need to come to terms with all of this.

Of course, what our smiling golden-haired cowboy seems to have forgotten is this: it's not me he needs to convince. And there are far scarier situations ahead of him that anything to do with spiders or snakes – like meeting his daughter for the first time ever.

Chapter 18

I'm not quite sure how to break this new and exciting news to Martha, and spend ages waiting in the car for her, staring numbly down the road through the village as I wait for the school bus to trundle back into view.

The drizzle has made a sneaky return, and it's now cool enough that I flick the heating on as I wait, listening to some *Motown Magic* on the radio. *Tears of a Clown*, which is appropriate, because I feel like having a little weep myself.

Cal's surprise arrival has taken me aback in a way I don't quite understand. I think I was starting to hope that Martha and I were just about finding our feet, here in Dorset. There have been small, warming signs of her coming out of her emotional deep-freeze, thawing in the heat of Lizzie and Josh's friendly advances, and the Cherie-patented cuddles, and the new college courses. Tiny signs – but definitely there. She's been less distant, less attached to her phone, more willing to at least ignore me politely rather than ignore me in a way that makes me feel like throwing myself off a cliff.

It's delicate, though, all of this. Fragile – because it's based on a bedrock of 'if only ...' Every new thing that she does – starting her A-levels, meeting the Budbury gang, even small stuff like discovering a new band she likes – is tainted by the deep and underlying wish that Kate was here to share it with her. That her mum was around to listen to her war stories, or give her a pep talk, or tell her that the new band she's discovered is actually crap and she should listen to some Jimi Hendrix instead.

I understand that – because I feel it too. Every time I sit on that bench and look down at the bay below, or eat one of Laura's creations, or see a bloody baby born – I wish exactly the same. Kate was more than my friend. She was my sister, partly my mother, and the most important connection I'd ever made in my life. I miss her every single minute of every single day. I'm lost without her, and the pain of that lives inside me, hidden away, beating next to my heart.

I try and hide all of this from Martha, and pretend that I am coping – the last thing she needs is my anguish dolloped on top of her own – but it's there. Always. My new friends are wonderful, but they are not, and never will be, a replacement for what I've lost.

So these tiny shoots and buds of hope that I've been seeing in Martha are precious. Important. Treasured beyond belief – and just as it seemed like we could at least try and steady our rocking ship, Cal has swum out into the wreckage, knocking everything off course again.

I'm also, I force myself to admit, a tiny bit worried about

Cal's role in Martha's world, and what it might mean for *my* role in Martha's world. This is such a selfish and petty thought that it makes me bite my lip hard enough to break the skin. If I was to look in the rear view mirror right now, I don't think I'd like my own reflection.

Because, being brutally honest, jittering along with the anxiety is a miniscule amount of jealousy. Kate always said I was Martha's second mum, and wanted me to carry on playing that part – but Martha's never seemed overly keen on the idea, and much as I've done my best, there is a sliver of concern that now her 'real' parent is here, I will be surplus to requirements. Who could blame her if she saw Cal as her knight in shining denim? She might even want to run off to Oz, and start a shiny new life with her dad.

And that, I realise, as I finally see the bus weaving its way towards the stop, is frightening: if I'm not looking after Martha, what use am I? All the roles that defined me are gone. I was Kate's friend, and she is dead. I worked in a book shop, but now I'm unemployed. I was someone's daughter, but I stopped thinking of myself as that long ago. Without Martha, what is the bloody point of me at all?

I'm spared further tortured soul-gazing by the bus juddering to a halt, belching exhaust fumes into the air and rocking slightly as young people stomp their way down the steps. *Tears of a Clown* is replaced by Diana Ross asking someone to touch her in the morning, which is just as mournful. I switch off the radio. It's too depressing.

I watch through the windscreen as the combined youth of Budbury all pile off the bus, a mass of purple uniforms and flannel. I smile as I see Lizzie and Nate scuffling over a bag of crisps, which eventually flies out of their fighting hands and crashes to the floor. It is immediately swamped by pecking seagulls, and they both stare at each other, as if to say 'that was your fault.'

I see Josh grinning at the hi-jinks, and nudging Martha, who is amazingly letting him. She even gives them all a small, tight wave as she walks towards the car, and shouts her good-byes as they head off to the cafe.

Her face changes from amusement at the seagull/crisp coup, to a carefully schooled blankness when she sees me and opens the car door.

She dumps her backpack on the rear seats, and immediately starts to fiddle with her earbuds.

"What are you listening to?" I say, pathetically. We've both always liked music – it's been one of the few ways we've stayed connected. Martha herself has a lovely voice, and could easily be a singer in a teenaged garage band. Although she's probably more of a tortured solo artist these days.

"Neil Diamond," she replies, shooting me a look that dares me to criticise. As if. The man is a God of easy listening.

"Cool. Sweet Caroline – best singalong chorus ever. So ... how was your day?"

I prepare myself for a snub, or a tirade, or even for her to pretend to fall asleep. These are all possibilities. Instead, she half smiles, and replies: "You know what ... it was okay. We started reading *Lord of the Flies*. I think Budbury's probably a bit like that over the summer, from what Lizzie's said. And, erm, how was yours?"

I am so shocked I grip the steering wheel, fearing that I might topple sideways and fall through the door. It sounded stiff and awkward coming from her mouth, as though the words were being spat out against their will, but she did actually ask how my day had gone. Miraculous.

"Well," I reply, not wanting to make too big a deal of it, "Becca's baby arrived. At the cafe. I'm surprised Lizzie didn't tell you."

"She did. Sounded pretty full-on. Kind of like *Call the Midwife* crossed with the *Darling Buds of May*."

Cherie has always reminded me a little of Ma Larkin, with her sumptuous bosom and plentiful hugs and the fact that she's constantly trying to feed everyone to cheer them up. I nod, and wonder how to broach the subject of the other new arrival – the one that's a lot bigger, hopefully doesn't need a nappy, and will make our own lives a lot more complicated.

"It was ... amazing. Did Lizzie mention the guy who turned up and actually delivered the baby?"

Martha frowns, as though trying to remember conversations she had whole minutes ago.

"Um ... I don't think so ... that sounds weird. Was he a doctor?"

"No," I reply, charging straight in, "he was your dad."

She twists her body around so she can look me in the eyes, her eyebrows up somewhere under her black fringe and a look of perfect shock on her face.

"My *what?*" she says, her voice so loud it echoes around the car.

"Erm ... your dad. Cal. He flew over from Australia to see you. He's staying at a guest house in West Bay, and he wants to meet up. If, you know, that's all right with you."

She is silent for a few moments after that, frowning and chewing the skin inside her cheek and fiddling with the wires of her earphones. Classic displacement activities, I think, wondering if I should get her some worry beads for Christmas.

"So, he turns up unannounced, from Australia, and just ... what, delivers a baby? In the cafe?"

She says this as though it's ridiculous – which of course, it is.

"Yeah. I know. It's all very strange – but that's what happened. I'm not making it up, honest – if I was making it up, I'd have had Poldark delivering the baby. How ... how do you feel about that, Martha? About your dad being here?"

More silence. More frowning. More chewing and fiddling and displacing. I can practically hear the cogs turning in her brain, processing it all, passing from shock to curiosity to something else.

"Hmmm," she says eventually, staring straight ahead, winding and unwinding the wires around her fingers, pulling them so tight I know they'll leave narrow red marks on her skin. "I'm not actually sure how I feel about that at all, which is a bit of a novelty. I can't believe he didn't tell us he was coming. I can't believe he's here ... what's he like? In the flesh?"

Lord, I think – how do I answer that one? It wouldn't be entirely appropriate to tell her he's super-hot, that Laura practically swooned into his lap, and that he looks like Pirate Cowboy Thor.

"He's ... nice," I say, lamely. "Good at delivering babies. Wears a cowboy hat. Really excited about meeting you properly. If you want to, that is. If you don't, then I'll deal with him."

She gives me an amused sideways glance, and finally puts the phone and earbuds in the glove box, maybe to stop herself messing with them.

"That sounded serious," she replies, a half-smile still on her face. "The way you said 'I'll deal with him' – like you might deal with him by beating him to death with a shovel after you've made him dig his own grave. You can be a bit scary sometimes, you know."

"Why, thank you," I respond, smiling back. "I have been told that before. And I think, given our location, it would make more sense to weigh him down with conch shells and float him out into the bay, don't you? So he can swim with the fishes?"

"You'd have to find the right spot. You wouldn't want him washing back up on the beach and scaring the fossil hunters."

"I know. I'm sure Sam could help us with tide times and currents and shit like that. Don't worry, I'll do it properly."

She's smirking now, trying not to actually laugh out loud. I know she's stalling for time while she lets this new scenario whirl through her brain, and I'm happy to assist her by talking as much nonsense as she needs, for as long as she needs.

She's quiet for a moment, then smacks her hand down on the dashboard so hard it makes me jump. Looks like she's come to a decision.

"Nah," she says, staring out of the windscreen, "not just yet. Maybe we should give him a chance."

I nod, and pat her hand, and start the car. The oracle has spoken.

"Besides," she adds, as I pull the car out into the main road, "we can always kill him later."

Chapter 19

In the end, it all goes much more smoothly than I could possibly have imagined. We arrange that Cal will come to dinner at Lilac Wine, meet Martha, and we'll see how it goes from there. Everybody is making a conscious effort to keep it casual, and not turn it into a huge drama.

I'm playing along with that, but the word 'dinner' sends me straight into a tailspin, as it seems unlikely that I can fit in a quick cookery course before nightfall. I grew up half-feral, and my domestic goddess has always remained on the shy side. I probably shanked her for looking at me funny. Cooking, cleaning, gardening … it all seems foreign to my nature, and such a waste of time when there are books to be read and songs to be listened to and box sets to be watched.

I do, however, manage a quick tidy-up, scooting around the cottage clearing up the detritus that two women living together tend to amass. Stray bobbles and hair grips; odd socks down the side of the sofa; Martha's school files; piles and piles of paperbacks; music magazines; stray shells and bits of driftwood I've collected on my walks; discarded earrings and gummy bottles of nail varnish.

Predictably enough, Laura comes to the rescue on the dinner front, an angel on my doorstep encased in a fuzzy blue sweater. She turns up, with Matt, about an hour before Cal is due to arrive – just as I am staring helplessly into the fridge, willing it to have created a gourmet feast without any assistance from me.

Midgebo is with them, and does a quick minesweep of the house, his big black nose snuffling around looking for treasures, his fat black tail wagging so fast it's almost a blur.

Matt gives me a little nod – he's a very self-contained man – and carries a load of foil-wrapped bowls into the kitchen. Laura stares after him, a peculiar mix of fondness and lust on her face as he takes his jean-clad self away. She's obviously over the Cal-swoon phase, and only has eyes for her man. And who can blame her? He looks like a young Harrison Ford, plays the guitar, and delivers pug puppies. Perfection.

"I hope you don't mind," she says, turning her attention back to me. "I just thought ... well, you had enough on your plate, without worrying about the catering as well. It's just a lasagne, which you can heat up, and some salad. And some red velvet cake. And some garlic bread. Oh, and some stuffed olives ... and some cider, donated by Scrumpy Joe ..."

She holds a bag up to demonstrate. It's made of brown paper, and bears the Scrumpy Joe logo. I barely know Joe, but one thing I've already learned about this place is that whenever there's a crisis – or anything vaguely resembling one – everyone soon pulls together, in whatever way they can. I know Laura's been over at Sam and Becca's, checking on them and Little Edie, but has still somehow made time to do all of this as well.

I give Laura a hug, overwhelmed by gratitude. For her kindness. Her friendship. And mainly, for the lasagne. I catch a glimpse of us both in the mirror in the hallway, and marvel at the sheer size of our hair. If we combined it and straightened it all out, it would probably reach the moon.

Matt emerges from the kitchen, and casts a glance around the cottage.

"This place looks nice," he says, after a quick visual inspection. "Like a real home, not a holiday let. I like the shell collection."

For Matt, that's quite a speech, and I reach out to pat his arm in thanks. He half-smiles, seemingly embarrassed at his own enthusiasm, and gestures to the door, raising his eyebrows at Laura. She nods, and gives me another quick hug.

"Good luck," she says, as Matt retrieves Midgebo from the kitchen, where he is attempting to stand on his back legs and sniff the food. "It'll all be fine. You know where we are if you need us."

"I do," I reply, gratefully. "And thank you, so much. At the very least you've just rescued Cal from a night of burned cheese on toast and stale chocolate Hob Nobs."

After they leave, I mooch my way up the stairs, and knock on Martha's door.

"Enter!" she shouts, in a mock-imperious tone, as though she's Darth Vader inviting a minion in to get his throat choked.

I push open the door, and see that she is sitting in front of her dressing table mirror, applying make-up. She's wearing a red tartan mini-skirt over black leggings, her Doc Marten boots laced up with red ribbon, and her hair is long and dark over the shoulders of her Guns N' Roses T-shirt. She's carefully painting on winged eyeliner, and has all of her various piercings in. She looks beautiful, in a scary goth chick way.

"You all right?" I ask, hovering in the doorway, arms folded in front of me to protect my vital organs from stray throwing knives. "Not nervous?"

"Yep, I'm nervous. I'm meeting my dad for the first time, and I'm screwing up my eye liner, and I'm wishing my mum was here. You?"

She lays down the eyeliner and turns to stare at me. I'm struck dumb by the fact that she's being so unguarded and honest, and find my eyes filling with sudden stinging tears. I screw them away, and let out a sigh.

"Yeah. I wish she was as well. Don't worry, it'll be okay. And your eye liner looks great …"

Martha lets out a 'hmph' noise and turns back to the mirror. She makes little shoo-ing gestures with her fingers, and I assume that I have been dismissed. Business as usual. I smile, and turn to leave.

"You might want to think about brushing your hair, or changing your top!" she yells at me as I enter my own room.

I bite down a sweary retort, and look in the mirror. Yeah. She's probably right.

By the time Cal turns up, bearing wine and flowers and gifts, I feel oddly calm. Maybe I've finally mastered my emotions, turned a corner into zen alley. Or maybe it's because I accidentally downed one of the Scrumpy Joe specials ten minutes earlier.

Cal and Martha stare at each other for a while, and I stand awkwardly to one side, not at all sure of my role in this and ultimately deciding that I don't have one – other than picking up the Martha-shaped pieces if it all goes horribly wrong.

He's dressed in jeans and a pale blue shirt, which sets off his bronzed skin and contrasts with his deep brown eyes. Brown and blonde – an unusual combination, and one that Martha would also have, if she didn't dye her hair. She has fair, pale skin, though, like her mum, whereas Cal looks like a burst of sunshine on legs. Long legs – so long that he's cautiously dipping his head to avoid the beams.

After a few moments of silence, while they size each other up, he breaks the tension by pulling a teddy bear out of his bag. It's fluffy and looks vaguely like a koala and is wearing a tiny red T-shirt that says 'I Heart Sydney'. He waves it in front of Martha's face with a flourish, and makes her laugh. I've not heard Martha's laughter for a while, and it's a wondrous thing, making her seem younger and simpler and ... well, happier. Laughter will do that for a girl.

"You do know I'm not 10, don't you?" she asks, taking the bear from his hands and squeezing it.

"No," he replies, handing me the flowers. "As far as I'm concerned, you'll always be 10. And I have no idea what 16 year old women like to get as gifts, so I was stuffed. Kinda like that bear."

"Cash is always good," she answers cheekily, her head angled on one side. "It's just so ... personal."

We all laugh, again. Mine may or may not sound slightly hysterical.

Cal sniffs the air appreciatively. "Wow. Something smells good. You must be a dab hand in the kitchen, Zoe."

Martha snorts and guffaws and generally makes it known to Cal and the wider Dorset community that I am, in fact, far from being a dab hand in the kitchen. I slap her legs with the tea towel I had hanging over my shoulder, and leave them to it. I am at the very least a dab hand at getting ready-made food out of the oven, and taking the tops off cider bottles.

Chapter 20

The night passes over, as nights will do, helped along by Cal's naturally outgoing persona and lashings of fine food and drink.

We eat at the big pine dining table, Cal only sipping his wine as he has to drive, me guzzling the cider while Martha looks at it longingly. If she'd been a normal 16-year-old, maybe I'd have let her have one, or watered some wine down for her. But she's not a normal 16-year-old – she's a 16-year-old who has passed out in her own vomit several times, and who has a tendency to drink herself into oblivion. I don't blame her for this – if I was Martha, I'd undoubtedly be even worse – but I also remain aware of it.

I can tell Cal notices that subtle underplay; her gazing at the chilled beer, and looking at me, and me shaking my head slightly. He doesn't mention it, which is wise, but I know there might be questions later. That's okay. He's her father, I tell myself, and he's entitled to know what's been going on – so far he's only been on the edge of her world, seeing what she wanted him to see, limited to the small rectangular shape of her laptop screen. Now, he's here, in real life, sitting at her dining room table – which makes it all very different.

For the time being, though, most of the questions are coming from her. Martha quizzes him about his life, his family, Australia. He tells us about his early years, in Canada, before his dad, an engineer, moved them all to Sydney. He tells us about his sister, Ronnie, and his brother, Jay, and his work on the farm in New South Wales. He tells us about the seven squillion acres he manages, and the animals that live there, and describes its combination of isolation and beauty so well I feel like I'm almost there.

He tells us about surfing, and his travelling, and his time doing jobs that seem to range from lifeguard to barman to sorting out scrap metal at a rubbish dump. He's an interesting man, and Martha has an expression of near-wonder on her face.

That tiny spark of jealousy I felt earlier is still there, but I stamp it down. There's no way I can compete with this man, and more to the point I shouldn't even try – he's her biological relative, he's handsome and funny and smart, and he's crossed the known world rescuing orphaned turtles and diving for pearls and living in fishing villages in Asia. He even delivers bloody babies, as I know first hand.

He's also, I realise, coming into her life at a time when she desperately needs someone new. Someone who will give her hope, and offer her potential. I'm sad that it isn't me, but it was never going to be me, was it? I know her too well. I'm too much part of the past; I know her flaws, and love her anyway – but none of that seems very important when you're a teenager. It's only when you're older and wiser that you realise how precious that particular combination is.

So, I resign myself to being the frumpy old woman who washes Martha's socks, and cooks her food (badly), and bosses her around. To being taken for granted, resented, and ignored. In short, I resign myself to the fate that mothers the world over have had to endure for millennia.

On the other hand, Cal is fresh and new and exciting. He hasn't ever had to scream at her to get out of bed, or been called in to see her head teacher, or caught her weeping in her sleep. As a result, she's loving every minute of him being there – and I need to let her.

She's more animated than I've seen her since Kate died, chattering away and waving her hands as she talks. She's enjoying herself, and not even noticing it. This might only last a few weeks – if he goes back to his real life – or it might last forever. Who knows? But for now, I have to just sit back, and let it unfold, and enjoy seeing the old Martha return, even if it is only for a limited run.

Eventually, as time wends its way towards midnight, I raise my eyebrows and point at my watch. She rolls her eyes, and does a dramatic teenaged sigh, but does at least stand up. She yawns, and covers her mouth with embarrassment – shamefully caught out being human.

"I know, I know …" she mutters, stretching her arms into the air. "It's a college night, and I need to get to bed."

She gazes at the table, which is scattered with used plates, and empty glasses, and haphazardly angled cutlery, looking as though someone has emptied a dishwasher on top of it in an act of guerrilla warfare.

"Shall I … I don't know … help you clear the plates away or something?"

I'm so shocked by this that I lean back in my chair, as though I've just been blasted with an unreality ray. Martha, not only noticing the mess, but volunteering to help tidy it away. Trying to be a good girl, or at least do a passable impression of one.

I glance at Cal, who obviously doesn't realise that this is an unusual turn of events, and grin. I'm so tempted to say yes, trap her in her own fictitious version of herself and make her do the lot – but even I'm not that evil.

"Nah, it's okay," I say, giving her a raised eyebrow to let her know this has all been noted and filed away for future mockery, "I'll sort it. That's what tomorrow's for. Get yourself off to bed."

She stands and looks at Cal for a moment before she leaves the room, and there is a slightly awkward sense of hesitation – like she's not sure if she should give him a kiss or a hug or something. Either would be weird, but somehow she's right – it feels even weirder to simply walk out of the room after spending your first ever actual, real-life face-time with your own father.

Cal correctly assesses all of this, and holds his hand up for a high five. She slaps his palm, and grins at him.

"You do know that's really lame, don't you?" she asks, hands on hips.

"Not where I come from, mate," he answers quickly. "It's the very cutting edge of social interaction. See you tomorrow?"

She nods, shrugs as though she doesn't mind either way, and struts out of the room. I listen to her clomp up the stairs in her Doc Marten's, and wait until her bedroom door slams behind her before turning back to Cal.

He's staring up at the ceiling, as though he's trying to see through it.

"Don't tell me you've got X ray vision on top of your other super powers," I say, standing up and starting to clear the table. I'd told Martha I'd do it tomorrow, but as I'm now feeling slightly freaked out by being alone with Cal, this seems as good a time as any.

Cal immediately gets up to help, scraping food and stacking dishes with the simple efficiency of a man used to looking after himself.

"No super powers at all, Zo," he replies, shortening my name in a way I usually find annoying – but as he's Australian, I'll let him off. "I'm just ... I don't know. A bit knocked for six by her, I suppose. And feeling stupid as well – I don't know why I waited so bloody long."

I nod, and finish off the dregs of my cider before taking

the glass and the salad bowl through to the kitchen. Waste not want not.

"I know. It must be very strange for you. But … well, you're here now, aren't you?"

He follows me through into the other room, approximately seventeen plates balanced on one long arm, and helps me rinse them off before stacking them in the dishwasher. It feels odd to have help with these boring and mundane tasks. Odd, and nice.

"Yeah, I'm here now," he says, leaning back against the counter and gazing around the room. "How did that go, do you think? I thought it was okay, but let's be brutally honest – I barely know the girl."

I grab another cider from the fridge, and think about my words as I pour it out. It's good stuff – I must thank Scrumpy Joe next time I see him.

"I'd say it went brilliantly," I reply eventually, offering him a bottle of water, which he takes and absent-mindedly opens. "Based on my extensive knowledge of the magnificent creature that is Martha, I'd rate that a ten out of ten on the success scale."

"Yeah?" he says, his face cracking into a huge grin as he speaks. I realise then how nervous he's been, which is only natural. He's hidden it well, but seeing how relieved he is now makes him seem so much more human. He's not a super hero after all – he's just a man, with flaws and vulnerabilities and tender spots, just like the rest of us.

"Yeah. Come on. I can finish the clearing tomorrow. Let's go and chill out for a bit before you leave. I'm sure you have questions."

He nods, and we move into the living room. He mooches around for a while, looking at the shells and the books and smiling sadly at the framed photo of me, Martha and Kate on the shelf, before settling down in one of the chintzy armchairs opposite me. He makes it look small, with his long legs spread out in front of him, his Timberland boots massive against the polished floorboards.

"I'm sorry I didn't know her better," he says, gesturing to the picture. "Kate, I mean."

"Some people would say you knew her intimately ..." I reply, smiling.

"Right. But that was ... God, it was one night. And it was so long ago. I mean, I always remembered her – she was so full of life, so much fun – but ... well, it wasn't a serious relationship, was it? And she never seemed to want one. Not with me, at least, which I don't blame her for – I was a 19 year old boy who was permanently drunk. Young, dumb, and full of rum, as the old saying doesn't quite go.

"She never shut me out of Martha's life – I've always been grateful she even tracked me down to tell me, I'd have been none the wiser if she hadn't bothered – but it was always made clear that I wasn't needed either. When I was younger, in all honesty, that was a bit of a relief – I was just a kid myself, wasn't I? Took me longer than your average idiot to grow up, as well. But now ... well. Now, I'm not a kid any more. And I want to get to know Martha, do what I can to help her, be around for her for as long as she needs me."

I nod, and sip, and realise that I am a bit drunk. Maybe more than a bit. I tell myself to get a grip – that this is a situation that needs some clarity and clear-headed thinking. I need to be wise and strong and sensible and say the right thing.

"How did you get that scar on your face?" I say, instead. Oops.

He laughs, and shakes his head. I didn't intend to ask, but he actually looks grateful for the distraction. Maybe he wasn't ready for a big, deep conversation either. He strokes the scar thoughtfully. It runs from the side of his eye to just above his jaw, noticeable but not disfiguring, well healed over, showing whiter than the rest of his sun-kissed skin.

"Ah," he replies. "That's quite the story. It was a shark attack."

He might be Australian, but something in his tone makes me doubt the veracity of that particular comment.

"It wasn't though, was it?" I say, pointing at him accusingly.

"Damn. Rumbled. Bar fight with Russell Crowe?" he asks, looking hopeful.

"Fat Russell Crowe, or *Gladiator* Russell Crowe?"

"*Gladiator*. Definitely. Will you settle for that?"

"If I have to," I answer, smiling. "Maybe you'll tell me the real story some time."

"Maybe I will. Especially if I'm ever here and not driving.

That cider looks tempting ..."

I swish it around in the glass, taunting him with its fizzy amber glory, before gulping some down in a manner that can only be described as deeply childish.

"So," I say, when I'm finished winding him up. "How long do you think you'll be around?"

"I honestly don't know. I can be flexible. At least a couple of weeks, but I can stay longer. I'm ... look, I know you've been around forever, and I don't want to step on your toes here. But I also don't want to be the crap dad, trying to cram a lifetime into a fortnight. She seems ... okay? Considering."

I let out a small 'ha!' noise, and put the cider down on the side table. It doesn't seem appropriate to have the next stage of this conversation while guzzling booze.

"She's ... better than she was," I say, screwing my face up as I try and find the right words. "But she's not okay, Cal. Not at all. The old Martha was ... well, she was a handful, don't get me wrong. A lot of spirit, a lot of character. But after Kate ... things spiralled. Drinking. Hanging round with a new crowd. Smoking. Dabbling in drugs. Staying out all hours. She changed – and don't get me wrong, I understand why she changed. She lost her mum, and got me instead – and I'm not being down on myself here, but I'm a pretty shoddy second best, to be honest. That's why we moved here."

"I got that impression when we spoke on the phone," he replies, leaning forward in interest. "It's one of the reasons I decided to come."

"I know, and I appreciate that. Don't worry about stepping on my toes – this does all feel a bit weird, but what I feel doesn't matter. It's Martha that matters. And although things here are improving, to be frank I need all the help I can get. If we work together, this could be good for her, I think. I hope."

He nods, and thinks it through. He's handling this well, considering everything I've just told him about his daughter – but he seems like a sharp guy, with plenty of experience of the world, so it probably doesn't come as much of a shock. Teenagers probably face the same temptations in Australia, but with less rain.

"Yeah. That sounds about right. We'll work together, and see if we can't just turn things around for her. I won't over-step, and you can tell me if I do ... I'm desperate to know more about her. To talk to her. To be in her life. But I'm also conscious that if I push too hard, she might back right off, like a nervous calf."

A spluttering laugh escapes me at that one.

"More like a nervous kangaroo," I say. "One that can punch your lights out without a second thought. But ... yeah, you're right. Is that why you sat and let her quiz you all night?"

"It is. I know she was putting a front on, but she must have been nervous. Weirded out by me being here. She's gone through a lot of change, and I didn't want to overload her, come across as the heavy-handed dad – because I have no right to do that anyway."

"It was the right call," I agree. "She doesn't respond well to heavy-handed anything. So ... look, let's just play it by ear, okay? Stay in touch. Have secret meetings. Code words. Whatever."

"I like that idea," he says, standing up and stretching. Looks like it's time for him to go, and it's definitely time for me to try and sleep off the cider.

He walks towards the door, grabbing his jacket on the way.

"Where's your cowboy hat?" I ask, trailing after him to see him out.

"Oh ... well, I left it in the car. Thought it was all alien enough without going full-on wild west around her. That can be our code word, okay? If ever you think I'm stuffing up, tell me to put my cowboy hat on."

"What if you already have your cowboy hat on?"

"Tell me to take it off. We'll improvise. Maybe I'll get some new hats. I always fancied a fez, or a sombrero ..."

We're both smiling by the time he's standing in the doorway. Both trying hard to navigate our way through a new and difficult situation.

It's cold outside now – autumn is well and truly starting to kick in – and I shiver a little. The sky is inky black, dotted with glittering stars that shine and sparkle so much more vividly than they do in the city. It's so much quieter too – no car horns or wailing alarms or drunk people singing in the street. Just the distant sound of cows in the field, nocturnal animals rustling in the undergrowth, and the gentle tinkle of the water feature in the middle of the green.

He pauses, and looks down at me. His hair is haloed around his head, and his eyes are dark and shining in the moonlight. I'm not quite sure how to leave this, feeling much as Martha must have done earlier – like it's been too significant to ignore, but not enough to merit a hug.

Cal sticks to his tried and tested method, and holds up his hand for a high five. I slap his palm, and he catches my hand in his, squeezing my fingers a little as he says goodbye.

I watch him walk away, boots crunching on the gravel as he heads for his car, and realise that I feel a bit strange. A bit giddy. A bit uncertain. A bit ... warm.

It must be the cider, I tell myself, as I close the door behind me.

Chapter 21

The next morning, I arrive at the cafe in search of some respite. Possibly some cake.

Martha woke up early, and was downstairs and dressed before I was – which made it all the more embarrassing when she found me standing outside her bedroom in my PJs screaming, 'get up, you lazy cow, we'll miss the bus.'

She just looked at me, one black eyebrow raised in silent judgement, while I scurried around looking for socks and shoes so we could finally leave the cottage. I ended up with odd socks, and my Crocs – a most excellent look.

She didn't talk much on the drive into the village, but she was definitely more bright than usual. I want to say 'bubbly', but that's not quite right – she was just less morose. I knew it wasn't because of my odd socks, so had to assume that it was because of Cal. His arrival had, I suppose, given her something else to focus on other than her own misery, and my shortcomings.

As she got out of the car, she poked her head back in, and

announced, "I'm looking forward to seeing him again. This whole dad thing is definitely not boring."

To Martha, 'not boring' is probably the highest form of compliment possible. I didn't get a chance to reply, of course, as she slammed the car door and marched briskly away. Listening to me would definitely fall into the 'boring' category.

I waved her off, looking on as Lizzie dashed over to her, keen to hear the gossip – handsome Aussie dad suddenly appearing seemed to be topping even the new baby – and sat in the car for a few moments, taking in deep breaths, as the school bus belched its way down the street.

I wasn't hungover, exactly – just weary. You know that feeling when you've had a bit too much to drink the night before, and not had enough sleep, and been kept awake by fitful dreams about your dead best friend and her former lover? Or a version thereof, possibly with different dreams? Well, that. I felt exhausted, like the inside of my brain had been scooped out and put in the recycling bin.

I was considering a lengthy snooze in the car – it wouldn't be the first time - when Edie knocked on the window. She was rapping away in a series of sharp taps that went on forever, and which I eventually recognised as a staccato form of the Strictly Come Dancing theme tune. If it'd been anyone else, I'd have told them to fox the trot off, but it's impossible to be snippy with Edie. It'd be like kicking a Labrador puppy.

I opened the car door, and gestured for her to get in – the sky was dark grey and the rain was gearing up to be something more serious than usual. Even the seagulls wheeling and turning above us looked worried.

"Off to the cafe?" she asked, her Vans backpack on her lap, her body wrapped up warm in a red puffa jacket. A knitted red bobble hat was perched on her tight white curls, and her glasses were speckled with raindrops.

I hadn't been planning on it, but as soon as she asked the question, I knew it was probably the best thing to do. At least then someone else would feed and water me, and it wasn't the kind of place that cared if your socks were odd. In fact, it was the kind of place that positively encouraged such things.

She chatted about the baby, and how Becca had escaped from hospital after only an hour, and how lovely it all was, and how she couldn't wait for the christening they'd be bound to have eventually, as it would be an 'absolute cracker of a party', and about Strictly, and about her great-niece Olivia who had just been named as Sausage Maker of the Year at an awards show. I try not to laugh at that one, as I can tell Edie's very proud.

By the time we arrive at the cafe, I am feeling utterly frazzled and in desperate need of coffee, toast, and possibly a couple of paracetamol as well.

Cherie and Frank are there, and Cherie is manning the cafe – Laura's parents are apparently on their way down from Manchester, and she's taken a few days off to help with the baby, and get ready for their arrival. Willow isn't in either, and apart from me and Edie, the only customers are a group of women in their 20s, who have pulled two tables together and are giggling over their granola. They're not local, and they're wearing walking gear – I decide that it's a hen party for an especially wholesome bride-to-be.

Cal has texted to say he is heading over, and that has done little to make me feel less frazzled. Last night, I'd said we could work together – this morning, I feel like that might be trickier than I thought. I'm only just settling into my rhythm in a new place, finding my feet with a new lifestyle, and now even that is changing up again.

I nod at Cherie, give Frank a wave, and head over to the corner. To the messy bookshelves, and the colouring books, and the board games. Edie picks up a battered copy of *Wuthering Heights*, and is immediately immersed.

Soon after, Cherie arrives, her hair tied up on her head in a messy bun, her face pink from the heat of the kitchen. She's carrying a tray, and the tray is laden with edible paradise – coffee for me, tea for Edie, warm granary toast, and freshly baked scones. God bless her and all who sail in her.

"Room for a little one?" she says, jokingly – as she is, of course, far from little. I scoot my chair around, and she sighs as she sits down next to me. She slips off her Sketchers, and stretches her long legs out, wiggling her red-painted toes.

"I'm getting too old for this work lark," she says, picking at a scone. "I keep trying to retire, but it never seems to take."

"That's because you're still a spring chicken, and too nosy to stay away from the action," pipes up Edie, not raising her head from the pages. I suppose, from Edie's perspective, that Cherie is a spring chicken – only in her early 70s and all. I'm starting to think that somewhere down on the bay, tucked away in a magical cave, is a small grotto – the kind of place that Indiana Jones might have discovered. And in that grotto is a fountain of youth – it's the only explanation for the sprightly seniors of Budbury.

"Missed the action yesterday, though, didn't I?" replies Cherie, sipping her own tea and grimacing slightly when she realises it's still too hot. "Can't believe that! And I've heard that was Martha's dad, who came along in the nick of time? And that he's Australian? And that he's staying in a hotel?"

I nod, and smile at her expression. I can tell she's desperate to know more, but doesn't want to appear too pushy. I consider toying with her and staying tight-lipped and mysterious, but there doesn't seem to be much point – Cherie always knows everything, eventually. She's like a benign Big Brother.

"Yep. All correct. Martha's never actually met him before, so it's all quite ... um, I don't know, exciting?"

"You say the word 'exciting' as though you actually mean 'terrifying', Zoe – didn't it go well last night, when he came over for dinner?"

See. She knows that already and it was only a few hours ago. Maybe she has secret cameras installed in all her cottages...

"It went fine," I say, trying to sound enthusiastic. "As well as it possibly could under the very weird circumstances. I just

... I got a bit Scrumpy Joe-d, I suppose ... and now he's on his way here, and I'm wearing odd socks, and everything just feels a bit ... wonky."

Edie breaks off from her reading to glance at my feet, shakes her head, and goes back to Cathy and Heathcliff. I bet Cathy never wore odd socks.

Cherie nods, and folds her arms over her plentiful bosom, and looks thoughtful.

"I can imagine. It's possibly good for Martha, but it feels risky – like you've only just got her settled and suddenly it's all change again?"

"Exactly! But she seems happy about it, and that's great. It's been a long time since she's seemed happy about anything. I don't know how long he's staying for, so we just have to make the most of it, I suppose. Get in as much dad time as we can before he jets off into the sunset."

"And be ready to mop up if it all goes wrong? Clean up on aisle Martha?"

I just smile. She gets it. Of course she gets it.

"Mopping up," she adds, her head angled on one side as she chooses her words, "can be very tiring work. Especially when you feel like you might need a bit of mopping up yourself. Look ... this is just an idea, and I'd never offer if you didn't agree, but Saffron is free. If Cal wanted to stay there, he could ... he'd be nearer to Martha, so they could properly get to know each other, spend more time together? Or would that be too much for you?"

I ponder that while I shove half a scone in my mouth. I feel bad that I'm not giving the scone my full attention, but I need to think while I eat.

The thought of having Cal on the doorstep is jarring. It makes me feel jittery and nervous and oddly threatened. But I need to put on my big girl pants, and think about what might work best for Martha. If Cal is only going to be here for a few weeks, then maybe this could work – it would definitely maximise the amount of time they had together.

"Thank you Cherie," I say, when I've finished with the scone. "That could be ... really good. Maybe we could talk to him about it when he arrives."

"He's here," chips in Edie, gesturing to the door with her silver head. She gazes at him for a few minutes, then goes back to her book.

Cal pauses in the doorway, shaking the rain off his cowboy hat, and stamping some mud from his boots. He spots me, and waves his hat like he's at a rodeo, before hanging his waxed jacket up on the coat hooks and making his way across to our corner.

"G'day, ladies," he says, laying the accent on a lot thicker than it usually is. Tart. I note all the hen party women staring at him as he crosses the room, taking in the hair and the tan and the snug-fitting Levis and the just-as-snug-fitting T-shirt and the big-buckled belt between the two. He looks like an exotic creature who's wandered into the room, unaware of how much of a stir he's causing. Or maybe entirely aware, I don't know him well enough to call it.

Cherie stands up and looks him up and down, hands on her hips.

"So this is the hero of the hour, is it?" she says, when she's finished inspecting him.

Before he can reply, she has him in a bear hug. Cherie's hugs can take you off guard, but he handles it well, and is one of the few people who isn't dwarfed by her Amazonian figure. He emerges from her embrace looking mellow and calm.

I stand up too, and feel like I'm a midget in a land of giants.

"Cal, you didn't get to meet everyone properly yesterday, in all the chaos. This is Edie. Big Edie, I mean."

Edie cackles in delight at that one. She's about four foot ten, so it must be the first time she's ever been known as Big Edie – she clearly likes it, clapping her hands together in glee.

"Edie is the hoola-hooping champion of all Budbury," I add, for some reason.

"That's right," she responds. "The hips don't lie ..."

I shake my head – pondering Edie and her hips feels wrong – and continue my introductions.

"And this is Cherie, who owns the cafe, and the holiday cottages, and ... well, most of Budbury, it seems ..."

"Yep. Just call me Mummy Warbucks," she says, grinning. "And you saw my hubbie Frank yesterday – you two will have a lot in common; he has his own farm, and his son and grand-children live in Australia."

"Ah. Well I probably know them, then," replies Cal, nodding in recognition as Frank holds up his hand in greeting. He's been immersed in the newspaper since we arrived, probably wisely deciding to let the women-folk get on with their gabbing, but now he makes his way over to shake Cal's hand.

"Nice to meet you," says Frank, also laying his Dorset accent on a lot thicker. What is it with these blokes?

"Well done yesterday, Cal – quite the welcome party, eh?"

"I've had worse," answers Cal, grinning. "Mum and baby doing all right, are they?"

"I hear so, yes. Not been round myself yet – give them the chance to get used to it all, I reckon. Bit of an adjustment, having a baby in the house."

A fleeting moment of sadness whisps across Cal's face as he replies: "I wouldn't know much about that; never been around babies much, unless they're covered in wool and destined for the dinner plate. I'm jumping in at the deep end with a teenager."

"You'll be grand, Cal," says Frank, thumping him on the back with a strength that belies his 80-plus years. "Nothing to it, and Martha's a great girl. Plus you'll have Zoe around to tell you how to do everything right."

I laugh out loud at that one – I just can't help myself. They all pause and look at me; even the hen party girls seem to be wondering what the noise is.

"Sorry," I say, embarrassed. "It just ... well, that amused me. As if I know what I'm doing – I'm making it up as I go along."

Cal gives me a lop-sided grin. Maybe he's wondering what he's got himself into.

"You're doing just fine," Cherie assures me, reaching out and squeezing my shoulder. "And we're all making it up as we go along, my love – some people just hide it better than others. Now, Cal, sit down, make yourself at home, and I'll go and whip up some breakfast for you ... we had a bit of a brainwave about your digs this morning. I'll leave Zoe to tell you all about it ..."

PART THREE

Modern Love

Chapter 22

"My legs are so fat, they'd make harem pants look like jeggings," says Laura, poking at her own thighs in disgust.

I glance at her legs, and see a perfectly normal, ever-so-slightly chunky set of limbs, encased in blue denim. Blue denim that is covered in floury handprints, from the damson and blackberry pudding she's been making. Laura and Matt have started a cottage garden at the Rockery, producing seasonal fruit and veg for the cafe, and this is one of her experiments.

The smell of the pudding is wafting around the cafe making us all sniff like starving urchins as we wait for it to bake, and I'm fairly sure that eating it won't help Laura's self-pronounced chubby leg problem.

She's not fat, Laura. But she's not thin either. I suppose she's just ... 'comfy' would probably be the best word. She looks like a mum should look, with enough extra on her to give good cuddles, but not so much she could be mistaken for Jabba the Hut on a night out.

"Don't be daft," I say, looking up from my mammoth pencil sharpening mission. "You look lovely. Matt certainly seems to think so. And it's better than being called a ginger boy."

"You don't look like a boy!" she utters in shock. "You're just ... petite!"

I grunt in thanks, and carry on sharpening. It really is the most chilled out of things to do on a rainy autumn day, and I'm getting through the colours at a speedy rate. I tell myself to slow down before I run out. I am one crazy cat when it comes to blunt pencils.

"I always wished I'd had more in the boob department," adds Edie, who is also sharpening. In fact, it was all her idea, and she brought along the sharpener – one of those old-fashioned metal ones they used to have in schools on teachers' desks. "Back in the days when I had any boobs at all!"

I find myself staring at Edie's frail looking chest, mainly because she's pointing at it with one bony finger, as though inviting me to check her bad boys out. I shudder and look away, quickly.

"Why is it," chips in Becca, Little Edie blissfully asleep on her lap, "that whenever a group of women get together, it is decreed that they will start moaning about their bodies? Comparing tits and whinging about arses and wishing for something different? We're all bloody perfect as far as I'm concerned!"

Cherie nods in agreement, pausing in her toenail painting. She has two chairs pulled together, her feet propped up on one, a bottle of something bright pink in her hand. She waves the little brush around as she speaks.

"That's true, Becca. We all are. Bloody perfect. And anyway, your size doesn't matter, it's the proportions that count – who came up with that quote? The one that says 'I have an hour glass figure, it's just a very large hour glass'?"

"I don't know," replies Becca, gazing at the baby's face. "Was it Confucious? I hear he liked a girl with a bit of meat on her bones ..."

We all laugh at that one, then stop abruptly as Little Edie starts to stir at the noise, waving a pink hand around like she's flagging a cab. It's always amazed me how something so tiny as a new-born baby can still completely dominate a room full of adults. It took Becca ages to get her to doze off, and none of us want to risk her wrath by waking her up again. Becca looks exhausted, in the way of all new mums – but also incredibly happy.

Little Edie is now three weeks old. Her tufty hair has lightened a few shades, and she is a chubby, round bundle of humanity. She's wearing a sleepsuit that says 'Surf Baby' on it, and one of her dimpled feet is bare. She looks even more scrumptious than a damson and blackberry pudding. Midgebo agrees, and is licking her exposed toes with affection until Becca gently pushes his furry snout away.

Technically, the cafe is open – but as there are no customers at all on this blustery October day, we're simply treating it as a place to hang out and chat. Cherie, I've been assured by

Laura, really doesn't need the money – which is a good thing, as the quiet season in Budbury now seems to have truly kicked in. There are some bookings at the cottages for the school half term, and apparently it picks up a bit near Christmas, but at the moment it's deadly quiet.

In fact, the only people knocking around the place are Laura and her kids, Matt, me, Martha, and of course Cal.

Cal, it seems, is staying a little longer than he originally intended. In fact, he's staying until New Year – a fact that fills me with both relief and fear.

Relief, because things with him and Martha are going brilliantly. They've developed their own routines and rhythms, and they're a damn sight better than her old ones. They're going for walks, swapping stories, teaching each other their native slang, listening to music, borrowing Midgebo for adventures, talking about their lives, about Kate, about work and college. About Martha's plans for the future – I'm delighted to hear her even admit to having one – and about which university she might go to. Cal has acquired a guitar from Matt, and I often hear him playing it as I pass Saffron, sometimes even accompanied by Martha's note-perfect voice.

She spends a lot of time with him, even staying over some-times, and I try not to be too much of a misery guts about it. It's not like sharing the house with Martha has ever been a wheelbarrow full of laughs – but when she's not there, I miss her. I even miss the door slamming and the sarcasm and the plates that suddenly find their way to the kitchen covered in dried-on pasta sauce that I have to blow-torch off.

Cal, in all fairness, is sensitive enough to realise that all of this is a big adjustment for me. He tries to include me – dragging me along on missions to collect fossils from Charmouth beach, tempting me out to the village pub for lunch, arranging video nights at Lilac Wine when we both get the chance to indulge in a few ciders. In fact, I see a lot of him – especially on those couple of occasions when we've both ended up in the swimming pool at the same time.

Those occasions have been kind of cringe-worthy, to be honest. I don't know why – I'm usually wearing an ancient costume I've had since I was 16 that is so modest a Victorian school ma'am could get away with it. It's not like I'm traipsing around in a thong bikini or anything – but it still leaves me blushing and mortified every time. I suspect it has less to do with what I'm wearing, and more to do with what he's wearing – or not wearing. I'm not used to seeing mostly-naked men in the flesh, and it makes my nostrils flare.

He has one of those bodies that's fit from work, from living on the land, rather than from the gym – solid and strong and long. I try not to stare, but it ain't easy, especially as he cuts through the water with such grace and ease, like a sexy dolphin. Luckily he doesn't make the weird clicky noises as well.

It's now reached the stage where I do a surreptitious check before I risk it, and if he's there, I tiptoe back to Lilac Wine, wrapped in my towel, hoping he didn't notice me peaking in through the steamy windows.

I have days where he always seems to be around. He'll turn up early to give Martha a lift to the village, and find me half-asleep in my coffee mug. Or he'll pop round to see if I fancy coming with them on a horse ride at the local stable, and laugh at my horrified expression. I'll be reading a good book, and he'll tap on the window. It's all very ... unsettling. He's not the kind of man you can ignore – he's too big for one thing – and I'm finding his presence in my life more of an irritant than I would have expected.

Some of that is because of my own screwed up need for solitude – but some of it is also to do with the fear I mentioned earlier. He's found a place here, Cal. He fixes things around the cottages for Cherie, and spends time with Frank over at his farm, looking at cows' bums or whatever, and goes for pints with Matt and Sam and Scrumpy Joe.

Laura still goes a bit moon-eyed when he walks into the room, and Cherie clearly loves getting him to change lightbulbs for her so we can all pretend we don't notice when his T-shirt rides up from his jeans. I suspect if I sneak into the cafe early one day, I'll catch her breaking lightbulbs on purpose.

He's kind, and funny, and likeable, and everyone seems to be half in love with him – especially Martha. This is the bit that worries me. It's highly likely that I'm over-thinking it all, but I can't help wondering about what will happen when he finally leaves.

Specifically, what will happen to Martha. Will she be cool with it? Will she have a complete breakdown at losing yet another parent, just as she's found him? Will she want to go with him? It's one of the reasons I've been resisting joining the Budbury branch of the Cal Evans appreciation society – I'm going to need to be fully prepared, and fully functioning, to deal with whatever life throws at us next.

I'm pondering all of this as I sharpen, lost in thought, the chatter of the women humming quietly away in the background like a gossipy Greek chorus.

"Earth calling Zoe, earth calling Zoe – are you receiving?" says Laura, prodding me in the side until I look up.

"Yes? What? Is the cake ready?" I say, looking around at their amused faces. "What did I miss?"

"Another ten minutes for the cake," replies Laura after a quick glance at her watch. "And we were just wondering what it's been like, having Cal around ..."

They're all staring at me expectantly. Even Little Edie, now awake again, is lolling in her mother's arms, fixing me with an eery blue gaze, like she's hanging on my every word. Midgebo is licking his own testicles now, so at least he's not interested.

"Um ... it's all right," I respond, weakly.

"Have you seen him in the swimming pool?" asks Laura, nudging me and grinning. "Bet he's quite the merman!"

"Yeah ... I suppose. I have seen him in the swimming pool. And in Lilac Wine. And in Saffron. And in the pub, and in here, and in my bloody dreams ... the man seems to be every-where. Can't get away from him."

"God, why would you want to ..." says Becca, rolling her eyes. "If I wasn't a taken woman, I'd be all over him."

Edie nods, then looks slightly embarrassed about it, while Cherie tells a story about asking him to fix the dishwasher, and enjoying the view as he crawled around on the floor to get a better angle. They all guffaw in response, while I feel increasingly awkward.

"What's up?" says Cherie, frowning at me. "Is it too much? Is it making you feel icky?"

"It is, for some reason. I mean, I know what he looks like – I've got eyes – but it just feels a bit wrong to be lusting after him like this. He's Martha's dad, for God's sake!"

"He's not *your* dad, though, is he?" asks Becca, soothing the baby as she speaks. "So that's okay."

I nod, because it's hard to explain. It's hard to put it all into words, the way he makes me feel – nervous and tense and happy all at the same time. Like if I let myself relax, I could enjoy his company a lot more than I should. That if I just allowed it to happen, Cal would make it onto the very short list of people who have made me feel safe and cared for in this life. The very short list that, until we moved here, only really featured Kate's name.

"I know ... but he's just there all the time. I'm used to living on my own, and had just about got used to living with Martha, and now there's someone else around. I feel a bit ... invaded!

Like I don't have anywhere that's just mine any more … I know it sounds pathetic and childish, but it's the way I feel. And no amount of muscle really makes up for that."

Becca stares at me while she processes all of this, and I see her thrash my words around in her mind. Until she met Sam, Becca also lived alone, in a small flat in Manchester, content with her own company and her own routines. I'm guessing she understands my outburst better than most – definitely better than Laura, who married her childhood sweetheart David when she was only 20.

Becca looks at Cherie, and some kind of unspoken conversation goes on between them, all wide eyes and smiles and nods.

"She needs an escape hatch," says Becca, grinning.

"You're right," replies Cherie, standing up and stretching tall. Her toes look gorgeous. "And it just so happens that we have one, doesn't it? Come on, Zoe – follow me, my lovely."

I shrug, and lay down my pencil – a bright shade of red.

"Don't do them all while I'm gone," I say to Edie, pointing my finger in warning. She lets out a horror-movie cackle in response, and mutters: "Mine, all mine …" as she scoops a pile of stubby pencils towards her.

I follow Cherie through the kitchen, where we both pause to inhale the tempting aroma of almost-baked pudding, and towards a door at the back of the room. She unlatches it, and we climb a flight of steep stairs that have bright yellow safety stripes on them.

"Fell down them a while back," she says over her shoulder. "Broke my poor hip. Frank's never let me live it down – he's still convinced I was high as a kite at the time."

Cherie, I have learned since I arrived in Budbury, is still at least partly the old hippie rock chick she used to be. She might not be following The Who around the festival circuit any more, but she still likes the occasional herbal cigarette – 'for medicinal reasons, obviously.'

We emerge at the top of the stairs into what I can only describe as a Cherie-inspired wonderland. It's a large studio flat that sprawls along the eaves of the building, flooded with what light there is today through large skylights in the roof. The walls are draped with Middle Eastern looking sheets and fabrics, vintage rock posters, and more of the framed pictures of the coast that she has on display in the cafe.

The furniture is an odd mix of new and old, light and dark, eccentric and functional, and the whole place is crammed with knick-knacks. Not the usual senior citizen parade of Royal Doulton figurines and scary porcelain dolls in lacy frocks – knick knacks that are similar to the strange objects downstairs. Shells and colourful glassware and ornamental gourds and mahogany carvings and a small gathering of antiquated snuff tins.

There are packed bookshelves, bearing photos of Cherie and the man I presume to be her late husband, Wally, in her younger days: she's gorgeous, hair still wild, feet still bare; he's smaller, with 70s sideburns and a grin that says he can't quite believe how lucky he is to have bagged this particular Goddess. There's a king-sized bed, draped in tie-dye sheets, and a huge collection of vinyl next to an old-fashioned record player.

"Welcome to my escape hatch!" she says proudly, gesturing around. "I moved in here after my Wally died. I floated around in misery for a few years, then decided to do something useful with the money he'd left me – I moved here, bought the cafe, and the rest is history. Been here almost 20 years now – funny how time passes. This was my haven – and I never thought I'd leave it, honest I didn't. I was happy here ... but then me and Frank came to our senses, and I started over again at his place.

"Then, it kind of passed on to Becca for a while – when she first came down here, it was her escape hatch, until she got together with Sam. It mainly sits empty now, which is a crying shame – so now it can be yours, too. Use it whenever you like. In the day, at night ... it's yours. I'll give you the spare keys to the cafe, and then you can come here and hide any time you want. You know, when the sight of Cal in his skivvies gets too much for you ..."

I roll my eyes at that one – it's already too much for me – and look around at the flat. As escape hatches go, it's just about perfect, and I can imagine myself burrowing away under those bed sheets, good book on the go, bit of Led Zep on the record player, completely and totally alone...

"It's perfect," I say, wondering if it would be rude to do all of that right now. "Thank you so much. I know it's stupid, needing a break from it all – but ... well. I am stupid, I suppose."

"No you're not. You're just human, sweetie. And you're welcome. But I must warn you, this place does seem to come with a curse ..."

I raise my eyebrows, and she grins and punches me in the arm.

"Everyone seems to start off here as a single lady," she says, giving it a little Beyoncé grind as she sings the last two words, badly. "But then they end up paired off ..."

Chapter 23

It's Parents' Evening.

Words that strike fear and sadness into my heart for a variety of reasons. Mainly, because I shouldn't be doing this – Kate should. Kate should be here to see her daughter growing up, and it is still insane that she's not. Nights like this always remind me of how completely screwed up this whole situation is; and I miss her even more than usual. In years past, I've simply heard second-hand from Kate how things went – the academic progress, the praise, the warnings, all wrapped up in Kate's amusing story-telling style. This time, it's all down to me.

As far as I know, her new college life has been going smoothly. I know Lizzie would usually adhere to the teen code of not snitching, but I also know she would have told Laura if anything serious had gone wrong. Like Martha actually getting off the bus after it left the village, and spending her days *Breaking Bad* in rural Dorset.

There have been no nasty letters or terse voicemails on my

phone from Martha's teachers, so I have been assuming that she hasn't burned down the drama studio, stolen anything, or punched the head master in the face. But what do I know? Maybe they've been saving it all up for tonight.

My interactions with Martha's educators haven't exactly been cordial thus far, so it's understandable that I'm feeling nervous. I'm also nervous because Cal is coming with me. Cal, who is her father, I remind myself – and thus has every right to come to Parents' Evening. Being, you know, an actual parent and all.

He'd asked my permission first, but I could hardly say no, could I? Especially when he paired it with a comment along the lines of, 'I've never had the chance before.' Laura thought it was a brilliant idea, but then again she would – despite the sadness of losing her husband a few years ago, I've never met anyone with such a belief in happy endings.

"It'll be lovely," she says, beaming. "Having him there to support you. The ones I did without David were awful – it was all I could do not to burst into tears while I was sitting on the naughty chair. It just felt so wrong to be there alone – and anyway, Martha will secretly be pleased."

I knew she was right, but I still didn't feel one hundred per cent good about it. Having Cal there for support was something I couldn't afford to get used to. Cal might currently be super-dad and the apple of everyone's eye – but Cal would be leaving. I can't let myself rely on him.

I try and hide my reservations, as Martha sees us off from

the cottages. She's arranged a sleepover with Lizzie at Hyacinth House tonight, which really does cheer me up. Her and Lizzie have a lot in common – they're both girls from big cities who were dragged away to live in the back of beyond; both have lost a parent, and both use way too much eyeliner. Despite her early resistance to anything positive in her life, Martha is finally allowing their friendship to bloom. That, at least, is excellent news.

Cal is dressed in his usual outfit of jeans, waxed jacket and cowboy hat, which I expect to cause quite a stir at a school in rural Dorset. I have attempted to look conservative and responsible, in leggings, a clean top, and my shiniest calf-high boots. The fact that Martha is sniggering at us detracts from my confidence levels, but I'm used to that by now.

"You two look so funny," she says, giggling in the doorway of Hyacinth. "Like you're one of those weird couples who auditions for the *X Factor* in fancy dress. You'd call yourselves the Texas Twosome and do awful country and western music while Simon Cowell rolls his eyes at you."

Cal promptly takes his cowboy hat off, and wedges it onto my head, where it floats on a sea of ginger curls.

"How's about that, then?" he asks, standing back to look at me. "Even better, yeah? I reckon we could do a mean Islands in the Stream ..."

Martha is now laughing out loud, and Lizzie is peering over her shoulder to see what all the fuss is about. She immediately takes out her phone and snaps a picture of us, the cow. I suspect my face looks like I've just encountered a huge pile of horse manure.

"Go on, get off with you!" shouts Laura from the hallway. "Ignore them. And have fun – don't worry about Martha, she's in safe hands..."

Just as she says this, there is a huge bang from the kitchen, and the smell of smoke. She darts off, yelling as she goes: "It's fine, it's fine ... Nate, what have I said about trying to dry your football boots in the oven? Did you even take them out of the carrier bag?"

The girls dash back inside – not wanting to miss a moment of the poor lad getting told off – leaving the Texas Twosome to make their way to Cal's jeep and head to the college. He used to have a rental car – a tiny Fiat 500 that he barely fit into – but once he decided to extend his stay, Frank loaned him one of the more weather appropriate farm trucks.

The rain has been coming down steadily for several days now, and the narrow country roads are mired in mud and mulched up leaves that the once green trees have shed. Some days are gorgeous and crisp and clear – others are foul. At the very least, Cal coming with me to Parents' Evening means that I don't have to drive, something I'm always thankful for.

We chat about the weather, about Martha, about incidents past, and about nothing at all important as we drive. As ever, I know I'm being friendly but distant with him – which seems to have developed into my default setting. I'm also tense about the night ahead, and finding out what Martha has been up to – literally nothing would surprise me.

In the end, I am a little surprised. But in a good way. All four of her teachers say she is bright, capable, and 'quite a character.' I've heard this description of Martha before, and it is usually a diplomatic way of saying 'she's an absolute horror' – but in this case, it seems to be meant as a compliment. Maybe she's working harder. Maybe she's changed. Maybe it's just different in sixth form, when they're given a bit more freedom and are actually studying subjects they're interested in.

Maybe, I think, as we get back into the car, still slightly shell-shocked by all the praise, I am a very bad person – I feel guilty that I expected the worst.

"Well," says Cal, as he heads back into the village, windscreen wipers doing an insane dance to try and cope with the downpour, headlights cutting a yellow path through the darkness, "that went well, yeah? I mean, I have no experience at all – but it sounded good to me. Settling in well, meeting her grades, homework in on time … nothing to worry about?"

I glance at him as we drive. Wisely, he's concentrating on the twisting roads ahead, his face shadowed, eyes focused. Strong hands on the steering wheel, cowboy hat on the back seat, sounding relaxed.

"I suppose so," I reply, wondering why I can't feel as relaxed as he seems to.

"You don't sound too convinced, Zo … what's bothering

you? I can tell there's something wrong. You always chew your lips when there's something wrong."

I immediately stop chomping, which I hadn't even noticed I was doing.

"No, there's nothing wrong – I'm just ... well, I feel bad. I was kind of expecting trouble, and now there isn't any, I'm a bit like a balloon that's been popped. And I feel crappy for assuming she'd have messed up. Kate would never have assumed that, and I'm sure you didn't."

He is silent for a few moments, thinking about what I've said, his fingers tapping rhythmically on the wheel the only sign that he's reflecting on it at all.

"I think," he says eventually, "that you need to give yourself a break. Kate was her mum for her whole life. You've only been doing it for a few months – and you definitely got the worst few months ever. And as for me, well ... Jesus, I've only just shown up! Easy for me to look like I've got it all right – but I'm not the one who's been keeping her safe. Looking after her when she's had a few too many. Worrying about her every time she's out of the house. That's been you, Zoe – you've given up your job and your home and your whole way of life to move here with her. *For* her. You've had to handle a lot of shit, and you've handled it well – so stop poking at yourself, and enjoy the moment."

I'm a little gobsmacked by this speech. Partly because he says it so definitely – in a tone of voice that clearly shows he wants no arguments. Partly because ... well, maybe he's right.

I've known Martha since she was born, and I can say whole-heartedly that our months together in Bristol were definitely the hardest. For both of us.

Now, maybe – if I work on the assumption that her college teachers are telling the truth, and not just scared because she's threatened to kidnap their children – we've turned a corner. Being here has helped. Lizzie has helped. Cherie has helped. Cal has helped. Perhaps even I've helped – if by 'helped' I mean 'not killed her or run away screaming into the hills.'

Possibly, I decide, looking back at the mothers I've known over the years – barring my own – that is the hardest part of all. The sticking around, even when you get no thanks, no appreciation, and no acknowledgement that you even exist.

I stuck around. I'm still sticking around – and even if Cal jetted home tomorrow, or Martha and Lizzie have a teenaged spat, or we have to move back to Bristol, I'll always be around. I don't have much to give Martha – but I can at least give her that.

It's a rare moment of peace, and I'm thankful to Cal for pushing me in the right direction. And in an equally rare moment of generosity of spirit, I decide to spread the love. I get out my phone – a message has landed from Laura, saying all is well and the girls are upstairs in Lizzie's room, plotting world domination. I compose a quick text of my own: 'Just been to Martha's parents' evening at her new college. She's doing really well, I'm very proud of her. Hope all is good with you two.' I pause for a moment, decide that adding kisses would be a step too far, and hit send – pinging the good news all the way to Barbara and Ron in Bristol.

Seconds later, a reply arrives: 'Thank you for letting us know. Ron has done the garden, and I've given the toilets a good cleaning. Will call soon to arrange a visit.'

I'm happy with some of that – I mean, who doesn't like getting the toilets cleaned for free? – but grimace slightly at the mention of a visit.

"Bad news?" says Cal, giving me a quick sideways look.

"Maybe. Depends on your point of view. Kate's parents are planning to come and see us. They'll probably want to meet you as well ..."

"Yikes. Do they view me as the dastardly cad who despoiled their daughter?"

"Probably, yes," I reply, grinning at the thought. A truly evil part of me looks forward to that – maybe Cal will finally encounter someone he can't charm. "Where are we going?"

I frown as he misses the turn that would take us back to the Rockery, and instead heads for the road straight into the village.

"I'm doing what all good Aussies do when they've had good news. Or bad news. Or been awake for a whole day – I'm taking us to the pub. No arguments, now, all right? Martha's safe with Laura and going to college with Lizzie in the morning, neither of us has to be anywhere, and I need a pint. You can't avoid me forever."

I stifle the urge to answer back, and claim that I haven't

been avoiding him – because of course, it's true. And as he's not a total idiot, he's noticed. Somewhere between that first night, when I said we could do this together, and now, I've retreated. Backed off into my shell. Seen that Cal needs no help at all – he has a better relationship with Martha after a couple of weeks than I have after years. I've never once had to use our 'danger, danger' cowboy hat code – he just seems to know instinctively how to communicate with her. The pig.

So I just nod, and decide to go with the flow. And anyway – we do have reason to celebrate. Not so long ago, I was pulling Martha out of nightclubs. Now, it seems, she's the model student.

When we park up by the Horse and Rider, the rain is torrential. Cal gallantly lends me his hat, and tugs his jacket up over his head as we make a dash for the door. I notice the light still on in Edie's little terrace, and wonder what she's doing – watching *Strictly*, maybe, or chatting to her dead fiancé. A couple of doors along is Sam and Becca's place, where all the lights are off – presumably they're trying to grab some sleep while Little Edie snoozes. It's a street full of Edies, at completely different ends of the age spectrum. Bless them both.

I follow Cal into the pub, him holding the door open for me, and am immediately engulfed in warmth and chatter. It's a proper pub, this – not a touristy, chocolate-box pretty pub, but a pub where real people come to celebrate and commiserate and talk about sport and flirt and wash away the cares of the day.

It's a long, narrow room, occupied by a long, narrow bar. Most of the tall stools next to it are taken by men wearing a version of what I now recognise as the rural uniform: check shirts, cords or jeans, warm sweaters, boots. People nod at Cal as he makes his way to get served, and I look around for a table. I see Matt and Frank over by the log fire, several empties already in front of them. Frank waves me over, and I shake the rain off the cowboy hat as I go.

"Don't be putting that on in here," says Frank, his face deadly serious. "You'll be living out many a man's fantasy. They're only flesh and blood, you know!"

I pop it onto his head instead, where it looks very fine indeed, his silver-white hair peeking out of the sides.

"How did it go?" asks Matt, pint of Guinness in hand.

"Erm ... strangely well. Not a bad word to be said about her. Glowing comments all round."

He nods, as though he wouldn't have expected anything else at all, and Cal arrives with our drinks. A pint of strange real ale called something like Black Badger's Bottom for him, cider for me. I gulp half of it down in one go, which attracts admiring glances from the menfolk. I've still got the magic.

"Looks like someone's got a thirst on," says Frank, gesturing at the glass. Oh boy, was he right.

Chapter 24

I end up drinking quite a few more pints of cider, and a Baileys 'for the road' Why is it that Baileys can hold such magnetic allure at the end of the night? You know it's a bad idea, but somehow it seems to be calling to you, in all its creamy goodness.

Matt and Frank leave at about ten – they both have early dates with various animals – but we stick it out until the bitter end. We get double orders in when the last bell rings, and we stagger back out into the rain at around midnight. By that time, Big Edie's lights are all out, but Little Edie's are all on again. New baby fun times.

Cal, although he doesn't look like it, has consumed even more beer than I have – I suppose he just has more room to store it. Despite the fact that he could probably walk in a straight line if he tried, there's no way he can drive, and neither can I.

The rain is lashing down, there's a wicked wind blowing up from the bay, and we're two miles away from the cottages.

It's at times like this I miss living in a city, where you can just throw yourself in front of a black cab and climb in the back seat with a kebab.

Cal is staring up into the rain, seeming to actually enjoy it as the drops splatter on to his face and pour down his neck.

"Better get a move on, then ..." he says, taking my hand and leading us towards the road out of the village. "Miles to go before we sleep, and all that."

I stop, and keep hold of his hand so he has to stop as well. I have had a brainwave. One of those perfect brainwaves that makes utter sense when you're drunk.

"We can stay at the cafe," I say, "I have the keys, and Cherie's kind of given me a flat to stay in ... it's only a few minutes away. At least we can dry off and wait out the rain. Plus the whole place is full of booze. And food. And records."

"Sounds like paradise," he replies, grinning a white-toothed grin in the moonlight. "Come on, I'll race ya!"

He may have much longer legs, but I'm nippy, and willing to cheat. I know all the shortcuts, and disappear off behind the Community Hall before he's even finished the last word of his sentence. Again, it's one of those things that makes sense when you're drunk – galloping along coastal paths on a dark, wet night, purely for the childish satisfaction of beating someone in a race.

As I don't plunge to a watery death or break my ankle, it all seems completely worth it – I reach the cafe door seconds before he does, out of puff but triumphant. I wave my arms in the air, dance around him, and chant: 'Loser, loser, loser …' while pointing at his face. It's all very gracious and sporting, the stuff that Olympic ideals were built on.

I am singing *We Are The Champions* by Queen as I unlock the doors to the cafe, and let us both in. It's a relief to be out of the rain, but also eerie in here at night – the weird objects and handmade mobiles hanging from the ceiling look slightly sinister, twisting and turning in the moonlight, casting shadows on the table-tops and looking as though they've suddenly come to life.

"Woah …" I say, pointing at the way the dangling seven-inch vinyl singles are rotating, "look at that! Do you think this place is haunted? Pirates? Smugglers? Jilted peasant wenches?"

"No," replies Cal, closing up behind him. "I think we opened the door and let a howling gale in, and that you read too many books."

"No such thing as reading too many books," I say, going through to the kitchen and swiping a few cupcakes from the chilled display cabinet. They're all made of chocolate sponge, and decorated with autumn themed toppings – golden leaves swirled in icing, fat blobby orange pumpkins, Halloween faces. Laura's been playing again.

I write a quick I.O.U, scrawling in lopsided letters that I'll pay for the cakes tomorrow, and gesture for Cal to follow me up the stairs to Cherie Land.

He emerges into the flat, and immediately grins as he looks around.

"This is brilliant," he says, taking in the wall hangings and pictures and weirdness. "Exactly the kind of place I'd imagine Cherie living. She's quite the girl, isn't she? Seems to have really bad luck with light bulbs, though ..."

"Oh! That's on purpose. She just likes watching you changing them. Hope it doesn't offend you to be objectified in such a terrible way."

"Ha! I thought something dodgy was going on ... and nah, it doesn't offend me. Being here, surrounded by all you gorgeous ladies, is a bit of a change for me. It's mainly smelly blokes back where I live, apart from the odd wife ... You're staring at me ... what's wrong? Seen another ghost?"

"No," I reply, looking him up and down. "You're dripping all over the place. Take your clothes off."

He pauses, and gives me a long, lazy grin that makes my tummy feel a bit funny. Or maybe that's the cider.

"Bit sudden, isn't it, Zo? I mean, I got the impression you didn't even like me much ..."

"What? Of course I like you! I'm just ... I don't know, I'm quite a private person, and you're only here for a bit, and anyway, this is all about you and Martha, not me ... and when I said take your clothes off, I meant so I could chuck them in the dryer. Don't worry, your virtue is safe with me. I'll go and find you something else to wear."

I scuttle away to the bathroom. I can feel a humdinger of

a blush coming on, and don't want to give him the satisfaction of witnessing it.

I towel-dry my hair, and then root around on the back of the bathroom door, looking through Cherie's vast collection of dressing gowns and lounge wear until I find one that I think will suit him perfectly. It's Chinese silk, hot pink, and decorated with exotic flowers and neon-shaded lily pads. Luckily Cherie is a statuesque lady, so he should be able to squash into it. For myself I chose a plain black towelling affair, which, when I shimmy out of my soggy clothes and into it, comes down to my ankles and flows over my wrists. I look like one of those Jawas from *Star Wars*.

By the time I come out, after a quick red-cheek check in the mirror, Cal is bare down to his white jersey boxers, and loading his clothes into the dryer. I pause to appreciate the view as he leans forward over the machine, then tear my eyes away – I'll be blushing again if I let my mind wander. I shove the Chinese gown into his hands, and add my leggings and top to the laundry.

He raises one eyebrow at the pink robe, but mercifully puts it on. I laugh immediately – it falls to his knees, but his brawny arms poke through about four inches lower than the sleeves, straining the material as he tries to wrap it around his chest.

"Whaddaya think?" he asks, giving me a twirl.

I trip over my own dressing gown on the way through to

the living room, which kind of serves me right, and reply: "Gorgeous. It's definitely your colour. Cake?"

He follows, and we settle down to give in to our munchies. The cakes are, obviously, divine, and Cal has also rooted out a bottle of brandy. I sit cross-legged on the bed, carefully arranging the folds of the robe so that everything is covered, and he sprawls on the sofa, slightly less covered. I take pity on him, and throw him a blanket – I don't need to be looking at that, thank you very much. The dusting of fair hair on the bronzed skin of his chest is way too distracting.

My phone pings, and when I check it, I see a message from Martha. I'd texted her earlier saying I was very proud of her, and she's replied: "I am printing this out and getting it laminated to use in future arguments."

I giggle, more than it merits due to alcohol and nerves, and sip my brandy. It fills me with instant warmth, and I bless the Gods of Serendipity that brought Cherie Moon into my life.

"So," says Cal, as ever looking a lot more relaxed than me, "alone at last. Talk to me."

"About what?" I ask, hoping he doesn't say world politics or climate change.

"Talk to me about Kate. Your version of Kate. Tell me what she was like."

I pause. Drink some more. Fidget with my dressing gown. Lean over to the record player and put on the album I'd been listening to yesterday: the appropriately titled *Wish You Were*

224

Here by Pink Floyd. We'd always loved this one, Kate and I – singing along to each other about how we were just two lost souls swimming in a fish bowl.

He's right, of course. I do have my own version of Kate. My Kate wasn't Martha's Kate, or his Kate, and definitely not Barbara and Ron's Kate. She was my very own crazy diamond, and I'd give anything for her to still be shining.

So, I talk. I tell him about my Kate. I tell him about the day we met in primary school. About the way we grew up together – teenaged years, boy crushes, layers of make-up over our spots, sneaking glugs of Barbara and Ron's whisky and topping up the bottle with water.

Her, desperate to break free from their benign dictatorship, stifled by their rules and regulations. Me, wounded by a lack of rules and regulations – nobody caring enough to bother telling me what to do. Us meeting somewhere in the middle, creating our very own safe ground.

Going to gigs and crashing festivals and nights in The Dump and being on first-name terms with club bouncers all over the city. Kate passing her driving test and us taking her ancient old Mini on a camping trip around Wales. Her going to Uni and me visiting most weekends. Endless nights on the beach near Aberystwyth, smoking weed and spotting whales in the moonlight.

The way she worried about me when she went travelling for a month, just after I'd started working in the book shop. The postcards and late night phone calls and me meeting her at the airport when she came home, her hair bleached blonde by the sun, her toenails neon pink in grimy sandals, rucksack full of memories.

Finding out she was pregnant, and spending the next hour laughing hysterically at the thought of either of us ever being mature enough to raise a child. Martha being born, and our lives changing overnight: a house, a mortgage, a proper job, family holidays. Listening to music in the kitchen, getting drunk in the house instead of the pub, dancing to Pulp and the Stone Roses while Martha slept.

Her coping with the Barbara and Ron Effect and the ways they screwed her up; me coping with the No Good Parents Effect and the ways that screwed me up; both of us determined to screw up Martha as little as we possibly could.

Life, moving on. Quieter in some ways, louder in others. Always together, always ready to deal with whatever got thrown our way.

Until the day she turned up on my doorstep pale and shaking, like a ghost that had seen a ghost. The day we got thrown the world's crappiest curve ball. The day she found the lump. The rapid-fire succession of GP-hospital-operation-chemo. The way she fought, the way she raged. The way she finally accepted, with far more grace and calm than I did. The day she died. Me by her side, Martha next to me, Barbara and Ron at the end of the bed, hovering, uncertain, broken and embarrassed at their loss of control, not knowing what to do or how to act.

She'd been quiet, eased into silence by drugs and kind hospice staff. Just once that day, she opened her eyes. Held out her hands for me and Martha to hold. Told us she loved us, one last time. One last time before she left us all.

I talk, and I cry, and he listens, and it feels ... liberating. I can't talk to Martha like this. I can't talk to anyone like this, and somehow, letting it all out is releasing a giant bubble of tension and grief that I've been carrying around with me for so long. Focusing on Martha, on her life and her pain, squashing my own down and hoping that it might just go away. It hasn't gone away. It probably never will.

At some point, Cal comes over to the bed. He holds me in his arms, and strokes my hair, and kisses my forehead. We lie down, and he comforts me while I sob, and eventually, exhausted, we fall sleep beneath the tie-dye sheets.

Two lost souls.

Chapter 25

When I wake up, he's in the kitchen. I can smell fresh coffee brewing, and hear bacon sizzling, and the sounds of toast popping from the machine. He has the radio on, very low, and is singing along to Lionel Richie's *Hello*.

I lie for a moment with one arm thrown over my face, unable to move. I have a hangover. My eyes are glued together and sore from all the crying. There is daylight pouring through the skylight, and I don't like it. The sound of rain clattering against the glass heralds the start of another beautiful day.

I groan and sit upright. My clothes from last night are neatly folded in a small pile on the sofa, and a glass of water is next to me on the table. Cal is clearly a man capable of looking after himself, and has kindly decided to extend that capability to include me this morning.

I'm not entirely sure how I feel about that. My first instinct is resentment, but I recognise that one as an old enemy: the 'I-don't-need-anyone' bullshit that I hid behind for years. The bullshit that comes across as me being bossy and independent, but is actually more about me being scared – scared that if I let anybody get too close, they'll let me down. They'll get caught selling knock-off video games in the market and get sent to prison; they'll decide there's no room for me in their home and send me to a new foster carer; they'll get diagnosed with terminal cancer and die.

Cal sees that I am awake, or at least doing a good imitation of it, and walks into the room with two steaming mugs in his hand.

"Hell-oooo!" he croons, in a bad mock-Lionel, "is it *tea* you're looking for?"

I moan, and reply: "Please tell me it's coffee instead!"

"It is," he answers, laying the mugs down on the table. "It just didn't fit the rhyme as well, so I adapted."

He's fully dressed in his jeans and shirt, and his hair looks damp from an early-morning shower. Unlike me, he seems to bear no physical evidence of the night before. I try not to hate him for it.

"So," he says, smiling at me, speaking gently to avoid hurting my aching brain, "I suspect we may have had a little bit too much to drink last night."

"Yes. Thank you, Captain Hindsight," I reply, sipping my coffee and hoping for a miracle. I tell myself that I've had hangovers before, far worse than this one. This one is just a whippersnapper of a hangover – I just need to pop a few pills, drink more coffee, go for a walk in the fresh sea air, and possibly amputate my own head. Then I'll be absolutely fine.

"What time is it? Is Martha all right?" I ask, as some of the fuzz starts to clear. Aaaah, coffee.

"She's fine. Called us dirty stop-outs, and seemed quite happy not to be the one behaving irresponsibly for a change. And it's half eight. I'm off to help Frank around the farm – need to keep my hand in, don't want to be turning into a city slicker ..."

"It's Budbury. Population less than 400. One bus stop. I don't think you're in any danger."

"Well, by my standards, that's a bustling metropolis, love. I've made you a bacon butty to help with your recovery, and now I know you're alive, I'll be off. How ... how are you feeling, after last night?"

I have a brief and fleeting moment of panic when he says that – what does he mean, after last night? Did something happen that I don't remember? Was there more than consolation and sleep going on under the tie-dye? Surely, I'd know...

He sees the look on my face, and correctly interprets it.

"I mean after our talk," he adds quickly, grinning. "Don't worry. I couldn't have penetrated that dressing gown even if I'd tried. It was like sleeping next to the giant marshmallow man from *Ghostbusters*."

Phew. Small mercies. I mean, I've not had sex for a year and a half, since an equally drunken encounter with a bloke with a green mohawk I met at a booksellers' convention. It would have been a shame to not even remember.

231

I nod, gratefully, and think about how to answer that question. How do I feel? Apart from physically hideous, that is.

"I feel ... all right," I reply, cautiously, as though trying it on for size. "I think it did me good. I needed to talk about her – to remember her. She was the most important person in my life, apart from Martha, and I've been so busy trying not to lose the plot, I suppose it had all been building up inside me. I never want to upset Martha by bringing the subject up, and neither does she, so we both tiptoe around it. So ... thank you. Thank you for asking about her, and thank you for listening, and most of all thank you for the coffee."

He smiles, nods, and stands up. He's so tall his head grazes the slope of the attic roof. He leans down and lays a gentle kiss on my curls, and grabs his hat.

"Good. Eat your breakfast before it goes cold. I'll see you later. I have a hot date with a heifer."

As soon as I hear the door close behind him, I drag myself out of bed, still wrapped up in the mighty towelling force field of Cherie's dressing gown, and stagger through to the kitchen. I lean up against the counter, and eat the sandwich. Not only is it perfectly cooked, but Cal has washed all the dishes, put the milk away, and stashed the brandy back in the booze cupboard. Damn him. He's just too perfect.

After a shower, a couple of emergency ibuprofen from my bag, and some fun times hopping round on one leg while I try and put my leggings on, I check all the lights and switches are off and head back downstairs to the cafe.

Laura is in the kitchen, pretending to be busy but very obviously waiting for me to arrive. She's not exactly a master of subterfuge, Laura – she'll have chatted to Cal when he left twenty minutes ago, and been waiting here in a state of suspended animation ever since, desperate for a chance to start the Spanish Inquisition.

I ward her off with a raised hand as she bustles over, already starting to talk.

"Stop!" I say, firmly. "I am in a state of severe hangover, and will not respond to questioning until I have imbibed more coffee!"

She clamps her mouth shut, and nods, dashing over to the coffee machine as I make my escape to a window seat. There's nobody else in yet, and I wouldn't be surprised if it stays this way all day. The sky is grey, and rain is falling in sheets so heavy it looks solid. The waves rolling into the bay look cold, dark water frothing with white, the beach dotted with a few dog walkers and the occasional die-hard rambler.

"So," says Laura, sitting down next to me, leaning her elbows on the table and resting her chin in her hands. "Here's your coffee. What happened? Did you ... you know, with Cal?"

Wow. She's straight in there. No small talk. No foreplay. Right for the gossip jugular.

"Well," I reply, lacing my fingers around the hot mug. "I wanted to. I really did. I tried every trick in the book. But it turns out Cal's actually *gay*!"

Her eyes widen, and her mouth forms a perfect circle, and she gasps out a completely shocked: 'Ooooooh!'

It takes her about five seconds to realise I'm winding her up – I give the game away by laughing – and she punches me none-too-gently on the shoulder.

"Ha, got ya!" I say. As I try and take my first sip of the coffee, my hand slips and I spill it all down my chin instead. Pure class. Laura, ever mum-like, immediately whips a napkin out of her apron pocket and dabs my face.

"Sorry," I say, sighing as I accept my humiliating fate. Some kind of coffee karma was in play. "I'm a clumsy oaf."

"It's okay," she answers, screwing up the tissue and leaving it in a ball on the table. "We're all a bit rubbish in the mornings."

"Speak for yourself – I'm rubbish all the time. And no – to answer your question, I didn't, *you know*, with Cal. We went to Parents' Evening, celebrated the good news at the Horse and Rider, and drank so much we ended up staying in the flat. He was the perfect gentleman. How was Martha this morning?"

She looks utterly crestfallen at this news, and has clearly been anticipating some titillating tales to brighten up a dull autumn morning in the cafe.

"Fine. Bit tired. I think her and Lizzie were up late, talking. I'm glad she's doing well at college, that must be such a relief for you ... are you *sure* nothing happened? Where did he sleep?"

"I'm sure. We slept in the same bed, but nothing happened."

"Did you top to tail? I hate doing that. You always end up with someone's big toe up your nose."

"Nothing happened, Laura. Not even an accidental big toe invasion. He got up bright and breezy, and left for Frank's farm."

"Yes, he said he was heading over. Do you know what I think? I think he'll get there, and Cherie will immediately discover eight lightbulbs that need changing round the house ..."

"Ha!" I reply, "you may be right. She's probably gone round with a broom handle, smashing them all. Although Frank's just as tall, I'm sure he's no slouch on the lightbulb-changing front."

"I said that to her – just to wind her up – and she said Frank was too old and frail to be doing such things!"

I laugh loudly at that one. Frank is about as old and frail as Rafael Nadal. He might be in his 80s, but he still looks like he could wrangle a cow and harvest a turnip field with one hand tied behind his back.

"She's an old lech, isn't she?" I ask, still smiling.

"She is, but I can't say that I blame her. Cal is ... well, it seems like such a waste! I mean, you say nothing happened. And I'm a taken woman. So is Becca, and so is Cherie. There's Ivy Wellkettle, and her daughter Sophie, but Ivy's never seemed interested in blokes, and Sophie's only 20 and away at uni. Katie's too busy with little Saul. Then there's Willow, but she kind of lives in a world of her own. And maybe you could count Tina Dorries down at the Community Hall, but ..."

Laura continues in this vein for some time, rattling off

the names of what sounds like every single female in the village, along with reasons why they'll probably never 'you know' with Cal. These reasons include being a lesbian; being married; having an imaginary fiancé; being more into horses than men; being under 20 and being over 80. When she finally judders to a halt, I pause to see if she's actually finished.

When it seems that she is, I reply: "Poor fella. Maybe we can ship someone in for him?"

Her eyes narrow slightly, and I get the feeling she is genuinely trying to think of whether that's possible. Maybe she's got contacts with some human traffickers in Sidmouth.

"Also," I say, interrupting her crazy train, "Martha's grandparents are threatening to visit. If they do, I might need your help. We're not ... well, not that compatible. Especially me and Barbara. I try and be a good person, and remind myself that she's lost her daughter, but at the end of the day, I'm not actually that good ... we've never liked each other, and only ever tolerated being in the same room for Kate's sake. And now Martha's, obviously. But this time, I'm going to really make an effort – she doesn't have much left, and I really want to make it all right for her, you know?"

Laura nods, her curly hair bobbing around.

"I know! Families are ... well, they can be hard, even in normal circumstances. But I'll help – we all will. We'll keep them busy, and help you avoid any flashpoints, and it'll all be fine. Things do tend to work out here better than other places ... must be something in the water. You heard about the party last summer?"

"Yes," I reply, smiling. "Because you told me about it. That's the one where you engineered the mass reunion, isn't it?"

Last summer had been Laura's first – and allegedly only – summer here. It was the year that Cherie broke her hip, leaving Laura in charge of the cafe and organising Frank's 80th birthday party. Being Little Miss Happy Ending, she'd also organised a few surprises. She'd arranged for Frank's son and grandson to visit from Australia, and for Sam's many sisters to come across from Ireland.

She'd also – and this was the biggie – tracked down Cherie's estranged sister, Brenda, who she hadn't seen since she was in her 20s. They're still in touch, making up for lost time, and it's given Cherie a whole new lease of life, getting to know her nieces and nephews and their children as well. It was quite the feat – but not one that surprises me, having known Laura for a short while. She's like a force of nature.

"It is. It was brilliant. What ... what about your parents, Zoe? You never talk about your family at all, beyond Kate and Martha. Are they still around?"

I know that by 'around', she means 'alive' – we have all reached that age in life where that could be a sensitive question. I stay silent for a moment, concentrating on not pouring coffee over my own face, and eventually answer as honestly as I can without needing a violin solo to accompany me.

"They are still 'around', as far as I know – but I've not had any contact with them for a long time. Many years. It's a complicated situation."

I'm hoping she'll leave it at that, but she raises her eyebrows and looks hungry for more. I can almost see the cogs turning in her brain, as she imagines some kind of heart-warming family gathering where we all cry and say we're sorry and move on to a brighter, stronger future. That's her way – but it's really not going to work in this scenario.

"I can see you playing with that one," I continue, looking at her firmly. "And I need you to let it go. There won't be a happy ending if you go down that route, I can guarantee it."

"But why won't there? They're your parents. Whatever you fell out about, surely it was a long time ago? Surely you'd like to see them again? You must have some happy memories of them?"

I sigh, and put my mug down on the table. Okay, I think – I need to nip this one in the bud, before Laura goes off on some internet odyssey to try and locate them.

"You know how I'm on the small side? Petite, as you put it the other day?" I say.

"Yes," she replies. "I'm very jealous."

"Well, I was always petite. Even as a child. Some of that might be down to genetics, some of it back then was due to neglect and malnutrition. I was tiny – short and bony and if I turned sideways, I disappeared. So this is one of my happy memories of my father, just to give you a taster: when I was about six, he was walking me to school. He didn't usually do that, so I was pretty excited. It felt like an adventure – like something a normal dad would do. He even held my hand and everything. I felt on top of the world – even now, I can vividly remember how nice it was. How secure it made me feel.

"When we were about half way along the route, he led me down into a quiet road. A nice road, all semi-detached houses and trees. Away from the estate where we lived. And after a while, we stopped, outside one particular house. He'd been looking at them all as we walked, and I thought it was funny – we'd talk about the cars outside, or what colour the walls were painted, or what they'd done with the gardens.

"Then, after we stopped – at a house with no car parked outside – he did a quick check of the street, and led us down the side of the house, along the pathway. I had no idea what was going on, but he was my dad, so I just followed along. My main concern was being late for school, but he told me that didn't matter. That school could wait. At the side of the house was a window, one of those with two sections. A big section, and a small section at the top. The top one was open.

"Before I understood what was going on, my dad told me he needed me to do him a favour. He needed me to get through that window – the one he would never squeeze through, but I could – and let him into the house. At this point it had started to feel wrong, but I was only a kid, not old enough to question him. So he hoisted me up, in my school uniform, and I slithered through the window. I fell onto the hallway floor, got up, and did as I was told – he was whispering to me by that stage, telling me to let him in.

"I walked round to the front door, amazed at how nice the place was. There were framed school photos of their kids on the walls, and flowers in vases, and super-soft carpets that your feet squished into. It smelled good, air freshener and flowers, and it was really clean. It felt like a different world to the one I lived in.

"I let my dad in through the front door, and he told me I was a good girl, and I should stay there and shout if anybody came home. I'm sure I don't have to paint you any pictures about what he was up to. I stood there, for about five minutes, getting more and more scared and upset – then I left. I just left, and walked the rest of the way to school on my own.

"I saw those kids, from the photos – they were in my school. One was two years above, the other was in the same year as me. I saw them, and I felt so ashamed, and angry, and upset. And I couldn't talk to anybody about it, or I'd get my dad into trouble. I was so freaked out, I was vile all day – starting fights, getting into trouble in class, generally being a pain in the bum. This was a pattern – I'd get upset, and act out, and nobody would have the slightest interest in figuring out why I was such a nightmare. I wasn't a likable child, it has to be said.

"That is just one of the many jolly moments from the showreel of my childhood, Laura. There are many more if you need them. I know you mean well, but please leave this one alone – I cut myself off from them for my own benefit, so I could live the kind of life I wanted to live. I don't often talk about all of this, and I'm not telling you to make you feel bad – just to explain why any kind of reunion wouldn't work. Not all parents are like you, Laura, more's the pity."

Laura has remained silent throughout this trip down memory lane, and I see with horror that she has tears in her eyes. I hate people feeling sorry for me, even though part of me acknowledges that it is a fair response – Laura is a mum. A kind, loving, responsible mum. She's been through hard times and always put her kids first, the way mums are supposed to.

Looking back on the way I grew up, I can see why it makes her cry. But if she cries, then I'll cry, and if I cry, I won't stop until I die of dehydration.

"Don't you dare start blubbing!" I say, in a no-nonsense tone of voice. "It wasn't all bad. Not long after, I met Kate. That made everything better. And I had some good foster homes too, with people who showed me the world wasn't made up entirely of twats. I chose to see myself as a survivor, not a victim – I've built a life for myself. I've never followed my parents down their path, or the path of a lot of the other kids I met in the system. I've followed my own – and that's not something to be pitied. But please, please, please ... do not go looking for a happy ending for me and my family, okay?"

She nods, and clenches her eyes so tight she squeezes the tears away, and pats my hand.

"Well, it doesn't matter anyway," she eventually says. "The past is the past. And now, you're here with us – and we can be your family. Me and Becca can be your sisters; Willow can be your weird cousin from outer-space; Cherie and Frank can be your mum and dad, and Edie's the best granny in town. You and Martha, you fit in here – and we'll always, always look after you."

Chapter 26

The next few weeks pass so quickly, I barely notice they're happening. November sees the weather settling into slightly calmer patterns: still cold, still blustery, but with brighter, crisper days and clear, star-studded nights.

Sam gives me a booklet on migrating birds, and I use that and my binoculars to spot the feathered friends who have made the journey from Scandinavia to their holiday home in the West Country. I see redwings and all kinds of geese and the awesomely titled red-breasted merganser. I am becoming a regular country girl, and wonder if I should start my own web show – a cut-price Autumn Watch without the experts or camera men or prime time TV slot. I could be an internet sensation – or just get spammed a lot by hot Russian babes looking for action. It could go either way.

I love these walks – and I don't always do them on my own. Sometimes I borrow Midgebo, who snuffles and wags and investigates everything in his curious Labrador fashion. Sometimes Laura comes along, or Becca, with Little Edie bundled up in a cute baby carrier on her chest. Sometimes even Martha deigns to accompany me, pretending to be cynical but secretly enjoying it.

And sometimes – in fact quite often – Cal is my walking buddy. He's used to living in the outdoors, and fills in his days around Martha time by working with Frank on the farm, and exploring the beaches and heaths in the area. He often looks at the freezing-cold water with something approaching lust, and it's easy to imagine him when he was younger: long blonde hair, surfer-dude, bumming his way around the world.

Since our night in the flat, we've become closer. Become friends. Much as he is a treat for the eyes, there's a lot more to Cal than the way he looks. He's funny and kind and down-to-earth. He has a high tolerance for eccentricity and a forgiving attitude to the quirks of human nature, which you definitely need when you live in Budbury.

He's quiet when I need quiet, and chatty when I need chat, and seems to have an unfailing instinct about which is appropriate. Perhaps that comes from living on a farm with a load of other men, where getting in each others' faces is always a risk.

He might have been immature when he created Martha, and I know he still feels regret about being an absentee dad for most of her life, but these days he's all grown up. I think Kate would have liked him, which is pretty much the biggest compliment I can pay someone.

We spend hours together, roaming the hillsides, exploring

the caves, collecting fossils washed up on the shore after a downpour. Every now and then, there is accidental physical contact – he helps me up a steep path, or holds out his hand to steady me as we climb. Gives me a hug to warm me up, or sits close to me on the bench to share body heat and a flask of coffee.

Now, I'm only human – and he is a deeply attractive man. I'd be lying if I said I never felt a spark between us, or wondered what it would be like to take things further. To kiss him, and be held by him, and to touch the smooth golden skin I know lies beneath his clothes. To wake up in his arms, safe and warm. To see if the spark turns into a flame.

I've felt all of that, and I think he has too. Sometimes I catch him looking at me, in the same way I'm looking at the redwings – as though he's trying to figure me out. Deciding where he fits into my life, and I fit into his.

I feel all of that, but I don't act on it. It would be easy, and I'm fairly sure it would be wonderful as well – but then there'd be the Aftermath. The awkward conversations about what it all meant; the difficult silences; the extra layer of tension that always seems to accompany my relationships with men. I tell myself I'm holding back because of Martha – because the last thing she needs, just as we've started to settle ourselves and just as she's getting to know her dad, is for me to jump into bed with him and mess it all up again.

I tell myself it's because of Martha, and that is true, but if I force myself to be honest, it's also because of me. Because

I'm scared of what might happen. Scared of getting close to him, making a space for him in my life, and then him leaving again. I don't feel strong enough to survive another loss, and it will be hard enough when he goes back to Australia as it is – never mind throwing sex into the mix. Sex ... well, it always complicates the shit out of things, doesn't it?

I've had my fair share of boyfriends, but none of them have ever been serious. Maybe it's because I never met the right person – or, more likely, it's because I was never willing to meet the right person. One guy I dated on and off for a few months eventually ended things because I was too closed off; too emotionally crippled. Because our booty calls left him feeling used, and he wanted more.

He left, and the main thing I felt was relief – relief that I didn't even have to try any more. Pathetic but true.

With Cal, it's different. We're already close. We already have a link that can't ever be broken – our past with Kate, and our future with Martha. He will always be in my life in some way or another, so I can't afford to jeopardise that. We've already come much further than I thought we would, and I'm happy about that – because it's good for Martha. The three of us are good together. She mocks us mercilessly, and I enjoy that – nothing like a good mocking to lift the spirits. I can tell she's starting to feel stronger – more confident, more grounded. More happy.

A lot of that is down to Lizzie and their friendship, to her new college and new relationships – but some of it is also because of Cal being here, and me and Cal creating our own slightly malformed version of a family unit to support her. Hopefully, by the time he does eventually leave, some of that newfound strength will have become permanent, and will help her through the next stage of her life.

Things are improving, but I know she desperately misses her mum. Occasionally, when I'm brave enough to venture into her room to dig for fossil-like dishes under her bed, I can tell that she has spritzed her pillow with the Burberry perfume Kate used. Her way of keeping her close, I suppose.

November is hard for us both – containing as it does the anniversary of Kate's cancer diagnosis. The first of a series of unpleasant anniversaries that are looming ahead of us – our first Christmas without her; the day she died, the day we said goodbye at her funeral. None of it is good, and I know there may be some bumpy times ahead. Cal and I do what we can – but we're not Kate. We never will be.

Martha herself has started to talk about her mum more, which I take as a good sign. Before, no matter how much I tried to get her to open up, she toughed it out – slammed the door in my face both literally and figuratively. Always resisted any attempts on my part to talk about Kate, and what she was going through.

I probably wasn't the best person to be doing it, really – I was still in pieces about Kate myself, and maybe a tiny part of me was relieved not to have to constantly talk about her. Now, though, things seem to be changing for both us. I've talked to Cal, and I know Martha has talked to Lizzie, and maybe that's exactly what we both needed – someone to talk to about Kate who didn't live through the loss, share the same pain at the same time.

Recently, I've noticed that she's able to laugh about silly things she remembers her mum doing; mention her name without crying, pick up the Terry Pratchett book her mum always told her she should read. Small steps, but significant. I even found her flicking through photo albums one night, curled up in her Glastonbury hoodie on the sofa as she turned the pages.

I'd sat down next to her, and we'd looked together – telling each other stories and sharing memories and shedding a few tears; her asking me more about Kate as a child, filling in the gaps that all teenagers have about their own parents' youth. Of course most teenagers get to ask their parents those questions themselves – but for Martha, I was as good as it got.

Apart from Barbara and Ron, of course – who were scheduled to visit the weekend after next. I tried hard not to look as though I was going to vomit at the prospect because, again, it might be good for Martha. They could tell her about their version of Kate, and it would be a chance for them all to help each other heal. Much as Barbara and I loathe each other, I never, ever doubt how much she loved her daughter, and how much she loves Martha. She might show it through obsessive amounts of toilet cleaning and Marks and Spencer gift cards, but the love is there – and it matters.

In fact, as I make my way back to the cafe after a particularly nice walk all on my lonesome, their visit becomes the subject of all conversation.

I walk through the garden and into the cafe, enjoying that wonderful sense of wellbeing you get when warm air first strokes ice-cold skin, and shrug my coat and scarf and gloves off. There are a couple of actual customers there, both scooping cream off the top of their hot chocolates with long-handled spoons, newspapers spread out on the table in front of them.

Cherie is manning the kitchen, as Willow is at a hospital appointment with her mum, and Laura's having a day off with Matt, doing some early Christmas shopping in Bath. Martha's college is closed for a staff training day, and she is here with Cal, foraging for food.

I join them, looking on in wonder at Martha's lunch – fish finger sandwiches on white bread, squished up exactly the way she always liked them when she was little. Exactly the way her mum always made them.

I glance up at Cherie, who is waving me over, a mug of the creamy hot chocolate on the counter alongside a slice of chocolate cake. I will turn into a woman made entirely of cocoa beans if I stay in this place much longer.

"How did you know?" I ask, looking at Cherie half admiringly, half suspiciously. Her long, fat plait is lying draped over her shoulder, and her cheeks are rosy from cooking.

"How did I know that you'd want chocolate?"

"No – that's not a challenge. I always want chocolate. I mean, about Martha and the fish finger butties ... it's what Kate always used to make for her."

I'd heard stories about Cherie's legendary ability to match people to their particular comfort food before – hence the name of the cafe – but this was the first time I'd really seen it in action.

"Oh, well, my love ... it doesn't take a genius. You just have to keep your eyes peeled and listen to what your instincts tell you. Ivy Wellkettle was in earlier, and that's what she always has – reminds her of when young Sophie was still living at home, it does. And I saw the way Martha looked at those sandwiches – like she might actually sneak over and steal them – and put two and two together. Everyone has a comfort food, don't they? Something that takes them back to happier times, or simpler times. Though beyond the chocolate, I've not yet quite figured out yours ..."

"That's because I'm an enigma wrapped in a mystery wrapped in a drunk person. And I'm perfectly happy with the chocolate, thank you ... what is this? It smells amazing!"

I scoop up a chunk of sponge with my fork, and can immediately confirm that it also tastes amazing.

"Laura's latest for the winter menu. Chocolate fudge cake, but made with some peppermint as well. Mint in the hot choc too – all very co ordinated, our Laura. Go on – go and sit down. I'll pop over in a minute for a chinwag before the rush arrives. And by that I mean Edie."

250

I nod – my mouth is stuffed full of cake – and take my goodies over to the table.

"Your face is blue," says Martha, looking at me like I'm an exhibit in a travelling freak show. "It's freezing out there. Are you trying to walk yourself to death?"

Cal smirks a little, and I shoot him half a dagger to shut him up.

"It's *beautiful* out there," I answer. "You should try seeing life beyond your phone every now and then. It's gorgeous. com."

She pulls a face that suggests I have just climbed onto the table and farted in her face, and replies: "Why is it that old people always think adding 'dot com' after something lame makes it hip and cool? It doesn't. It just makes it evenmore-pathetic.com."

"And you're a rudecow.com," I say, sipping my hot chocolate and pulling my own face – one that possibly resembles an orgasm. It's that good.

"I think you're both totallyawesomechicks.com," chips in Cal, which earns him a dirty look from both of us. United at last.

"So," says Martha, leaning back and narrowing her eyes at me. "Guess what?"

"I can't possibly guess what – just tell me."

"You'll like it."

I can tell from the look on her face that I won't like it. I make a 'wind it on' gesture with my hands, and note that Cal has carefully schooled his expression into something unnaturally neutral.

"Gran and grandad are coming down this weekend instead of the one after. Isn't that completelymarvellous.com?"

I try and emulate Cal, and keep my face neutral, but I suspect from the fact that Martha bursts out into witch-like cackles of laughter that I'm not entirely managing it.

Suddenly, I've lost my appetite. Even Laura's most divine creations would probably taste like ashes in my mouth right now.

I'd got used to the idea that they were coming. In fact, had even persuaded myself to welcome it, for all the right reasons – it would be nice for Martha, it would give Cal the chance to meet them, and it would hopefully also reassure Barbara that all was well. Seeing Martha in the flesh might actually convince her that we hadn't actually run away to join some kind of hippy commune to smoke dope out of specially crafted wellington boots.

But I'd got used to the fact that they were coming many days from now. It was the tomorrow that never comes – the disaster on the horizon that you still had time to prepare for. Time to stock up on tinned goods and fix the air filtration system in your underground survival bunker, that kind of thing.

The news that I now only have one night to do all of this completely unhinges me.

"Oh," I say, quietly, laying my spoon down on the table and

taking some deep breaths. "Oh … right. Gosh. I have so much to do. I have to clean the bloody toilets. And change the bedding. And dust, and hoover, and hide all the booze, and buy some food, and learn how to cook it, and … and …"

I am hyperventilating slightly by this point, and Cherie has come over to see what's going on. I sense her hovering above me, but my vision has started to cloud as I panic.

I don't know why I feel quite this bad. I knew they were coming. It's not that big a deal. But suddenly, I feel completely overwhelmed – threatened, and pressurised, and exposed. I think it's because I know that no matter how much I clean the toilets or scrub the cottage, it won't be good enough. In Barbara's eyes, I was never even good enough to be her daughter's friend – never mind her granddaughter's guardian.

Since we've been here, in Budbury, with all these strangely delightful people, I've been so much more relaxed. When you're hanging round with Amazonian geriatric rock chicks and surfer dudes and space princess waitresses and women in their 90s with life-long delusions about their fiancé, you start to feel less weird. Weird becomes the new normal, in fact.

Now, Barbara and Ron are on their way, to show me that it's not. To judge me, and find me wanting.

I only calm down when Cherie and Cal launch a double attack. Cherie lays her arm around my shoulder and squeezes, and Cal reaches out across the table and takes both my trembling hands in his. Martha, to be fair, is now looking slightly guilty about winding me up so much, shuffling round on her chair, eyes wide as she watches me go into my meltdown.

"It's okay, Zoe," says Cal, his voice deliberately low and gentle and monotone, like he's trying to calm down an anxious animal. "It'll be all right. You're not doing it on your own, you know? We're all here. We'll all help."

Cherie nods, and squeezes me some more. I suspect I may be bruising like a peach by now, such is her insistence on reassuring me.

"That's right, my love," she says. "You don't worry about a thing. We'll get everything shipshape, and we'll have them over here for dinner, and we'll show them the sights – it'll be grand. There's no need for you to worry so much. We'll all look after you. You're a member of the tribe now, and we're good at protecting our own, you know."

I look up at her – almost six foot, built like a warrior, encased in an apron that says 'Kiss the Chef' – and I nod. I'd lay good money on Cherie being the best defender on the planet. And Laura, and Willow, and Edie, and even Cal. Becca could probably win a street fight even with a baby strapped to her chest, and Sam and Matt will be with me too. They're like my very own Dorset Avengers, and I know they'll assemble when I need them.

Cal is stroking my fingers, and brushing wind-tangled strands of hair away from my face, and I start to breathe a little more easily. Even start to feel borderline embarrassed about my drama queen attack, because it's really not like me at all – at least not in public.

I feel my heart rate coming back within normal human levels, and try on a grateful smile for size.

The smile becomes slightly more genuine when Martha finally decides to speak. She doesn't meet my eyes, and is fiddling with her black hair as she says it, but it's the thought that counts.

"Don't worry," she says, quietly, gazing at a spot somewhere over my shoulder. "I'll clean the toilets."

Chapter 27

Watching Barbara endure her weekend in Budbury is a bit like watching a car get squashed up in a scrap yard. You know, when it starts off all big and strong and solid, and ends up as a small corroded block of crushed metal? It seems to defy the laws of physics, but it happens.

Except Barbara's not being crushed by some giant steel claw – she's being crushed by the unfailing niceness of absolutely everyone she encounters during her three nights here. Even Barbara cannot withstand these superhuman levels of kindness.

With every soft word; every compliment on her hair and clothes; every slice of home-made cake; every comment about how proud she must be of Martha; every inquiry about Ron's golf handicap; every astonished gasp of surprise when listening to stories about their last cruise, her resistance is weakened a little bit more.

Cherie is the welcoming hostess and respectable small business-owner; Laura is the responsible mother helping to keep an eye on Martha's progress; Frank is twinkling-eyed charm itself; Matt is a vet (appealing to snobs the world over); Edie is so old nobody can resist her; Becca has a baby and is therefore a star attraction, and Sam takes them on guided beach walks. Willow might look a little odd, but she constantly plies them with hot beverages and home-made food, so also becomes a force for good in their eyes. Even Scrumpy Joe, not one for difficult social situations, presents them with a gift-box of his very finest 'artisan ciders.'

It's kind of astonishing to see. It's like my friends here – my bonkers, eccentric, law-unto-themselves friends – have collectively decided to put their communal best foot forward on my behalf. They're still *them*, but slightly more sanitised versions.

Becca never swears, not even once, not even when the baby vomits all over her hair for the third time that morning. Lizzie and Nate are model teenagers. Cherie appears to forego all tobacco products for the weekend. Frank makes not a single comment that involves animals or their digestive systems, which is unusual for him. Even Edie fails to mention her fiancé – just giving me a sneaky wink as she packs the extra portions of food into her Vans backpack. As charm offensives go, they're completely nailing it.

As promised, the day before Barbara and Ron's arrival, pretty much everyone helped out. Willow, who runs a little cleaning service for holiday lets in addition to her other roles, turned up in her dinky white van, and started transforming

Lilac Wine into a palace, with some assistance from Martha. She had her own rubber gloves and everything, and got stuck right in, Bella Swan trailing around after her, one of Willow's classic rock playlists echoing around the cottage. I helped too, scrubbing the shower while singing along to Jefferson Airplane's *Somebody to Love*.

Laura and Cherie stocked my fridge with enough food to feed a small African republic, and Matt made sure the gardens were in tip-top shape and the cottage was drenched with wildflowers.

The whole place looked and smelled fantastic, and I was almost in tears of gratitude by the end of the day. Even Barbara, arriving in a cloud of ready-prepared disapproval, could find no sarcastic comments about our new home. She did her best – casting a beady eye over the bathrooms, surreptitiously running her fingers over the shelving looking for dust – but it was all beyond reproach. Willow had even used a special hand-held steam cleaner on the bloody curtains – who knew such things existed?

Cal had turned up later, bearing a bottle of posh whiskey for Ron and a box of chocolates for Barbara, and endured it all with amazing grace while she carried out a similar series of tests on him.

I was used to it, of course – the subtle and non-too-subtle questioning, the elegantly raised eyebrows, the slightly sneering tone in even the most innocuous sounding questions. He wasn't, but he didn't seem to let it get to him at all. He simply carried on smiling, carried on charming, and eventually, she seemed to relent. Barbara might sometimes give the impression of being a space alien with perfectly coiffed hair, but she was still female – and Cal has this perfect mix of charisma, good looks, and old-school manners that seems to affect all women like a dose of opium.

The main factor in these small victories was, to be fair, Martha herself. She seemed genuinely pleased to see them; genuinely keen to tell them about our life here, and genuinely concerned that they got on with Cal as well as she did. And while I have not often had kind words to say about Kate's mother, I've always known that she would do anything for Martha – even tolerate her strange choice in guardianship.

Between the walks on the bay and trips to the cafe and ready-made meals I was able to miraculously whip out of the oven for them, there was barely any time for bitching at all. On either side. Every time I felt tense and imagined some kind of insult heading in my direction, something else would happen – Midgebo would come charging in and try to steal pudding, or Cal would suggest a game of Scrabble, or Martha would want to show them a piece of her college coursework.

And every time Barbara narrowed her eyes at me, or seemed about to utter some cutting piece of criticism – if all else failed, she could always have a go at my hair – someone would intervene. Cherie would ask about the golf club, or Frank would offer to take them on a tour of the farm, or Becca would pass Little Edie over to Barbara to hold for a few minutes and everyone would descend into coos of adoration.

The whole visit was a masterwork of distraction and deflection – spotting flashpoints in advance and nipping them in the bud. After two days of this, I finally started to relax – realising that perhaps I was, potentially, just as childish as Barbara sometimes. The two of us had such a long and unpleasant history that we were both struggling to see around it – but with a little help from our friends, we were at least able to try.

On their last night in Budbury, after hot chocolates at the cafe and a strangely peaceful communal walk on the beach with Cal and Martha, they were taking Martha out for dinner in Dorchester, the nearest metropolis. Cal and I had both been invited, but I could practically hear Barbara's teeth grinding as she uttered the words – we may be experiencing something of a detente, but she'd still rather have her granddaughter to herself.

So we did the decent thing, and cried off. In fact, I cried off the whole evening – Cal had already offered me his spare room for the night, and it just felt like the right gesture to make. We'd kept Barbara busy, and she had had literally no time at all with Martha without someone else being around. Part of me felt nervous – like she might kidnap her, shove her in the trunk of their Skoda Octavia and driver her back to Bristol.

But part of me knew I had to respect their relationship.

Give them time together. Let Barbara decide for herself that Martha was actually well and truly happy. Or as happy as a recently bereaved teenager can be.

I wave them off at the gates, and wander around to Saffron, Cal's holiday cottage across the green from ours. It's slightly smaller, in a three-strong row of mellow-stone terraced homes, the front of the building draped in climbing vines and hanging baskets that are now in hibernation for the coming winter.

The nights are drawing in, I think, which immediately makes me feel about 700 years old – that's such an old person concept. The weather has been cold but glorious for the last few days, those chilly, light-drenched days that make you feel glad to be alive. Now, at just after 6pm, it's already almost complete dark – the sky a deep indigo, studded by stars and the flitting outline of bats performing their evening acrobatics. As ever, it's perfectly quiet out here – not even the sounds of distant traffic once Ron navigates the Skoda down the gravel driveway, beeping his horn in farewell as they leave.

I knock on the cottage door, and hear Cal shout: "Come on in, it's not locked!" This is a countryside thing, the non-locking of doors, I've noticed. And I suppose it would take a pretty determined burglar to trek all the way out here and break in. Still, I've lived in a city too long, and read too much crime fiction, to be that trusting – Lilac Wine is well and truly secured, just in case anyone takes a fancy to my priceless collection of crappy paperbacks and the DVDs I've swiped from the Rockery's games room.

I make my way through to the lounge, hearing the sounds of the shower from upstairs. I mooch around the room for a few minutes, looking at his reading material, plinking tunelessly at his guitar strings, inspecting the general tidiness with a sense of wonder. I always thought bachelor dudes were supposed to be messy, but Cal puts me to shame. Again, I know it's because of his communal lifestyle back in Oz – sharing a farmstead with a group of other human beings has taught him these ways. It still freaks me out though.

When he finally emerges, head bent to avoid the beams, he is fresh and damp and smelling of something masculine and woodsy that makes me feel a bit giddy. His T-shirt is clinging to him in all the right places, and his hair is a shaggy mass of multi-shaded blonde. Yikes.

"You all right?" he says, giving that hair a quick rub with the towel he's carrying and looking at me in concern. "You're looking a bit off, there."

"No! I'm not off. I'm fine. I'm just a bit tired I suppose. It's gone better than I expected, but it's still bloody exhausting."

"Yeah," he drawls, padding barefoot into the small kitchen and pulling two cans of lager out of the fridge. "She's pretty full on, old Barb, isn't she?"

"Don't ever call her that to her face. Old or Barb. Either is likely to get you kneecapped. But yes, she is ... always has been. In fact, much as she's never accepted this, it was partly her fault Martha even exists."

He raises his eyebrows at me, looking confused, as I gratefully crack open the beer – is there any better sound in the world than the gentle fizz of freshly popped lager? – and collapse onto the squishy floral sofa.

"I don't mean literally. I am assuming she wasn't there that night in Bangkok. I mean ... she was always so controlling. Crazy strict. Kate had curfews on her curfews, wasn't allowed to talk to her friends on the phone, got taken to and collected from school even when she was 16. Boyfriends were definitely not allowed, and going to gigs or festivals or clubbing was cause for a public stoning. As a result, of course ..."

"Kate got even wilder," he completes for me, sitting next to me on the couch. It's a small couch – a two-seater to fit into the tiny lounge – and his long thighs are squashed up against mine, his legs stretched out in front of him.

"Yep," I reply, nodding. "Exactly. She probably would have dumped me as a friend within weeks if not for the fact that Barbara tried to ban her from seeing me."

"You're probably doing both yourself and Kate a disservice with that one, Zo," he answers. I chew my lip for a few seconds and decide he's right – there was much more to our relationship than rebellion, but it definitely was a factor.

"That's true. But in a way, it's part of why we were drawn to each other – she had too much structure, too many rules, and I didn't have enough of either."

"And between you you made an almost normal human being?"

"Exactly! Anyway … enough of this. I don't feel in the mood for deep and meaningful tonight. I'm worn out by being nice to Barbara."

"I think everyone is," he answers, downing half his lager in one big gulp. "I've never seen this lot on their good behaviour before. The look on Cherie's face the other day, when Barbara suggested the cafe could use a good sort out … God, I thought she'd swing for her!"

I giggle, and drink, and reply: "I know. That would be a clash of the Titans wouldn't it? My money's on Cherie, but Barb wouldn't go down without a fight. So … it's good to have a night off from it all, anyhow. I have beer. I have fine company. And I have Netflix. All the perfect ingredients for a very pleasant night. What do you fancy?"

He gives me a comedically leery grin, worthy of a *Carry On* film, and I nudge him hard in the ribs

"Ouch!" he squeals. "That hurt! But you're cute when you're angry …"

"Don't call me cute, it's patronising."

"Okay … you're a scrappy little thing. Is that better?"

"Absolutely not. It makes me sound like one of the cast of Scooby Doo."

"That's not a bad thing. I have a lot of time for those meddling kids. Anyway … I'm going to grab us a couple more beers, and turn the lights down low. You're blushing again, and I don't want to embarrass you by commenting on it all night."

Before I can respond, he's up and gone, leaving me holding my own cheeks, wishing the red away. He's right, of course – and I do welcome it when he flicks on a small lamp and turns off the overheads.

He passes me another lager as he sprawls next to me, in the newly-dimmed cinema lighting.

"What do you want to watch? Something mushy and sad?" he says, pulling a face.

"God no. I want to watch something with lots of guns and explosions and sexy men."

He nods in approval, and I silently wish I'd actually asked to watch *Terms of Endearment* or *Me Before You* instead, just to see the look on his face.

Eventually, after doing the usual TV-remote shuffle through an endless supply of rubbish shows and second-rate movies, we decide on *Casino Royale*. Plenty of guns, and one of the world's sexiest men – James Bond.

We sit next to each other in the dark, faces patterned with the flickering action of the screen, getting quietly but steadily drunk. It doesn't sound very exciting, but I realise how much I've missed this – companionship. Having someone to watch telly with. Having someone to banter with. Just ... having someone around, I suppose.

Since Kate died, I've been pretty much alone. Coming to Budbury has helped, but it's not the same.

Martha's better now – she does condescend to engage in small talk with me, and recently suggested we should watch

Better Call Saul, which was a huge victory – but she's usually in her room, or out. I like my own company – I always have – but it was so much easier to enjoy it when I didn't have it forced upon me. There's a huge difference between spending a quiet night in on your own, knowing that your best friend is there across the road, and spending a quiet night in on your own because it feels like nobody else exists in the entire universe.

This – the simple pleasure of sitting and drinking and watching a movie with another human being – feels so good. I've missed it so much, and I know I'll miss it when he's gone. But hey, I remind myself as Daniel Craig shoots his way through Venice, that's a worry for another day.

By the time the film finishes, we've worked our way through several cans of lager and munched our way through bags of crisps, popcorn and nuts. If that had happened at my place, of course, the empty tins would be lying at our feet, spilling out their last dregs and tripping us up every time we went for a wee. They'd still be there the next morning, stinking the place out, shaming me in their metallic glory – because I am completely rubbish with things like that. Cal, of course, isn't – he picks them up and puts them in the recycling as we go.

By the end of the film, I am a bit tipsy, and a bit teary. That bit where Vesper Lynd meets her watery grave gets me every time. I sigh out loud as the credits draw to a close, and find myself leaning my head on Cal's shoulder.

"Are you crying, you big baby?" he asks, sounding amused.

"No. Yes. I don't know. It's just so ... sad, isn't it? Poor James. Poor Vesper. He's never the same again ..."

"I know. First time I watched it, I felt a bit of a blubber coming on myself. But I was in a big cattleshed in a field in the Australian bush, surrounded by twenty-five macho blokes, so none of us dared let on. It'd be social death to cry at a movie, especially a James Bond movie. You all right down there? You want another drink?"

"Nah ... I've had enough already. I just want to be still and quiet for a minute. You're really quite comfy, you know."

"I have been told that, yes. It's one of my many godlike skills."

He slips his arm around my shoulders, and I snuggle right in, burrowing into him until I find just the right spot for both me and my hair. Don't want to make him sneeze with a stray tangle up the nostrils or anything.

"So, tell me about your other godlike skills," I say, realising as I do that I sound a bit flirtatious. Four cans of lager, and I forget all my own rules.

"Well," he replies, seeming to give it some thought. "There's surfing. I'm, like, super ninja level at that. Sheep-shearing is also a speciality. I'm a dab hand at horse riding, and lager-drinking, though I try not to mix the two. I can make a mean spaghetti carbonara. I can walk on my hands for at least three steps. I'm a bit of a dog whisperer on the side. I'm ... hang on, give me a minute ..."

"You're very tidy," I butt in. I say it like an accusation, which makes him laugh.

"I am, yeah. Comes from the farm, and also from living out of a backpack for years on end. I think that's it, though – can't think what else I'm good at. That you'd be interested in hearing about, anyway, being a lady and all."

I snort a little at that – I am possibly the least lady-like person I've ever known – but know what he means.

"You forgot one thing," I reply. "You're a good dad."

He's quiet for a few moments after that, his fingers gently stroking my upper arm, chin resting on my head.

"Thank you for saying that, but I don't think it's true," he eventually responds, sounding uncharacteristically serious. "I left it so long. I can say it was because Kate didn't want me to come, that she didn't need me, that you guys were doing fine without a bruiser like me waltzing in – but it wasn't just that. It was me. I wasn't ready. Kate gave me an easy out, and I took it. Can't tell you how much I regret that now, letting Martha grow up without me."

I reach up and take his hand in mine, squeezing his rough fingers in reassurance.

"We've all done things we regret," I say. "Or regretted things we haven't done. Nothing can change that – and as you're actually only a man, not a god, you're going to have to accept that. You were a kid yourself. Martha didn't grow up feeling rejected or unloved, and Kate never felt like you'd let them down. And now you're here – and you're doing your best to make up for lost time."

I feel him nod, and feel his grip on me tighten slightly in

thanks, and then hear what I think sounds suspiciously like a sniffle.

"Are you crying, you big baby?" I ask, trying to lighten the tone by repeating his earlier question to me.

"No," he says quickly. "I just got some of your hair stuck up my nose. But, well ... yeah. Thanks for that. Good pep talk. This is nice, isn't it? Just the two of us, all on our own?"

"I've had worse evenings," I reply. In fact, in the last year, I don't think I've had one as nice, but I don't tell him that – it might go to his head.

There's a pause. A beat. I can feel his heart thudding from my cosy-hole on his chest, and I can tell he's grinning as he says: "So ... about my godlike skills. There are a few I didn't mention. You want to make out? I can put a white shirt on if you like, we can go and sit in the shower like James and Vesper?"

I can't help but laugh at that whole speech. I have no idea if he's serious or not, but the man is bloody funny.

"They ended up in that shower because James had just brutally killed a machete-wielding maniac in front of her. All you've brutally killed is a six pack of Fosters and some dry-roasted peanuts," I reply.

"God, woman, you're demanding! I saw a spider in the bath earlier ... want me to tear it limb from limb with my bare hands? Will that be enough to impress you?"

"Not enough to get me into the shower, that's for sure. I'm happy enough here, thank you ..."

I am a little bit drunk, so it seems perfectly natural to match that comment with wrapping my arm around his torso, and tucking my legs beneath myself so I'm well and truly comfortable. He scooches me up closer, and we settle into the shape of each other's bodies. We sit like that for a few more moments. It's peaceful, and quiet, and eventually, starts to feel alarmingly like it could turn into something more.

Maybe it's the booze. Maybe it's the gentle flirting. Maybe it's the aftermath of *Casino Royale* – but I'm definitely starting to wonder how much of a disaster it might be if I let my hand drift beneath his T-shirt to touch the taut skin of his belly; or what would happen if I turned my face up towards his, and our lips finally met. His fingers are twining themselves into my hair as I'm wondering this, and I know he's wondering it too.

I can feel the muscle of his chest beneath my cheek; the firm line of his thighs next to me; the persuasive touch of his hands in my hair. Neither of us seems to be breathing, and it's as though we're in suspended animation: poised on the precipice of change. Of transforming our relationship into something else entirely. Something my body definitely seems to want, but the rest of me isn't ready for. Might never be ready for.

I pat his chest with the palm of my hand, and lean myself upright again. He's looking at me with interest – not wanting to push, not wanting to force the moment. I meet his gaze, and smile, and shake my head.

"I know. I feel the same. But I just can't … we just shouldn't. You're Martha's dad, and Kate's ex, and it just isn't right."

He looks a little confused by this statement, and also – understandably – slightly frustrated. I feel his pain. I'm frustrated too.

"You do know I was only with Kate for one night, 17 years ago, don't you? It's not like we were engaged," he says.

"I know, I know … but it still feels a bit … icky, to use a technical term. Or maybe it's just me, using that as an excuse."

"An excuse for what?"

"An excuse to avoid all of this. To keep my hands off you when I really don't want to. To say no to that shower when I really want to say yes. An excuse to make sure things between us don't get complicated. Because you'll be leaving, won't you? You'll be leaving, and I'll still be here, and life will go on. I'm already going to miss you enough, you big lug – I can't let you start giving me multiple orgasms as well."

"Ah," he replies, grinning in a way that tells me that although he might not agree with me, he's letting me off the hook – for now at least. "You *have* heard about my godlike skills, after all …"

Chapter 28

We share a final lunch at the cafe before Barbara and Ron head back to Bristol. Martha and the other young people are in college, so it's grown-ups only, and the cafe is usually closed on a Monday – they've opened up specially to celebrate the grand departure.

We sit, and eat the shepherd's pie that Laura has cooked for us, and talk about nothing at all, until the time draws near. The blessed time. The time of much glory. The time when I will wave the two of them off, and breath a vast sigh of relief.

"This is almost as delicious as your shepherd's pie, Barbara," I say, trying to end things on a good note. In reality, it's actually better – but that wouldn't be diplomatic. Barbara's shepherd's pie was often grudgingly served to me, but when it was, it was also often the only food I'd had that day – certainly when I was still living with my parents.

"Yes, I remember you always devoured that," she replies,

eyes narrowed slightly as she casts her mind back. "Like a starving little tinker, you were. No table manners at all."

I catch Laura's expression as Barbara says this, and see her nostrils flare in barely-contained anger. I think if a starving little tinker child turned up on Laura's doorstep, they'd get a slightly different reception than the one I got at Kate's house. I'd probably have been adopted immediately. I shake my head very slightly to tell her to stand down – it's almost over, and it would be a shame if we blew all our good work now.

Instead, she scurries off to the kitchen, muttering to herself and wringing her hands on a tea towel. Perhaps she's imagining it's Barbara's neck, who knows?

Cal looks similarly annoyed, but you'd have to know him pretty well to notice the signs. The smile has faded from his eyes, and one of his fists is curled up in a ball, tapping away against his thigh. It feels good, having these cheerleaders – in fact, having them gives me the strength to simply not care about Barbara's snippy comments.

"I know," I say, shoving a whole wedge of bread into my mouth at once. "And I'm not much better now."

The last few words are distorted by the fact that I'm talking with my mouth full, and I may well choke on them, but it's kind of worth it to see her horrified reaction as I splutter bread all over the place.

Ron, looking from his wife to me and back again, decides that this is the perfect time to check his watch. Can't say that I blame him.

"Come on, Barbara," he says, standing up. "We'd better make a move – don't want to get caught up in rush hour, do we?"

As it's only one pm, that seems unlikely – but I'm grateful for the diversion. We all stand, chairs scraping and bowls clanking, and everyone makes their farewells. Cherie, usually first on the scene to dispense hugs for any occasion, refrains from this, and instead shakes their hands. Frank gives them a polite salute, and Cal sticks with a simple: "It was good to meet you." Liar, liar, pants on fire.

"Thank you so much for your hospitality," says Barbara – redeeming herself slightly – "and please say goodbye to the others for me. I'm sure we'll visit again sometime soon."

I walk with the two of them down the winding cliffside path to the carpark. It's another crystal clear day, the breeze gently ruffling the air rather than beating it up, and the sunlight is shimmering on the bay. It's so beautiful here, and I make a vow to never let anybody ruin that for me – I refuse to associate this place with anything other than positive vibes.

We reach the Skoda, and Ron unlocks the doors, hovering at the side of the car. He gives me a genuine-looking smile, and says: "It really was nice to see you, Zoe, as well as Martha. Lovely place you've got here."

He's okay, Ron, I remind myself. Lacking in backbone, but okay.

He climbs into the car and starts the engine, and it's

Barbara's turn to hover. Her hair is perfectly frosted and her make-up is perfectly in place and her clothes are perfectly respectable. She could actually make a decent living as a Margaret Thatcher impersonator, although I'm not sure how much call there is for that. The only thing less than perfect is the expression on her face – it's one of uncertainty, which is definitely not an emotion I associate with this particular Iron Lady.

I stare at her, wondering what she's waiting for – surely she's as keen to get away from me as I am to get away from her? She looks nervous, unsure. Like she's considering doing something crazy.

Turns out, she is.

"I'm sorry, Zoe," she says simply. For a few moments I am so confused I don't even respond, just stand there with stray strands of hair flying in front of my face, gaping.

"Sorry for what?" I eventually ask.

"For everything. For that comment back there about your table manners. For not … not helping you more when you were younger. I know I should have. I was just … well, this isn't easy for me to say, but I was always a little bit scared of you. You were everything I was trying to protect Kate from – you were wild and unpredictable and strong-spirited. But you were still a child, and much as I've denied it to myself over the years, you were a child in need. Kate always saw that more clearly than I did. And now you're here, and you're looking after Kate's own child, and you're doing it well. Better than we could. We love Martha, just like we loved Kate – but we don't understand her the way you do. She needs you. So ... thank you."

I am utterly horrified to see that Barbara's grey eyes are swimming with tears. I don't know whether it's because she feels guilty, or because she's just broken her cardinal rule and admitted to weakness, or simply because she's missing her daughter.

I don't know, but I desperately want her not to shed them. Seeing tears on Barbara's face would be one of those great, prophetic signs that the world was coming to an end. The kind of thing the Mayans would have predicted. Such a thing simply could not be allowed to happen, for all our sakes.

I grab hold of her arm, not sure what I'm going to do with it, and it turns into a kind of awkward half hug, neither of us at all comfortable with the physical contact, but both perhaps needing to at least make some kind of gesture. We pull away from our horrible dance, and she daintily wipes the tears away with one finger. Phew.

I know I need to talk. To say something wise and under-standing and spiritual, something important. Sadly, I can't think of a damn thing.

"It's all right," I say, when the silence stretches into some-thing oppressive. "You were a bit of a cow, but I know you can't help it. You created Kate, and Kate created Martha, so I have a lot to thank you for as well. We're both older and wiser now, aren't we? So, let's just ... start again. Or at least do the best we can."

She nods abruptly, obviously as embarrassed and over-whelmed as I am. We've been playing cat and mouse with each other for so long, neither of us really knows how to do it any differently.

"Right. Yes. Well. Better be off then ..."

She climbs into the car without a backward glance, and I see Ron looking at her with concern. He reaches out one gloved hand, and gently pats her knee, and eventually starts the engine. With a cheery honk of the horn and a wave through the window, they're gone.

I stare after them for a moment, before walking – very slowly – back up the hill to the cafe. I need a few minutes to gather myself after that unexpected encounter. I know I should be feeling happy about what just happened – but bizarrely, I only feel unsettled. Like something I've known and understood for a very long time has just transformed into something new and confusing before my very eyes.

I mean, I know how to handle Bad Barbara – but what the heck am I going to do with Good Barbara? I can only hope she has a change of heart on the drive home, and sends me a vile text to put my mind at rest.

I push open the cafe door, and am met by Cherie, Frank, Laura and Cal all looking at me in concern.

"Has she gone?" says Cherie.

I nod, and Laura starts dancing around the room singing 'Ding Dong the Witch is Dead' from the Wizard of Oz.

Cal just looks at me, obviously sensing that something's wrong, and walks forward to take me into his arms. He's big and he's strong and he smells good and I really need a hug, so I stay there for a while, him stroking my hair and making reassuring noises. I'm not at all used to being looked after, and it feels good.

"Was she a complete bitch to you?" he whispers into my ear.

"No," I reply. "It was much worse than that. She was nice to me."

"You're a nutter, you know that?"

"I do know that, yes ... and thank you."

He lets me go, and I feel suddenly full of energy. It's like I've been holding my breath for the last few days, and now I can finally relax.

"I need to do something fun," I announce to the room.

"Want to bake banana muffins with me?" asks Laura, looking hopeful.

"I've got some pigs that need mucking out ..." adds Frank.

"Want to sit outside and listen to music and get drunk?" says Cherie, clapping her hands together.

Cal just raises his eyebrows at me, grins, and murmurs the words: 'godlike skills ...'

Wow. I guess we all have our own different definitions of fun. Including me.

"No ... thank you all, but no. I know what I want to do ... Cherie, would you mind if I sorted out all these paperbacks? Those bookshelves have been driving me mad since I got here!"

She bursts out laughing, and nods.

"Go crazy, my love. Alphabetise to your heart's content."

Chapter 29

It's during the second week in December that I start to notice there's something wrong with Martha. Well, not something wrong exactly – but something less right than it was.

It's small things, really. She starts cycling to college instead of going on the bus, which is weird as the weather is freezing and every day seems to bring with it the threat of snow. Claiming she wants to get fitter, she teeters off down the driveway every morning, bundled up like an Eskimo, her bike wheels leaving patterned trails as they crunch through the frost.

She also starts coming home later, and seems both exhilarated and exhausted when she does. When I query where she's been, I get told she's been doing course work, or attending an after-school club, or doing Christmas shopping. None of these things is an outrageous claim, but none of them quite rings true either.

I also notice that she's eating a lot more than usual – or at least appearing to. She makes extra sandwiches for her packed lunch, and takes multi-packs of crisps to her room, and piles apples and pears into a carrier bag every time she leaves the house. This gives me a momentary panic that she's pregnant, and leads me into a very undignified privacy invasion where I check her bathroom for tampons or stray pee-sticks. I find the former, and thankfully not the latter, and have to hope for the best.

It's all so bizarre, and all of these things alone are so small, that I am almost convinced that I'm going mad. Teenagers need their secrets, and I'm probably worrying too much.

When I raise the issue with Cal, during one of our walks along the beach with Midgebo, he gives it some serious thought before replying.

"Well, when she was round at mine the other day, I did notice that my lager supply had gone down a few notches. I know you were worried about her drinking when you left Bristol, but I've not seen any signs of that, have you?"

I ponder this, and shake my head, my bobble hat wobbling around on top of my head. It's so very cold – I have my hat tugged down, and my scarf tied around my chin, and only my nose is peeking out to greet the chilly air.

"No, I haven't," I reply. "And I'm always pretty vigilant about it. I know the signs well enough to get a panic alert pinged straight to my brain about that kind of stuff. I haven't even seen her smoking. That's partly what I'm worried about – that she's somehow managed to hook up with Budbury's answer to a rebel without a cause, and is sliding down the same slope she was on before. Am I being mad?"

He laughs, and throws an arm over my shoulder, bundling me closer as we traipse along the damp sand, our footsteps accompanied by Midgebo's insanely circuitous paw prints.

"Well, the answer to that question is usually yes," he replies. "But in this case, I'd say trust your instincts. You know her better than anyone else, and if your gut is telling you there's something wrong, there probably is. Have you asked Laura? Or spoken to the college?"

These are both very sensible suggestions, and bizarrely I have actually done both.

"Yep. Laura talked to Lizzie for me, and after a bit of subtle probing managed to glean that there is something going on, before Lizzie invoked the Teen Code and shut her down. Laura reckons that if it was anything, you know, life-threatening, she would have blabbed – but teenagers can be weird about this stuff, so that didn't completely put my mind at rest.

"I spoke to her learning mentor at college, and she said things were basically fine – but she has been leaving early when she has free periods, and she's definitely not joined any after-school clubs, so that one was a fib."

We pause in our walk, looking on in amusement as Midgebo – a big, full-bodied black Lab – is merrily getting humped by a Chihuahua wearing a tartan coat. Midge just seems a bit confused by it all, which is fair enough.

"Well," says Cal, once we rescue our pooch and walk on,

"it sounds like you've done everything you can apart from one thing."

"What's that?" I ask.

"The hardest thing of all. I think we need to actually talk to Martha."

Chapter 30

That, of course, proves to be a lot harder than it sounds. Martha is a bright girl, and can be as slippery as an eel when she wants to be. Plus, you know, I'm not exactly the world's biggest expert at this whole mothering lark, and probably go in with as much subtlety as a bulldozer.

"You would tell me if you were in trouble, wouldn't you?" I say, gazing at her over the cornflake box the next morning.

"What do you mean, in trouble?" she answers, narrowing her eyes at me in suspicion. "What do you think I'm up to?"

"Well, that's the thing – I don't know. But my spider senses are tingling, Martha, and I need to know that you're all right."

She shovels a huge spoonful of cereal into her mouth, and I recognise it for what it is – an attempt to buy time while she comes up with an answer that will get me off her back.

"I'm not in trouble. I'm working hard at college, I'm not smoking, drinking or doing crystal meth, and I'm not pregnant with Eminem's love child. I am, in fact, the model citizen – so give me a break, will you, SS Grupenfuhrer?"

She's gone a little far in the Nazi comparison, I feel – which actually only serves to confirm to me that she's hiding something. This is Martha doing what teens do so well: going on the offensive to stop them appearing defensive.

She drinks the milk from her bowl, gives me a Hitler salute, and goose-steps into the hallway, where I hear her putting on her seventeen layers of clothing ready for her cycle to college. I take a quick peek into her backpack, which she's left lying on the floor by the table, and see three bottles of water and a random assortment of snacks in there. No crystal meth, or love tokens from Eminem.

After she's gone, I spend a lot of time thinking about it all. Wondering if I'm overreacting. Being a drama queen. Trying to stir up trouble where there is none. This, combined with an illicit search of her bedroom and randomly googling phrases like 'teenager secrets' and 'what to do when your teen calls you a Nazi', takes up a lot of my day.

Eventually, I find myself sitting on the couch, staring at the framed photo of Kate in desperation.

"What do I do next?" I ask. Luckily, Kate doesn't answer – but I realise that I have access to the next best thing, and I decide to turn up on Laura's doorstep. I'm distracted, and forget to put socks on, and realise after about three steps that bare feet and Crocs are not appropriate footwear for winter.

I am shivering and possibly turning blue by the time she answers the door, Midgebo hot on her heels in case it's someone with bacon, the sounds of domestic chaos wafting through from the cottage. I can hear Nate playing something loud and shooty on the X Box, and Lizzie is clearly upstairs, as the delicate sounds and intricate melodies of thrash metal are booming down the steps.

"Come in, come in ... you'll catch your death!" she says, ushering me into the hallway.

"I've always found that a weird saying, haven't you?" I reply, grateful for the warmth that immediately engulfs me. "When I was little, I had a teacher who used to say it all the time, to the point where I was convinced that death was actually some kind of contagious disease ..."

"I suppose it is weird, now I come to think of it," Laura answers, heading straight into the kitchen to put the kettle on. As ever, there is the fragrant smell of baking hanging in the air, and I realise as my tummy rumbles that I kind of forgot to eat today.

She hears the rumbling – possibly passing Russian satellites also hear the rumbling – and stares at me with a probing gaze.

"Hmmm. You look like crap."

"Why, thank you."

"Go and sit down – I'll bring supplies."

I do as I'm told, and perch by the big dining room table. It's battered and scarred and made of oak, scattered with magazines and recipe books and car keys and the detritus of modern family life. Nate gives me a little wave of acknowledgement at the far end of the room, before going back to his game.

Within minutes, Laura is sitting across from me, wrapped in a bright pink fleece that damages my retinas, and I have a mug of coffee and cheese on toast in front of me. Aaah, cheese on toast – so perfect, in all its gooey yellow simplicity.

She refuses to engage in any conversation at all until I've eaten a slice, which takes approximately seven seconds. I feel so much better after that, and give myself a telling off for being such a dick.

"You have to look after yourself," she says, her voice concerned. "I know it's hard when you're busy looking after someone else – but there's not enough of you to be skipping meals, Zoe. I'd be all right for a month or two, but not you. Now ... what's going on?"

"It's Martha," I say, pushing my hair behind my ears in preparation for tackling slice number two.

"Well I could have guessed that. Are you really worried about her?"

"I am! I really am ... but I don't know if I'm just being paranoid. I mean, it's nothing I can quite put my finger on. Having a healthy appetite and riding a bike and needing time alone are not crimes, are they? But I just feel like there's more to it, and I'm ... well, I'm completely out of my depth. I do my best, but I'm not her mum, and I'm convinced I'm doing everything wrong ..."

I feel quite weepy and emotional as I say all of this, and

she reaches out to pat my hand, smiling gently as I half wail my woes.

"It's okay. We all feel like that. It's one of the secrets of motherhood – none of us know what we're doing, no matter how much practice we've had. Every kid is different, and they're always changing – just when you think you've got the hang of it, they evolve into something completely different, and you have to start all over again. It's normal. But if you're sure there's more to this than meets the eye, you need to trust your instincts."

"That's what Cal said," I mutter, glancing over at Nate, wondering if he's listening in.

"Cal's clearly a wise man. And don't worry about Nate – he's liberating some slave planet in a fictional solar system or something. He has no interest at all in what two boring old women are blabbering on about."

I can tell from the way he's leaning forward on the sofa, eyes focussed, limbs jerking around as she shoots, that she is right.

"Now, what can we do about all of this?" she asks, gazing off into the distance and twisting a strand of green hair around her fingers as she thinks.

"Have you tried talking to her? It seems obvious, but sometimes we skip that step."

"I have. This morning. She called me a Nazi and gave me a Hitler salute as she left the house."

"Ah. Nice. And you have no clue where it is that she's disappearing off to after college?"

"Not at all. It's not an after-school club, I've checked. And she's not on the college bus any more. I know I should leave it alone, let her have her privacy, but ..."

"But that's impossible sometimes, isn't it?" asks Laura, her eyes looking upwards, as though she can see Lizzie through the ceiling. "Because you love them, and you want to protect them. Look, I've got an idea ... are you on Snapchat?"

I blink, and try and remember what that is. I fail miserably.

"No. I barely manage normal chat, never mind anything snappy."

"It's just one of the countless ways kids today communicate with each other. And it has this feature, where they can all see where they are – like a virtual map, with their little icons spread around it. Lizzie's too savvy for such things, and knows that I know about it, so she's gone into this thing called ghost mode, so she's hidden. For when she's round at Josh's and told me she's at school, or whatever. No big deal – as you say, sometimes you have to let them have their privacy.

"But if Martha's on it, and she knows you're a bit of a retard when it comes to social media, she might not have turned it off. That might be a way we can track her. That or tracing her phone, if she's on android ... but then you'd need her google account details, and ..."

I am staring at Laura in astonishment by this point. Not only is she speaking a foreign language, she seems fluent in it.

She notes my confusion, and laughs.

"You've got to stay up with the times, kiddo! You don't want to be one of those grannies who can't even figure out how to work TiVo, do you?"

I stay quiet at this point. I am way ahead of her. I've never been able to figure out how to use TiVo.

"Okay," I say, after mulling it all over. "So that might work. But I'm definitely not on Snapchat, whatever it is, so how does that help us?"

She makes a 'top secret' tapping gesture on her the side of her nose, like a superspy giving me a signal, and walks quietly into the hallway. I hear a few rooting sounds, and Laura shouting up the stairs: "Lizzie! Are you still in the shower? When do you want your dinner?"

There's a pause, no response, and Laura dashes back into the room grinning from ear to ear. She's brandishing an iPhone, and holds one finger to her mouth, pointing at Nate with the other. Ah. This is a stealth mission. Message received and understood.

She sits down, and swipes a pattern on the front of the screen, watching as the phone comes to life.

"She didn't answer, which means she's still in the shower," she whispers, her head bowed as her fingers fly over the phone screen.

"She has Snapchat on permanently, just in case something amazing happens ... they're all suffering from bad cases of FOMO, these teenagers ..."

I don't ask, but she says anyway: "Fear of Missing Out.

Right, here we go ... user name MarthaMoo. That's got to be her, I think. Okay, let's check ... yeah. She's here. I've found her."

She stares at the screen, frowning, and I feel a quick sting of panic. What is the map showing her? Has she run away? Is she back in Bristol? Is she living in a cardboard box under an archway in London?

"What?" I say, still whispering, but loudly. "What is it? Where is she? It's bad, isn't it? Is she with Eminem in a sex dungeon?"

Laura is taken aback by that one, which is fair enough. Crazy even by Budbury standards.

"Erm, no ... not unless Eminem has chosen to locate his sex dungeon in Dorset. She's down on the beach. Along a bit, by that old boat shed. Here, look."

She passes me the phone, and I look at the screen. It's a brightly coloured map, dotted with various illustrated figures. I see Josh – a giant brown beanie hat – at the Cider Cave, and Nate, a blonde lollipop head, located exactly where he is, and I see MarthaMoo. MarthaMoo has a solid helmet of jet black hair and looks a bit like Lego Batman. I take in the spot where she's pinned, and know exactly where it is.

I pass Laura the phone back, and stand up.

"Right. Thanks for that. I hope you don't get it in the ear from Lizzie – I feel bad for making you sneak round behind her back."

"Don't worry about it," replies Laura, accompanying me to

the door. "Sometimes, as a mum, you just have to do what you have to do – they can't always like you, can they? That's why we're mums and not friends. Besides, hopefully, she'll never know ... good luck! Let me know how it all works out. I'm sure it'll be fine."

I see her slipping the phone quietly back into Lizzie's bag, and wave goodbye.

I'm heading straight home for some socks, proper footwear, and a bloody big coat. Then I'm going to find Cal. And then we're off on a Mission Impossible.

Chapter 31

"So," he says, as we stomp along the beach, "how do you want to play this? We should have a plan."

He's right, of course – we should. The sad thing is that I can't think of one. We drove straight down to the bay, as soon as I explained what I'd found out, and now we're almost there. It's nearly five pm, and already the sky is an ominously dark shade of grey. The beach is completely deserted, and there's a brutal blast of wind cutting its way up from the sea. I've forgotten my gloves, and my fingers are so numb they could get chopped off by a passing guillotine and I wouldn't even notice.

"I know. But at the moment, my plan is to march up to the boat shed, and burst through the doors like something from *The Matrix*."

He ponders this, and it seems to be amusing him.

"What?" I say, annoyed, "what are you smirking at?"

"I'm imagining you in a long leather coat, doing body swerves to avoid bullets and running up walls."

Well, yes. Fair enough. That is quite a funny image. Hopefully there won't be any bullets, but who knows?

"We could pretend we were just passing ..." I reply, narrowing me eyes as I try and picture how that one would work out.

"Just passing and accidentally went into the old boat shed? Why would we do that?"

"I don't know – because we're keen boating enthusiasts? Because we're cold? Because we need a secret place to talk?"

He pulls a face, and I know I'm talking nonsense. But that's never stopped me before, so I plough ahead.

"We could say we saw a light on, and came to investigate, or ... damn, we should have brought Midgebo! We could have blamed him ..."

I'm saved further speculation by the fact that we are almost at the shed itself – and as we draw close, I see Martha slipping out of the door. There are two big, wide doors that open enough to presumably let boats out – back in the days when it was in use – and a smaller one cut into one of them, to let humans in and out more easily.

Martha is, as usual, all dressed in black, and she looks like a ghostly shadow in the darkening light. It's definitely her, though, blowing on her fingers as she walks towards the bike, which is perched against the wooden sides of the shed.

According to Laura, the building hasn't been used for years, which you can see in the peeling paint and generally slightly haunted vibe it gives off. It would be a great place for a

Halloween party, and I'm amazed that Cherie hasn't thought of that already.

I speed up as I see Martha start pushing the bike away in the wet, compact sand – she wouldn't be able to do that in the summer, when it's loose and powdery. She's heading back towards the village – and, although she hasn't realised it just yet, towards us.

She's heading our way, ear buds in, listening to music, living in that completely shut-off world that teenagers can transport themselves to so easily. You see it all the time in Bristol – teens crossing busy roads without engaging at all in any sense of reality, barely escaping death by car, not even noticing when horns are blaring at them. It's a miracle the human race has survived.

I'm half walking, half jogging, towards her. Cal is right by my side, though he just looks like he's taking a casual stroll. By the time our paths finally cross, she still hasn't spotted us. We're both wrapped up like mummies, and she's not paying attention, so she doesn't actually notice we're there until I physically stand in front of her bike, blocking her path.

I stand there, with my hands on my hips, trying to come up with some kind of snappy comment and failing. There is one very brief, very hilarious moment, where her shock registers. She stares at me, stares at Cal, and glances back at the boat shed. It only lasts a few seconds, that look – but it's there. It's the look that says 'shit, I've been rumbled!'

"What are you two doing here?" she eventually asks, pulling

her ear-phones out and raising her voice to be heard over the wind that's whirling around us. It's a fine recovery, and I'm almost proud of her.

"Looking for you," I reply. So much for the 'pretend we're just passing' plan.

"Well, you've found me ... look, I'm freezing my tits off, I'm going to head home, all right?" she says, gripping the bike handlebars and trying to set off again. I move in front of her each time she tries to wheel it away, like some kind of insane dance partner, blocking her escape route. After the third block, she's getting completely exasperated, and I fully anticipate her ramming me with a full body charge any second. I will be left winded and tearful on the wet sand, bike wheel patterns over my face, like a cartoon character who has just been flattened.

She mutters a few choice words that start with 'f', and then yells at me: "What are you *doing?*"

"I'm stopping you from leaving, until we've looked in that boat shed," I reply, simply. Cal, I see, has already made his way there. She turns round, notices him, and even in the dull evening shade I see her face go pale. Like I said, she's been rumbled – and nobody likes being rumbled.

"It's not what you think ..." she mutters, dropping the bike to the sand and running after him. "Don't go nuts, okay? Please don't go all psycho on me!"

Cal has the door open, the wind blasting it back so it thuds and rattles against the frame, and I jog after Martha.

We all stand in the doorway to the shed, gazing inside. I have no idea what I expect to see – but it's not a scared-looking teenager, huddled in a sleeping bag, a tattered paperback in one hand and a torch in the other.

For some reason, the first words out of my mouth are: "Why are you reading *Fifty Shades of Grey*?"

He looks embarrassed, drops the book, and replies: "It's really funny. I needed cheering up. I'm sorry!"

I don't know whether he's sorry for being there, for getting Martha into trouble, or for his dubious taste in reading materials – but he looks terrified. Martha is casting desperate sideways glances at me, and Cal is looking to me to take the lead. Suddenly, I seem to have become the nominated Grown-Up in this situation.

"We can talk about sorry later. Come on. Let's get out of here."

Chapter 32

Less than an hour later, we are all back at Lilac Wine. Never has a place felt more warm and cosy and welcoming – the weather outside is now elemental, and I fear for Cherie's roof tiles and chimney pots as the wind whirls and twists outside. I've switched the lamps on and drawn all the curtains, both for privacy and to make us all feel more safe.

The Boy in the Shed is sitting in the flowery-patterned armchair, looking madly out of place with his spider-web tattoo and nose ring, but also looking pathetically grateful. He's clasping a hot mug of cocoa in his hands, and his teeth are still chattering slightly. Jesus. It was bad enough being out there for half an hour – he's been living in that shed for almost a week. I've given him a fleecy blanket, and he's tucked up inside it, big black biker boots popping out at the bottom.

I recognise him now, of course – from that night in The Dump. The night when Martha and I had Rebel Rebelled, and I'd taken her home in tears. He'd given me a bottle of

Peroni, I remind myself, and didn't try and stop me when I made Martha leave.

He looks a lot more vulnerable now. His previously spiked black hair is floppy and lank, and he looks less like a tough kid who could cause trouble and more like a 10-year-old who needs a cuddle.

Cal is back at Saffron, rooting out some spare clothes for the boy, and Martha is sitting on the floor by his side, like a mini-Goth guard dog. She's glaring at me like I'm the enemy, which is a look I'm not unfamiliar with, so it doesn't bother me at all. I can almost see the thoughts tumbling through her worried brain: How much trouble am I in? What will she do next? How can we get out of this? What's the best way to play it?

"Right," I say, sinking into the comfort of the sofa and realising how tired I am. Not just by today – but by the days running up to it; the days when I was worried that Martha was descending back into a pit of angst and grief and self-destruction, and even more worried that I wouldn't be able to drag her back out again. I'm so tired, and I need sleep – but first, I need to at least start sorting this mess out.

"It's time to tell me what's been going on ..."

I have my own mug of cocoa, but have taken the liberty of splashing some brandy in it. One of the few perks of being the nominated grown-up.

Martha starts to speak immediately, and I hold up one hand to silence her.

"No, Martha, not you. I can already figure out your part in all of this, and we'll talk about that later – but now I want to hear from ... what's your name, anyway?"

"Uh ... Peter," he mutters, looking terrified. I don't blame him – last time he saw me I was on the warpath and threatened to pull his nose ring out, and this time I probably don't look much more friendly. I make an effort to smile, to get him to relax – he's just a kid, after all, just a poor lost kid whose life is clearly not going well. I can spare some kindness, no matter how tired I am.

"Your surname's not Parker, is it?" I ask, immediately. What can I say? It's just the way my brain is wired.

He looks momentarily confused, and then his fingers go to the skin of his neck, and the spider web tattoo that criss-crosses it. Boy, he's going to regret that one when he's 60.

"Oh! I get it! Peter Parker! No, it's not ... look, I'm really sorry," he says, sounding genuine. "For coming here. For dragging Martha into this. I just ... I had nowhere else to go. I was desperate."

I hear the sound of the front door opening as Cal returns, the brief howl of the storm outside before he closes it again, and nod at him as he walks into the room bearing a small pile of clothes. Spider Man is tall, like Cal, but super-skinny, in the way of these young men today – the gear will swamp him, but it's the best we can do at short notice.

Cal assesses the mood, and simply sits next to me so we can present a united front. That's good – I'm sure Martha's

303

Machiavellian mind has already been hoping she can divide and conquer.

"Go on," I say, after a sip of my cocoa. "Tell me about it. Why were you desperate? And be honest. I am completely unshockable, I guarantee it."

Peter still looks shaky, and pauses for a moment, looking from Martha to me to Cal.

"It's all right, son," says Cal, firmly. "You're safe now. We might look scary, but we won't bite. We've all been young, and we've all made mistakes – and maybe we can help you."

The boy gazes at Cal with something approaching adoration, nods, and finally begins to speak. He has a thick Bristol accent, and was clearly born and raised there.

"Yeah. Well. I suppose it started with my step-dad. My real dad … well, he went away when I was a kid. Don't know where. It was all right – my mum was all right. But then when he moved in, the step-dad … well, it wasn't all right anymore, so I left."

I ponder asking him why it wasn't all right, but decide that that would be too much. He looks as though he might clam up on that particular subject, so I let it lie. There'll be time for the whole story to come out eventually, and it's not exactly an uncommon one, is it? Might be that the step-dad was a wife-beating arsehole who deserved a slow and painful death. Might be that Peter was just a stroppy teen who couldn't accept his mum had a new man in his life. Either way, the end result was the same.

"So, where did you go?" I ask, already suspecting I know the answer to this one.

"I bummed around for a bit, you know? Sofa-surfing. Spent a bit of time crashing in the park when the weather was good. Eventually, I met some people. They had a place ... well, they'd kind of taken over a place, an old shop that had closed down. It was all shuttered up, and nobody was using it anyway, and we weren't really doing any harm ..."

He sounds defensive, and I know why: I've lived in those 'places' as well, and they invariably end up less as a blissful socialist co-operative and more as a drug-infested pit of squalor. It often starts well, starts hopeful, but there's usually someone in there who rakes up trouble – someone with more of a habit, someone who's got issues, someone who is just a bit of a twat and likes bullying people. For anyone vulnerable – young, weak, in less than robust mental health – it's not an ideal environment.

"I can imagine," I respond, not wanting him to stop now. "So. Why did you leave?"

"Well. It was okay to start with. Martha knows a lot of that gang, and honestly, they're good guys. Not, like, in the normal sense – but decent people, no matter how they look. So it was all right. But then this new guy moved in, and he wasn't so nice. Things started to change. He ... he'd come back with stuff. Stuff that wasn't his. Phones and iPods and sometimes wallets. He always had cash, and he was generous with it, so nobody really asked too many questions. Except ... well, it just didn't feel right, you know? Not to me, anyway.

"It was last week when I decided I couldn't do it any more. He came back to the shop with a big bag full of toys. Still in the Toys R Us bag. I mean, they obviously weren't his – it's not like he'd been there and bought them. He'd nicked them. And they were probably some kid's Christmas presents, and some mum had probably worked really hard to buy them ... my mum always did, she saved up through the year ... and ... well. I just couldn't stay. And I had nowhere to go, and nobody to ask for help, and I had Martha's number ... so I hitched my way here. Took ages as well."

I can imagine that it did. He doesn't exactly look like the kind of person you'd stop for at the side of the road on a cold winter's night.

He's tearing up slightly as he talks, and his nose is running. Probably partly because of the emotion, and partly because he's been living rough for so long – that lifestyle isn't easy on the health and wellbeing front, and spending the last few nights on a windswept beach in an abandoned boat shed can't have helped. I bite down my frustration – if only they'd come to me, asked for help instead of sneaking around shrouded in mystery, he could have been here, and safe, and warm.

But I remind myself that they are just kids. That Martha is only 16. That at that age, things have their own sense of logic – one that defies anybody over the age of 30. Sneaking around always seems like the most sensible solution.

"Okay, I get all that – and don't worry, all right? You'll be fine with us for the time being. But when you say you don't have anywhere to go, is that really true, long term? You're, what, 19, 20? Your mum sounds like a good person. She must be worried sick about you. Are you sure you can't go home?"

He shakes his head, so vigorously that he spills cocoa on his fleecy blanket, and replies: "No! No, I can't. I try and stay in touch with her, every now and then, just so she knows I'm okay. But I can't go back, no."

"Is there anyone else? Any family at all?"

He pauses at this one, and I know that there is. That it might not be easy, but that there is at least a possible way out for him.

"Well, I have a brother. But he's ten years older than me, and he lives in London, and he's just had his first baby, and his girlfriend doesn't like me much ... I can't turn up there. He wouldn't want me."

"Have you asked him?" I say, as gently as I can. "Have you given him the chance to say yes or no, or have you decided for him?"

His silence tells me that it's very much the latter. That Peter has done what lots of kids in his situation do – rejected himself in advance, to spare himself the trauma of someone else doing it.

I'm self-aware enough to realise that at least some of my sympathy is based on my own experiences, and tell myself not to get too carried away – he needs help, and I will help him. But he's not me, and nothing short of a time machine is going to change my childhood.

"Can he stay with us? Please?" asks Martha, pleadingly. I suppose, ultimately, that is the main question that needs to be answered right now. We don't have a spare bedroom, but I'm guessing he'd be happy enough on the sofa...

"He could stay with me at Saffron," replies Cal, following my train of thought. "I need to check with Cherie first, though."

It's a sensible idea, and I hope she says yes. I don't know what I'll do otherwise – and having him in Saffron with Cal is better all round. He seems like a decent enough kid that's fallen on hard times, but until I know him better, I'd also prefer it if he wasn't sharing a house with Martha. Harsh, but true – she has to be my priority. She's at that weird age where she's responsible enough to want to help a friend, but not mature enough to see the potential pitfalls. I guess that's my job – and much as my instincts tell me Peter is okay, I can't risk her sliding back into her old ways. She's still vulnerable, still grieving, still only just working her way through life. It's a delicate balance, and I need to help her maintain it.

Cal has left the room to speak to Cherie, and I use the time to dispense chocolate HobNobs. It's definitely a chocolate HobNob kind of night. By the time he returns, we're all munching away, and covered in crumbs.

"She says it's fine," he announces, "as long as he doesn't steal the silver candelabra or pee on the Persian carpets."

I laugh as he says this – of course there are no silver candelabra or Persian carpets in Saffron – but it's such a Cherie thing to say.

"I promise, I won't!" says Peter, taking it seriously, which makes me laugh even more.

"Okay. Well, short-term, we're sorted. Now we all need to have something proper to eat, and then Peter, you can head over with Cal. Then me and Martha can have a nice talk ..."

She grimaces as I say this, and had obviously hoped she was off the hook. As if.

I stick a couple of pizzas in the oven, manage not to burn them, and we all eat from plates on our laps. Peter puts it away like he's starving – no table manners at all, just like Barbara remembers me – and says 'thank you' approximately twenty thousand times during the course of the evening. Eventually, after hugging Martha so hard I fear her head might explode, he takes off to Saffron. Cal even lets him wear his cowboy hat, which makes him look like something from the Walking Dead as they battle their way through the wind.

As soon as we've waved them off, Martha makes a smart exit – scrambling up the stairs doing a theatrical series of over-emphasised yawns, just to let me know how absolutely exhausted she is. Way too tired for a conversation, of course.

I grin, and clear away the plates, and spend a few minutes pottering around downstairs before going up. I am lulling her into a false sense of security, just for fun. I have the urge to let out a demonic evil-villainess cackle as I climb the stairs, but show super-human restraint.

I knock once on her door, but go straight in. I catch her unawares before she can even pretend to be asleep. She's in her PJ trousers, but sleeping in my David Bowie T-shirt, I see. Honestly, the girl's a magpie. Her phone is on her lap, and she's propped up against the headboard. I can smell the rich scent of Kate's Burberry perfume, and I inhale as I sit down next to her, on the edge of the bed. She looks nervous, and twitchy, and is obviously anticipating a huge bollocking. Maybe I was even anticipating dishing one out – but the perfume has killed that idea.

"You know," I say, taking the phone from her hands and placing it on the bedside cabinet so she can't get distracted, "that you should have come to me, don't you?"

She nods, and chews her lip, and considers what she's going to say.

"Yeah. I suppose I do. But it was a weird situation, and you brought me here to get away from that gang, and ... and well, you can be a bit scary sometimes, can't you?"

"This is true. I can. Mainly because I'm scared – I'm scared for you, Martha. I know we don't do deep and meaningful very well, but maybe we should at least try. I love you, babe – so much. Not just because you're Kate's daughter – but because you're you. I was there when you were born. I was there when you started walking, and talking, and even when you started swearing, which wasn't much later. And I didn't just move us here to get you away from 'that gang' – I moved us here so we could both have a fresh start. We both needed it, didn't we?"

She nods again, and mutters something that sounds suspiciously like agreement.

"And with Cal turning up like he did, it's turned out to be even more of a fresh start than we expected," I say, reaching out to stroke her hair while her guard is down. "How do you think it's all been going, honestly? Are you happy here?"

She scoots her pillow from behind her back, and holds it to her, cuddling it. She looks about 12, and it breaks my heart.

"I am, happy ... or as happy as I can be right now. Cal is great. Lizzie's great. This place is great. But ... I just miss her so much, you know? Mum. Some days it's worse than others. Some days I don't think about her for ages, and then I feel guilty, like I'm forgetting her, so I make myself remember things that I know will upset me, like I deserve to be upset for forgetting her ... it doesn't make sense, does it?"

"It does, sweetheart. It makes perfect sense. I do it all the time. Neither of us will ever forget her – but she wouldn't want us to live the rest of our lives in pain, would she? She'd want us to at least try and be happy, even if we don't quite manage it."

Her eyes are closed, and I know she's fighting away tears. So am I. We're a useless pair, really – we should probably just both give in and have a good sob. It'd probably make us feel better.

"You're right. I know you are. And she told me that, before ... before she died. But it's not as easy as it sounds, is it? Sometimes I can't even go round to Lizzie's because I feel so jealous of her having her mum there with her. That's so mean and horrible of me, but I can't help it. So I just stay away until it passes – it always does, eventually."

"That's because you're basically a good human being who doesn't have it in you to be mean for too long. And Lizzie maybe feels the same way when she sees you with Cal, you know – sad about her dad?"

Martha looks at me with dark, shining eyes, and I can see that she's never considered this possibility before. It seems to make her feel better, and she gives me half a smile. Half is better than none.

"Maybe. It's weird here, isn't it? In a good way. It's like we've all got various parts missing, but between us, we have everything – Lizzie has a mum and no dad; except an almost-dad with Matt, and I have a dad and no mum, except an almost-mum with you. And Cherie has no kids of her own, but she's adopted us all ..."

She's right, of course, now she points it out. This place is more than the sum of its parts. I came here with no friends, and no-one to turn to – and now I feel love and support at every turn.

"And now Peter's here as well," continues Martha before I

can respond. "I'm really sorry, you know. That I didn't tell you. Partly I was worried about it, but if I'm honest, it was a bit exciting as well …"

"Yeah, I know," I say – because I do. Me and Kate were terrors for intrigue and drama. "Sneaking around, stealing food, being all Miss Mystery Teen 2017. I get it, I do. But … well, I don't know how much your mum ever told you about my childhood. Enough, I'm sure. I understand what he's going through, and I'm proud of you for trying to help him. He needs help. We all need help sometimes. For me, that came from your mum – and she taught me not to always expect the worst from people. Sometimes, you just need to reach out and see what happens. It isn't always bad."

Martha thinks it over, and eventually replies: "I know. And it must be awful for you, not having her here anymore. I've never thought about that. I hope … well, you're not on your own now, are you? I know I'm not much use, but there's Laura and Cherie and everyone else, and Cal's here for now anyway, so … you're not on your own."

"No," I say, kissing her on the forehead and standing up. The scent of Burberry is all around us, and I feel Kate closer than ever – through the perfume, through Martha's words, through my own memory of her kindness and the gifts she brought into my life.

"I know. I'm not on my own, and I will always be grateful for that. Now get some sleep, super-girl."

Chapter 33

Peter spends the next two weeks with us, and the transformation is astonishing. Part of that is due to being well-fed, warm, and feeling safe for probably the first time in years.

But part of it is due to Cal, who comes into his own when he's tasked with looking after him. Martha is still at college, dragging herself towards the end of term, and we are all trying to keep her focused and ensure that the arrival of her old friend doesn't distract her.

Being Martha, she's aware of this campaign, of course, and lets us know exactly how aware through a series of sarcastic comments and exaggerated eye-rolls. Teen wrangling – it's a barrel-load of laughs.

Cal keeps Peter busy in a way that leaves him too tired to worry. They spend hours on Frank's farm, doing hard graft, and hours walking, and even hours at the local stables, where he makes friends with a mare called Bessie. He eats well, and gains weight, and his cheeks pink up from all the fresh air, and eventually – after a while – he even stops saying 'thank you' after every single sentence.

It's kind of heart-warming to see, and for me, especially so. We've given Peter a second chance, and I count it as a victory. Small kindnesses can make a huge difference if they come at the right time, I know.

With his permission, I've spoken to his older brother, Mark, who works as an IT consultant in London. Peter was right – his girlfriend doesn't like him much – but she's willing to give him a chance. They've both agreed that he can come and stay with them for Christmas and New Year, and they'll see how it goes from there. Baby steps, but steps at least.

Today is the day that we are taking him to the train station in Dorchester, and saying our goodbyes. Cal and I are waiting for Peter and Martha at the cafe, giving them some alone-time before we drive into town.

The cafe is looking extremely festive, draped in random streamers and strips of glittering tinsel, baubles dangling from the mobiles, windows decorated with spray-on snow and silver-sprayed pine cones.

Laura is on duty, with Willow, and both of them are currently a bit tipsy on the mulled wine they've been making – testing it for purely scientific reasons, I'm told. The wine has filled the whole place with the rich scent of cinnamon and cloves, and it feels like the Comfort Food Café has opened up a Marrakesh branch.

They have Christmas tunes playing on Willow's phone, and

the two of them are doing that strange leg-kicking dance to *I Wish It Could Be Christmas Every Day*, arms around each other's shoulders. They're giggling away furiously, and I suspect it's only a matter of time before they're twerking on the tables to *Hark the Herald Angels Sing*.

"Maybe that's their turn for the show on Christmas day," says Cal, laughing at them as he sips his coffee.

Ah. The Big Show – the event of the decade, and one that I am secretly dreading.

This year, the various freaks, geeks and cake-making wonders of the village have decided that instead of buying each other presents, we will all chip in to pay for a big party at the cafe. Cherie has proclaimed that it will be in the format of a TV talent show, with Edie May taking the coveted role of head judge. Her very own chance to be Len Goodman.

Nobody *has* to get up and perform, but the implication is clearly that anyone who doesn't is a giant wuss and will be mocked for life. For annoying people like Cal and Martha, who can sing and play guitar, that's fine – but the less creative amongst us have been left flailing. Becca, who is famous for her Grinch-like attitude to the festive period, and who proudly wears a T-shirt with the words Bah Humbug on it, is dreading it – but says even she has got something planned.

Laura looks slightly flustered every time it's mentioned, so I'm pretty sure she's not come up with an idea, and I'm completely out of options. I may just hide in the toilets for the whole night, locked in a cubicle with a vat of mulled wine and a good book.

"Who knows?" I reply, looking on as Laura careens into a chair after an especially exuberant leg-kick." Literally anything could happen, Budbury's Got Talent. I'm looking forward to the top-secret act that you and Martha are working on ..."

He nods, and winks, and is clearly not going to tell me any more about it, damn him. They've been practising for days now, hiding away in Saffron, me banned from even walking past in case I accidentally hear or see anything incriminating.

Cal glances at his watch, obviously hoping, like I am, that the kids turn up on time. It started snowing this morning – just lightly, and it's not settled properly yet – but we'll need to allow a bit of extra time for the drive.

"They'll be here, don't worry," I say, perhaps sounding more reassured than I feel. "And before they get here, just let me say – you've been brilliant. With Peter. I don't think he's ever had a man in his life like you before, and it's made a huge difference."

Cal looks marginally embarrassed, and tries to brush it away. It's kind of cute, him looking embarrassed – especially when it comes packaged the way it does with him, all big and tough and outdoorsy in his Levis and navy sweater and boots.

"Nah, it was nothing. He's a bloke, he just needed another bloke to give him a few pointers. I know I've not exactly been around for Martha – and she still confuses the shit out of me – but he's a young lad. I'm used to them, we get a lot on the farm. Young lads who've left home for whatever reason, come walkabout to the bush looking for an adventure. Some of them take to it straight away, but others ... well, they're a bit like puppies that got taken away from the litter too early, you know? Need a bit of support. That's all it is with Peter, right enough."

"You're really bad at taking compliments, aren't you?" I say, grinning at him. I don't get the chance to mock Cal anywhere near often enough.

"Well I learned from the master, love! The other day when I told you your hair looked nice, you punched me in the gut!"

"Yes, well ... that's different. My hair's a touchy subject. I was just waiting for the follow-up comment about Duracells, or being dragged through a bush backwards. Anyway. You've done good. And I like your hair too."

He idly reaches a hand up to touch his own locks, and ponders it.

"If we had kids," he says, slowly, "they'd be strawberry blondes. I'm never sure how I feel about them. I always find it confusing, not knowing if they're blondes or gingers, you know?"

"If we had kids," I reply, feeling myself blush as I speak, "it would be an immaculate conception, and perfect for this time of year ..."

"I know," he says, giving me the lazy half-smile that does nothing for my red cheeks. "You've so far managed to find me highly resistible, which is miraculous in its own right – but maybe I'll trap you under the mistletoe at some point. Then you'll be in trouble."

I probably would be, and I make a silent vow to myself to sneak into the cafe at night, and burn all the sprigs that are hanging at various weird locations all around the room. There's even a branch hanging by the door to the loos, which is potentially disastrous – what if you were desperate for a wee and someone collared you for a snog as you went past?

"Well, I don't have long to go," I say, making light of it. I can't engage in a flirt battle with Cal – he'd definitely win. "I only need to protect my virtue for a little while longer, and you'll be jetting off back to the land of Oz on January 3."

He nods, and looks serious.

"Yep. I suppose I will. How do you feel about that? About me leaving?"

That, of course, is a question I've avoided thinking about for a long time. The truth is that I will be devastated. He's become my walking companion, my TV buddy, my drinking partner, my glamorous assistant in all Martha-related issues.

He's boosted my confidence and made me feel good about myself; he's tolerated my eccentricities and shared his own. He makes me laugh, gives the best hugs, and isn't exactly hard on the eyes. Basically, I realise, he's become my best friend – filling at least some of the void left by Kate's passing. Without him, I've no idea how I will fill my days. And as Martha and

I are due to return to Bristol in February ourselves, there is simply too much change on the horizon for me to be able to deal with it in a mature fashion.

"Oh, you know," I say, trying to sound casual. "I'll miss you, but I suppose I'll cope. Battle bravely on ..."

He's nodding, looking vaguely deflated, and I suddenly feel bad. I'm not being fair, here – glossing over things that have actual emotional weight, just because I'm a coward. I reach out, and slip my hand into his, squeezing his fingers.

"Truth? It's going to be really hard, Cal. I've got used to having you around, and there'll be a big, Cal-shaped hole in my life, and in Martha's. But in case you hadn't noticed, I'm a bit of a screw-up when it comes to this relationship stuff, and I never seem to know how to express myself properly, or deal with heavy emotions.

"So I have this imaginary file, in my head – it's not got a name, but if it did, it would be something like *Stuff I Don't Want to Think About Right Now*. And every time something flitters across my mind that upsets me, I add it in, just so I can get through the day. You leaving? It's one of the main contents of that imaginary file – it'll be bad enough when you actually go, without torturing myself with it before it happens. One day at a time, and all that. Anyway ... what about you? How do you feel about it? Surely part of you will be looking forward to getting home?"

I try to remove my hand from his, but he's having none of it, keeping a tight enough grip to hold me in place. He's stroking the skin of my palm with his thumb, and it's not doing much for my powers of concentration.

"Looking forward to the sunshine," he says, glancing out of the window at the snow, "but not much else. Home is where the heart is, they say – and I'm starting to think that's true. I'll be sad to leave this place, and all the people here. Sad to leave Martha. Sad to leave you, Zoe …"

I'm feeling hot, and bothered, and as though I'm wearing too many layers of clothing. The Christmas music has moved onto *Band Aid*, but I can practically feel Laura and Willow watching us, sitting here holding hands, waiting to see what will happen next. I'm quite keen to know that myself, as this feels like a strangely important moment – one where what I say will matter. Where what I do will count.

Luckily, I'm saved from the monumental disaster that I usually make of such moments by the arrival of Martha and Peter. They burst into the cafe in a whirl of noise and young people energy, completely disrupting the old people Magic Moment – which is fine by me.

I snatch my hand away from Cal's, but know that Martha has noticed by the way she raises her eyebrows at me. I feel naughty, caught out, as though she's the mum and I'm the misbehaving teenager. My blush levels reach critical mass, and I should probably start warning people to run and hide in their nuclear fallout shelters round about now.

"What have you two been up to in our absence?" Martha

says, throwing herself into her chair, Peter next to her. "You look fabulously guilty."

"Nothing!" I snap back, sounding so fabulously guilty that everybody laughs, even Laura and Willow in the background. It breaks the tension, and I decide to focus attention on someone else – anyone else will do.

"Peter," I say, "how are you? Are you feeling all right?"

It's a distraction – but it's also something that needs to be asked. This is a big deal for him, making this move. Reaching out to his brother. Looking for change – putting himself in a position where he is vulnerable. God knows none of us like that.

He gulps, and nods, and hesitantly replies: "I'm okay ... bit nervous, you know? I haven't seen Mark for ages. And Lucy isn't too keen. And ... well, who knows?"

"It'll be fine," Martha says, firmly. "He's your brother. He loves you. There's nothing to worry about."

She's trying to be kind – but as my eyes meet Peter's, I see his frustration.

"That's easy for you to say, Martha," he replies, not sounding angry, but definitely rattled. "It's different for you. I know you've gone through your own crap, but you've always had so many people who love you. So many people who would welcome you into their lives, instead of seeing you as a burden. People who want to look after you, not cross the street to avoid you. Zoe's here for you. Your grandparents would love you to live with them, even though I know you'd probably top yourself after two days. You could even move to Australia and live with Cal, couldn't you?"

Her face changes with that last sentence. Her eyes flicker from me to Cal, and it's her turn to look guilty. I know, in that one moment, that it is something she's considered – maybe even discussed with him. It makes me feel hollow and anxious, so I refuse to engage with it. I whisk it away to that file of avoidance I was telling Cal about, and hide it.

"Well," I say, not meeting anybody's eyes and trying not to let it show that I even heard that last comment, "try not to worry, Peter. Give it your best shot. Don't expect them to be perfect, none of us are. But if it really doesn't work out, then for God's sake, call us – don't just move into the boat shed! We'll always be here if you need us."

Peter nods, and puffs out his cheeks in relief, and I hope that saying that has at least made him feel less desperate – less trapped. The more secure he feels going into the next stage of his life, the more likely it is to work out.

"Okay," says Cal, decisively, sensing the change in mood at the table. "We better get a move on. All aboard the Dorchester express, guys!"

Chapter 34

It's Christmas Day, and we're having a barbecue. In the snow. Cal insisted, saying he wanted to give us a taste of his homeland, and who was I to argue? It saved me having a showdown with a turkey, at the very least.

We've already exchanged gifts, which was a much more pleasant experience than I anticipated. For me, waking up at Christmas without Kate was really hard – and I'd been worried about how Martha was going to deal with it as well.

With a hefty dollop of relief, I soon realised that she had clearly decided to at least try and enjoy herself. Neither of us was crying – and avoiding our own version of *Oh Come All Ye Tearful* was a real plus point as we began our festive celebrations. That might come later, I knew, but to start with at least, we were holding it together. Maybe for each other's sake – but if it works, it works.

Cal called over early, bearing parcels in a sack and wearing a hat with reindeer antlers sticking out of the sides, and we sat in the living room in front of the fire, opening our presents.

Martha had compiled a play-list of alternative Christmas songs, and in the background we had the likes of The Pogues doing their *Fairytale of New York*, Chrissie Hynde belting out The Pretenders' version of *Have Yourself A Merry Little Christmas*, and Sonic Youth singing *Santa Doesn't Cop Out on Dope*. Festive but weird – just like us.

Martha's gift to me was my own David Bowie T-shirt – but a quick sniff test told me she had at least washed it first, and there was also a pair of cute peacock feather ear-rings hiding inside the folds of the fabric, as well as the latest Jilly Cooper book. She knows my guilty pleasures too well. Cal gave me a totally orgasmic antique copy of *Tess of the D'Urbervilles*, which I sat and stroked for a while, and a couple of paperback crime thrillers set in the Australian outback. I've always suspected that a pack of hungry crocodiles would be the perfect way to dispose of a dead body.

My present-buying has been a bit hit and miss this year. Martha is at that age where there isn't much to get her that she doesn't want to choose herself. I gave her some cash, which always goes down well, plus some books. Because it wouldn't be Christmas without books. Thanks to the wonders of the internet, I've managed to find a teenager-sized Postman Pat onesie, complete with feet, which she adored and immediately put on, posing for photos while she did the traditional heavy-metal rock sign with her fingers and stuck her tongue out like Ozzy Osbourne.

Cal also donated some folding money to the Martha

Fund, plus a pair of new Doc Marten's with tartan ribbons that she flipped over. They look great with the Postman Pat onesie. And between us, me and Cal have bought her some fine additions to her vinyl album collection – some Pink Floyd, Velvet Underground, and a selection of Motown and Stax classics like Marvin Gaye and Otis Redding and Booker T and the MGs just to make sure she doesn't get too miserable.

She's bought him socks with Simpsons characters on the sides, and a selection of Australian snack foods that pretty much had him salivating immediately – chocolate biscuits called Tim Tams, some kind of coconut bar called Cherry Ripes, and crisps called Cheezels, which are like a cross between Hula Hoops and Wotsits. Nothing quite says home like a delicious spread of junk food, I suppose – I'd probably miss Jacob's Clubs if I was deprived of them for long enough.

I'd struggled with what to get Cal, eventually deciding on a leather belt I found in a vintage clothes place in Bournemouth. It's thick, tan, and has a huge metal buckle on it in the shape of a mightily-horned bull. For all I know, it was made in Taiwan, but it looks old and genuine, and like the kind of thing John Wayne would have used to hold his jeans up on a cattle drive. I matched it with a new cowboy hat – a plastic one, with Kiss Me Quick written on the front.

We are all wearing our new finery – onesies, ear-rings, boots, belts, plastic hats – as we pile outside for the food, as well as extra gloves and scarves and padded jackets. The snow has well and truly settled now, making the green in the middle of the Rockery look like someone snuck out in the middle of the night and coated it with thick layers of icing sugar. The trees and bushes are frosted and white, and the water in the little fountain is frozen solid. The sun is bright and the sky is a vivid blue, but the temperatures are low enough to leave our breathe clumping out in steamy clouds as we talk.

Cal has set up his barbecue in the middle of the grass, and is struggling to handle the tongs with his skiing gloves on. He remains determined, though, adding steaks and chicken breasts and burgers to the top of the grill, teeth chattering as he turns them, the smoke spluttering in the breeze. Totally bonkers.

"This," he says, muttering under his breath, "is a lot easier in the sunshine, on the bloody beach ..."

Within a few minutes, the smell of the cooking meat wafting around the gardens, doors start to open. Black Rose, Matt's cottage, is the biggest of all the buildings here, and this Christmas has been playing host to pretty much everyone. He and Laura cleared out most of the furniture to create a big space for tables and chairs, and she's been in her element cooking for her parents, Becca and Sam, Edie, Katie and Saul, and Cherie and Frank.

Predictably enough, the teenagers emerge first, all kitted out in what looks like new Christmas clobber, eager to let off steam after being cooped up with a bunch of adults all day. Lizzie has on the exact same Doc Martens and tartan ribbons as Martha, but hasn't been lucky enough to win the Postman Pat onesie jackpot.

Nate, Lizzie and Martha immediately blow any pretence at being cool teens by starting a snowball fight, running round in the white stuff, clomping their footprints into the ground, shrieking and laughing as they chase each other. Little Saul toddles after them, and Midgebo starts to give pursuit, before standing perfectly still, big black nose quivering in the air. Correctly, he scents food, and instead gallops over to us in case something delicious accidentally falls off the barbecue. The smell of the steak means that he sits at Cal's feet – in fact on Cal's feet – and looks extra-pathetic for the next twenty minutes, literally giving him the puppy-dog eyes and pretending that he's not been fed that day.

Laura has brought out a bottle of Champagne and some plastic glasses, and is merrily dispensing bubbles to us all, everyone milling around wishing each other a merry Christmas and enjoying hugs and kisses and sharing oohs and aahs over gifts. Her parents, who have travelled down in their motor-home to see their daughters and grandkids, are dressed in matching green gilets, which for some reason makes me laugh. They look like characters from an 80s sitcom.

Even a few of the actual holiday-makers edge bravely out from their cottages to see what's going on, one family with young kids who immediately join in the snowball fight, one with a pair of Boxer dogs who do some balletic twisting leaps through the snow before adding themselves to Midgebo's barbecue vigil, sitting on quivering hind quarters, stubby tails thumping away. Poor Cal is completely fenced in by hungry dogs now – one false move and it'll all be over. Possibly even better than the crocodiles.

Cherie stomps through the snow in her bright red moon boots, and engulfs me in one of her super-hug specials. She's wearing an ankle length padded coat that makes her almost entirely spherical.

"Happy Christmas, me lovely!" she says, when she finally lets me up for air. "I love your earrings. Christmas pressie? What else did you get?"

She fingers the peacock feathers as she talks, making them twist and turn until they tangle up in my hair.

"Mainly books," I reply. "I'm easy to buy for. Can't go wrong with a good book."

"You do love your reading, don't you?" she replies, eyes narrowing in thought. Laura passes by, gives me first a quick kiss on the cheek, then a plastic glass full of fizz.

"I do," I answer, sipping the Champagne and grimacing slightly. I'm not sure chilled wine was what we needed on a day like today – it's more of an Irish coffee day – but hey, it's alcohol, so I'll drink it.

"I think it's from when I was a kid," I continue, smiling as I watch the young people frolic. Nate has been pinned down outside Saffron, and is getting a thorough pummelling from the older girls. "It wasn't exactly an Enid Blyton-style childhood, and books were always my escape. I just couldn't get enough stories – and that's never changed."

She nods, and says: "I can understand that. And I've been thinking ... I know you two are only supposed to be here until February, but if you wanted to extend that, I'd be happy to keep Lilac Wine for you. Or one of the bigger cottages, if you needed more space ..."

She looks at Cal as she says this, and raises her eyebrows expectantly. Ah, I think – here it comes. The Budbury Happy Ending pitch. This place changed Laura's life, and Becca's, and now it seems like I'm next on the hit-list.

"That's really kind of you, Cherie, but I'm not sure ... I couldn't just stay, without making some changes. Finding a job. Sorting out the house and flat back in Bristol. It's a big decision, and I'm not especially good at those."

"No pressure – just an offer," she answers, patting me on the hand. "You and Martha seem so settled here is all. And as for a job, that's another thing I've been thinking about ... the book shop in the village closed down years ago, just wasn't the demand I suppose, so I was considering setting up something at the cafe. I'd keep the bookshelves for people to read for free obviously – but I was thinking that a little concession wouldn't go amiss. Like you say, you can't go wrong with a good book – some mainstream fiction, local authors, poetry, photography collections for the tourists, maps and guides ... even a cookery book or two!"

As she speaks, my mind automatically conjures up the

images to go with it: the counter displays, the Budbury Book Chart for the most popular titles; a whole section on fossil-hunting and local history; nature guides; a Thomas Hardy shrine ... they could even hold events, readings by local writers, poetry evenings. There's not much to do around here, they'd be a highlight of the social calendar ... and the cafe should produce its own cook book, crammed with Laura's recipes and Lizzie's photos...

The thoughts are coming thick and fast, and it opens up a whole new world of opportunity. I've loved my time here – but I've missed my job as well. What if I could combine the best of both worlds? What if we could stay? What if February didn't have to be the end?

I feel excited, and nervous, and scared. It's a big change. I'd have to talk to Martha about it, see what she thought. I glance across at her, and see that she is lying on the ground, making snow angels in her Postman Pat onesie, screeching with laughter as Nate gets his revenge by pelting her with snowballs. She looks and sounds so happy – but would she want to stay? Without Cal? I have no idea.

"I'll leave you with that food for thought," says Cherie, dragging me out of my dream world. I realise that I've been completely silent, not responding at all, and splutter my apologies.

"Yes, thank you, Cherie ... I'll definitely think about it," I say, as she moves off to chat to her holiday tenants.

The tenants look happy but confused, and I can see why.

There is an air of controlled madness out on the green, between the kids and the dogs and weirdness of having a barbecue in the snow and the fact that both Little Edie and Big Edie are dressed as elves. Matt is doing a second round with more Champagne, and Katie actually looks relaxed for once, as little Saul helps Lizzie to roll up the body of what might end up being the world's biggest snowman.

Becca strolls towards me, cradling Little Edie in her arms, hardly any of the actual baby visible between the dangling green elf hat, the pointy green elf shoes, and the seven-inch thick clothing she's wearing between them. Her eyes – Sam's shade of dazzling blue – are open and alert, her tiny face creased into the cutest smile as she gazes up at me.

"Wow. She's a complete heart-breaker," I say, holding out one gloved finger for Little Edie to grab on to.

"I know," replies Becca, grinning. "I say this with absolutely no bias as her mother, but I don't think a more beautiful baby ever graced planet Earth. How are you holding up? With all this ... Christmas?"

She kind of sneers a bit as she says it, and I am reminded that this is very much not her favourite time of year.

"Okay," I reply, steadily. "I mean, it's Christmas – what's not to like?"

"I'll write you a list," she answers. "One day. When I have time. But ... I suppose it's not too bad. In fact certain aspects of it are pretty amazing. This time last year, I had no idea what was going on in my life. Now here I am – all loved up and playing mama bear. Never would have predicted that one. But hey ... things have a habit of sneaking up on you sometimes, don't they?"

As she says this, Cal promptly sneaks up behind me, grabbing me into a bear hug and making me squeal. Becca laughs, in a slightly evil way, having obviously watched him tiptoeing towards me for the last few seconds.

I deliver a swift slap across the head to Cal, and only refrain from dishing out the same to Becca because she's holding the most beautiful baby that ever graced planet Earth. I scowl at her instead, and she scuttles off, still giggling.

Cal wraps his arm around my shoulder, and squeezes me into him.

"Good day, isn't it?" he says, dropping a kiss onto the top of my curls. "Even without the sunshine or the beach. Don't think I'll have enough stuff to go round this lot, but Laura says she'll bring out turkey sandwiches if anyone gets hungry."

Of course she will, I think. She's probably planned for the feeding of the festive five thousand already.

"It is a good day," I say, liking the feel of his solid mass next to me. He's second only to Cherie on the hug front, is Cal. "And your daughter seems to be enjoying herself as well. I wonder how Peter's getting on ..."

"He's doing great," replies Cal, as we stand and watch as Martha clambers up, dusts the snow off her legs, and heads towards us. "Sent me a photo earlier, of him holding his little niece. So far, so good."

Martha strides through the now churned-up snow in our direction, just as Cal dashes off to deal with a small barbecue emergency. It seems to have set on fire. So much for his native skills.

"You okay?" I ask, as Martha performs an elegant skid, stopping right next to me. Her pale cheeks are streaked with pink, her black hair is dripping, and she seems to have forgotten to paint on her eyeliner this morning.

"Yeah. Good. This is … all completely mad, isn't it?" she says, holding out a gloved hand to indicate the scene in front of us. The dogs are whooping and jumping as Cal scoops charred bits of meat off the grill; Big Edie is hula-hooping in her elf outfit, and Laura and Matt are having a sneaky snog outside Black Rose. The devils.

"Completely and utterly mad," I reply.

Martha pauses, and a flicker of pain ghosts across her face. She turns to me, and gives me a sad smile.

"She'd have loved it, wouldn't she?"

"She would," I answer, nodding. "But in her absence, I suppose we'll just have to love it enough for all three of us, won't we?"

Chapter 35

Cherie and Frank bring the house down. They're dressed in matching suits and bowler hats, and have just finished a slapstick Laurel and Hardy routine that involved a lot of arse-slapping, falling over each other's feet, accidentally knocking each other's hats off, and comedic dancing. They both end it with a chorus of 'that's another fine mess you got me into', to tumultuous applause.

Edie, who has been set up on a mock judges' table at the front of the space that's been cleared in the cafe, is literally in tears of laughter. She holds up one of the *Strictly*-style paddles that Nate and Lizzie made her from cardboard, and gives them a Ten From Len.

So far, she's been a very generous judge – in fact, everyone has received a ten. I'm beginning to suspect that everyone else will as well – Edie is definitely a little on the tipsy side, and her sherry glass is never empty for long.

Budbury's Got Talent started at around seven pm, with Becca, who doesn't drink, ferrying everyone over to the bay in her mum and dad's motorhome. They're staying at Black Rose looking after Little Edie, which is as good an excuse as any to get out of performing. I should have thought of it myself.

We're all sitting at tables that have been decorated with teeny-tiny Christmas trees, and there are possibly ten thousand crackers strewn around, ready to be pulled. The room has been draped with twinkling fairy lights, and the main ones switched off, so the whole place looks like a fairy tale cavern. If anyone is walking on the snow-covered beach below, it must look like something magical is happening up here on the cliff's edge.

Laura and Willow have set up a buffet area off to one side, trestles laden with cold meats and breads and pies and cakes and a whopping great bowl of trifle. Scrumpy Joe's been in charge of the booze, and there is a half a cash-and-carry's worth of beer, cider, wine, spirits and bubbly to keep us all merry and bright, as well as soft drinks for the younger crowd. Edie has her very own bottle of Harvey's Bristol Cream on her judging table.

So far, the acts have been hilarious. Scrumpy Joe, his wife Joanne, and son Josh, did a routine that involved blowing across the tops of cider bottles filled with different amounts of liquid – managing to decently replicate *Silent Night* in resonant puffs of air.

Willow and her mum Lynnie, who is lucid and charming tonight, do an act that is part yoga, part acrobatics, with head-stands, hand-walking, and some scary looking moves that end with them both landing in the splits. They're wearing matching black leotards and tights, as well as flashing cat ears – because, why not?

Ivy Wellkettle, who I don't know that well as I've luckily not had any call to visit her pharmacy, is joined on the 'stage' by her daughter Sophie, who is home from medical school for the holidays. The two of them perform a bizarre 'pin the tail on the donkey' type game, where the donkey is actually a full-size picture of the human body, and each time the pin lands, Sophie gives us an educational talk on that particular organ.

Luckily they avoid any willies or boobs – it's a rowdy crowd, not calmed any by the fact that Martha and Lizzie have tied a sprig of mistletoe to a broom handle, and are using it as a mobile device. They're sweeping through the crowd with the Kissing Stick, as they call it, and encouraging random encounters – anything from full on snogs for Becca and Sam, enjoying their first baby-free night out together, to chaste pecks on the cheek between Edie and Matt. I knew I should have followed through on my death-to-all-mistletoe plan, and keep a careful eye on their wanderings.

Lizzie abandons the mistletoe broom when it's her turn to get up and perform. This one's a bit of a family affair – Matt on guitar, Josh on bass, Nate on bongos, and Lizzie on vocals. They've taken pity on Laura, and given her a pair of maracas, which she shakes at completely inappropriate times throughout their show.

The band is called The Dead Tulips, and as Lizzie is at the helm, decked out in finest Emo black, I'm expecting something with a tinge of Nirvana, or a hint of death metal. Shows what I know – instead, they launch into a fast, furious and occasionally entirely tuneless rendition of *Barbie Girl* by Aqua.

Lizzie ends it with a particularly menacing 'come on Barbie let's go party!', before saying 'thank you Budbury – we were the Dead Tulips, and you've been a fabulous audience!' She drops the mike like a true diva, and struts off the stage to equal amounts of laughter and applause. The rest of the band follow her off, Laura still jauntily shaking her maracas and looking relieved that it's all over.

Cal, sitting next to me, is creased in two with it all, as Edie combines all of her cardboard paddles and gives them every score between 1 and 10.

Next up is Becca and Sam, who have actually changed costumes for their turn. Becca is in a slinky dress slit to the thigh, still a bit of baby belly left, but looking sexy as hell, face made up, dark hair wild and sprayed with something glittery. Sam is in a tuxedo, but with the tie hanging loose around his neck, tall and blonde and surfer supermodel handsome. Nate, in charge of what might loosely be called 'lighting' – it's a big torch – creates a spotlight as they walk up.

They strike a pose, and within seconds Cyndi Lauper's *Time After Time* is playing. Sam sweeps Becca into his arms, and they perform an extremely graceful and outrageously sensual dance. If I watched *Strictly* as much as Edie, I'd probably know the name of it, but I don't. They swoop and whirl in and out of shapes, spinning and pausing and spinning again, ending with Becca in Sam's arms, one long leg wrapped around his waist.

Edie is beside herself with glee, clapping her tiny hands, on her feet applauding.

"Oh my darlings!" she squeaks. "That was the most beautiful rumba ever! Even better than Jay and Aliona the other year!"

"Just for you, Edie," says Becca, giving her a cheeky wink as they return to their seats.

Wow. That's going to be a hard one to follow – which is a shame, as according to the set list that Cherie has chalked up on the board usually used to display the day's specials, it's now my turn.

"That was hot," whispers Cal into my ear. "I'm feeling strangely aroused ..."

"Don't worry," I whisper back before I get to my feet. "I have just the cure for that."

I walk up to the stage area, taking deep breaths as I go, and pick up the microphone from its place on Edie's table.

"Okay ..." I say, clearing my throat nervously. "This is hard. I can't sing. I can't dance. I can't act. I have very few talents, in fact – but this is one of them. I hope you enjoy it."

Everyone is looking at me expectantly, a sea of happy and semi-drunk faces all smiling their encouragement.

One more deep breath, and I'm ready to go. I perform one

of my very few specials – one I've been practicing for many years. I belch-sing the whole of *Away In A Manger*. Using skills I developed as a young and unpleasant child, I've completely mastered the art of swallowing in enough air, and expelling it in the right way, hitting just about enough of the notes for it to be recognisable as the carol.

As I'd hoped, it makes everyone laugh – there's really no other response to a performance like that, and before long, the guffawing sweeps the whole room like a Mexican wave of amusement.

I nod, and drop a small curtsy, before exiting to applause, my face a fetching shade of beetroot. Edie flashes her ten paddle as I leave, which makes me strangely proud. Funnily enough, the teachers at school never used to like it that much when I did it during Christmas services. No wonder they all hated me.

I walk back over to Cal, and raise one eyebrow.

"Feeling less aroused now, stud?" I say, as I sit back down next to him.

"On the contrary," he replies, in a deep-voiced James Bond-style delivery, laying one hand on my thigh, "that was magnificent ... I never knew you had such hidden talents ..."

It's dim in our corner of the cafe, but I can see his eyes shining, and the half-smile forming, and the paler shape of the scar on his face. He's drop-dead gorgeous, and for some reason, burping my way through a Christmas carol has left me on an adrenaline high.

342

"Oh I do," I reply, laying my hand over his. "Talents you can only imagine."

I say this in such an outrageously flirty voice that is so unlike me, it actually makes us both burst out laughing – which is probably for the best, all things considered. I've had way too much to drink, and it's been an emotional day, and we're both still ruffled by the rumba. I probably shouldn't trust my judgement right now. Or possibly ever.

"We'll continue this discussion later," he says, still grinning. "So hold that thought. But right now, duty calls ..."

Duty, I see, feeling bereft as he moves his hand from my body, comes in the shape of Martha. She's not wearing the Postman Pat hoodie tonight – it is a party, after all. She's fished out a black dress that I know was Kate's, but is wearing it with deliberately tattered black leggings and her new boots, making it look more grunge than LBD. Her hair is pouffed up into a semi-beehive, the love child of a can of hairspray and some furious back-combing, and her eye liner is now well and truly in place. She's wearing red lipstick, vivid against her pale skin, and she looks truly beautiful.

She's perched on one of the high stools that usually line up next to the cafe serving counter, holding the mike in her hand and looking not at all nervous – though I know she must be. Cal has grabbed his guitar from its case, and is jogging over to join her. He's kind of dressed up too, in well-worn Levis and a black shirt, the belt I gave him between them.

He sits on another stool next to Martha, and nods at her, letting her know he's ready. I'm excited to see this – I know they've been rehearsing hard, and it's got to be better than my Sing-Along-A-Belch.

Martha holds the mike to her face, and Cal starts to strum, and it takes me a few seconds to recognise it. When I do, when I understand what I'm about to hear and see, I feel tears immediately sting the back of my eyes, and know that I am going to be helpless to resist. I grab up a napkin from the table, hoping it's not coated in trifle – because I'm going to need it over the next few minutes.

Cal is playing the song in a way that's super slowed-down, an artful acoustic version, done at about half the pace of the original – but those opening chords are still uniquely recognisable as he expertly plucks the notes. The opening chords of David Bowie's *Rebel Rebel*.

Martha comes in, her voice slow and pure and absolutely note perfect, drawling out the words and phrasing it in a way that has the whole crowd suddenly silent and awe-struck. The two of them work it perfectly – her singing, his playing, the power of the song itself. It's easily the best thing we've seen all night, although I may be biased.

I was right about the tears, and don't even try to stop them. I just let them roll, let them come, let them gather in a pool at the bottom of my neck. This performance – this song, and all the memories it holds, of Kate, of Martha, of the past – deserves some tears, and I don't really care how soggy I get.

I knew they were going to come at some point today – and this seems like the perfect moment. I'm overwhelmed: the singing, the playing, missing Kate, loving Martha, loving our new home here, even loving Cal, I admit to myself.

I do love him, there's no doubt about that – I'm not quite sure how I love him, but I do. He's watching me as he plays, a gentle smile on his face, knowing the effect this is having, concentrating on what he's doing but also on me. I try and smile back, but it's a crooked thing.

They play on, and in an obviously rehearsed move, when she gets to a certain line, Nate turns the spotlight of the torch onto me, and everyone's eyes follow it.

"Hot tramp," she sings, slowly, achingly, pointing at me in exactly the same way we did that night in The Dump, seven hundred years ago, "I love you *so* ..."

Cal picks up the famous guitar riff from there, and Nate mercifully moves the spotlight away again. I see, as it wanders over the faces in the room, that I'm not the only one crying. Not the only one moved by this. Laura has given into it completely, leaning her head on Matt's shoulder and weeping; Becca is holding her face in her hands and blinking away tears; Cherie is spellbound, her face damp and shining, gripping Frank's hand in hers.

Well done Martha, I think – you've reduced the entirety of Budbury to emotional rubble. I almost laugh – almost, but not quite. I'm still flooded with emotion, and don't really know where to put it all. I'm sad and happy at the same time; proud and moved and raw. Mainly, though, I feel lucky – lucky to be here, with these people, with Cal and Martha. To have them in my life. To enjoy the privilege of being Martha's fake mother, and Cal's friend, and of carrying Kate's memory with me.

We've come a long, long way since the last time we danced to that song – and I'm incredibly grateful.

The performance draws to a slow, perfect close, and everybody gets to their feet. They stomp and clap and cheer and wipe away tears, and Edie holds up her paddle – she's used a marker pen to change the '10' to a '100', which seems about right.

Martha gives me a jaunty salute as she walks off stage, but doesn't come over – I suspect she's feeling a bit emotional as well, and can't take the mush overload. Instead, she heads towards Lizzie, who wraps her up in a hug and sits with her quietly for a few minutes while she calms down. I'd like to run over there and give her a big kiss, but I know I need to give her space. She's not alone, and that's what matters.

Neither, I remind myself, am I – as Cal looms over me, a sheepish grin on his face, guitar in hand. I stand up, and kiss him on the cheek.

"Thank you," I say. "Really. That was ... well, it was amazing."

"Are you sure? Because it looks like you've been crying."

"I have. But in a good way. It was beautiful – the best Christmas present ever. Kate would be so proud of her – and of you."

He looks flustered, makes a kind of 'aw shucks' face, and puts his guitar back in its case. Budbury's Got Talent has drawn to a close, which is probably a good thing – nobody was going to top that last act.

Someone has put music on, and tables are being cleared off to the side to make a dancefloor. Edie is on her feet, Becca at her side, doing a lively bop *to Santa Claus is Coming to Town*. Cherie joins them, and starts shaking her wild hair around like the rock chick she is.

Cal slips an arm around my shoulder, and I slide into him, wanting to savour every moment. I have no idea what the future holds – whether we'll stay here or go back to Bristol; and even less idea of how my world will look once Cal leaves for Australia. But for now, tonight, in this one moment, everything feels as perfect as it possibly could. I wish I had some kind of magic pause button that I could press, to hold everyone in the here and now. Frozen in time, hanging in a glittering capsule of loveliness.

I don't have that magic button, of course – nobody does – so instead I look at all of these people, at my new friends, and try and lodge everything about them in my memory banks, ready to whip out and smile about when I'm feeling down.

Cal seems to feel the same, and we stand there for a few moments, surveying the madness of our current kingdom, enjoying the spectacle of a group of drunk people celebrating the coming of baby Jesus in their own special way.

"Come on," he says, as we both hear the distinctive opening sounds of *Last Christmas* by Wham!, "they're playing our song ..."

"I got my heart broken to this at a school disco in 1993 ..." I protest, as he drags me towards the dancefloor. "I still haven't got over the trauma."

"What happened?" he asks, ignoring my objections and pulling me in for a slow dance. The pace has calmed, and there's actually a distinctly old school disco feel to the cafe right now – Becca and Sam getting all handsy with each other; Laura actually being lifted off her feet by Matt as they smooch around; Frank and Cherie moving together under the fairy lights. Even Edie is in on the act, doing some kind of ballroom-type shuffle with Scrumpy Joe.

"Well," I reply, settling into his arms, letting my face rest against his chest, "I had the hots for this kid called Jason Doyle. He was so handsome – tall, hunky, way less acne than most of the boys that year. Looked a bit like Robbie Williams, which was as cool as it got back then. He asked me to dance to this very song, and we had an extremely bad teenaged snog during it – you know the kind, all tongues and enthusiasm, no skill at all, like two snakes trying to swallow the same mouse?"

"I know the kind," he says, laughing. "We've all been there."

"Well, I was ecstatic – thought this was the beginning of a whole big love affair. Kate was sitting it out, watching from the PE benches, giving me the thumbs-up and making rude gestures behind his back. I was already thinking that I'd maybe let him get some over-the-bra booby action on the walk home – don't know about your adolescence, but during mine, everybody seemed to get their early sexual awakenings either on the walk home, or in the park ... anyway. Even after that snog to Wham!, he didn't walk me home – he walked Sally Aimes home instead! Would you believe it?"

"My God!" replies Cal, sounding horror-struck on my teen-aged self's behalf. "The bastard! How could he? So, what happened?"

"Well, I walked home with Kate, which was probably more fun anyway, especially as she didn't stick her hand up my top. And the next day, I Superglued Jason Doyle's bike wheels to the concrete floor of the bike shed. They had to cut it off, and there were bits of rubber left there for the rest of term."

"So ... ultimately a happy ending, then, Zoe-style?"

"I suppose so," I say, smiling at the memory. Funny how things that happen to you at that age seem so big, so enormously important, that you don't realise that a few years on, today's trauma will be nothing more than tomorrow's amusing anecdote. Maybe it's that way until you're 90, who knows?

We dance our way past Laura and Matt, and I see her eyes widen as she notices us. Her Mills & Boon mind will be going into overdrive now. I laugh, and relax, and enjoy the moment. Cal is big and solid and warm, his arms have me squeezed comfortably into his body, and I can feel his heart beating beneath my cheek. He smells good, and feels good, and it's all a damn sight better than 1993, without a doubt. I'm guessing that Cal's a better kisser than Jason Doyle anyway – he certainly knows how to hold a woman on a dancefloor, that's for sure.

I'm blushing slightly as I ponder this, my hands on his back, where I can feel the lean muscle of his body bunch and release as we move, the press of denim-clad thighs against mine, and am grateful for the dim lighting. My body is enjoying this a whole lot more than I'd like it to.

Just as poor George is vowing that next year, he'll give his heart to someone special, Cal stills. He stops dancing, and freezes solid on the spot. I drag my face away from its cosy spot on his chest, and look up at him, wondering what's going on. He's grinning, his gaze falling behind me.

I turn around to see what's happening, and am confronted with a now fully-recovered and mischievous looking Martha – the Kissing Stick gripped solidly in her hands. Lizzie's next to her, giggling, and together they look like the embodiment of pure evil.

I open my mouth to say something – possibly something that involves swearing – but before I can get any words out, she's thrust the broom handle towards us, the mistletoe branch dangling above our heads. She stares at me challengingly, and I return the stare with interest. Little minx.

I'm fully prepared to break with tradition and ignore it, but Cal has other ideas. He smiles at me, slow and slightly dangerous, dark eyes flashing, and says: "Looks like it's time to put the ghosts of 1993 to rest ..."

He tilts my chin up with one hand, gently brushes my hair back from my face, and leans down to kiss me. It's an absolute killer of a kiss – long, slow, deliberate, and very, very effective. One hand bundled into my curls, another on the small of my back, crushing me into him, he takes his time – and there's nothing at all platonic about it.

I momentarily forget that I am standing on a dancefloor in front of a cafe-full of people; forget that my teenaged almost-daughter is looking on, steps away; forget that I'd sworn this would never happen. I forget everything, apart from the touch of Cal's lips on mine; the feel of his broad shoulders beneath my fingertips; the joy of his hands in my hair and his heat engulfing me. I am filled with sudden need, and mould myself into his body like liquid.

When he finally lets me go, I gasp slightly, from excitement and nerves and the need for oxygen. His eyes meet mine, intense and for once serious, and the rest of the world seems to disappear as we somehow manage to speak without words. The cafe disappears, the people disappear, even George disappears ... there's just me, and Cal, and the lingering sensation of the spark that still seems to be leaping between us.

We might have spoken, eventually – once either of us was able – but we didn't get the chance. I'm still in his arms, trembling and slightly terrified, when the whole room bursts out into riotous applause. I glance around, and see that everyone else has stopped whatever they were doing, and is clapping their hands and whooping and stamping their feet. Becca's fanning her face in a 'wow, that was hot' gesture; Martha is laughing so hard she's dropped the Kissing Stick, and Edie has retrieved her scoring paddles, holding up a 10.

Cal keeps me in his arms, correctly sensing that I might flee in panic, and laughs along with them. Laura walks over, and punches me lightly on the arm.

"Well," she says, clearly delighted, "it's about bloody time ..."

Chapter 36

Eventually, the party winds up, and just after midnight, Becca finishes her tour of Budbury with her final stop at the Rockery. The journey has been hilarious, all of us crammed into the motorhome, sitting on each other's laps and perching on tables. We possibly broke some over-crowding laws, but the roads are completely empty, and Becca is completely sober.

Still wearing her slinky ballroom outfit and full face of make-up, but now with chunky trainers on her feet, she drives us through the glistening snowscape like a pro, giving us fake tour guide commentary as she goes. Highlights include 'the famous spot where Midgebo once did the world's biggest poo', 'the world-renowned bus stop where Lizzie once appeared without eye-liner', and the cornfield where 'respected vet and pillar of the community, Matt Hunter, first snogged my sister.' Of course, being a bit drunk, we all find this totally side-splitting.

She drops off the Jones family at the Cider Cave, Edie, Sophie and Ivy Wellkettle in the village, Willow and Lynnie at their tiny cottage on the outskirts, before making a detour to Frank's farm and then home. She parks up, and we all crunch our way through the snow back to the houses, saying our goodnights and sharing farewell hugs.

It's a beautiful evening – absolutely freezing, but beautiful, the sky clear and dark and studded with brilliantly shining stars; a perfect full moon hanging in the sky like a giant cheese; the fresh layers of snow glistening in its yellow light. The snowman the kids made earlier is still there, wearing Cal's Kiss Me Quick hat, its carrot nose slightly wonky, its mouth-of-sprouts grinning at us.

I pat him on the head as we pass, and all troop back inside Lilac Wine. It's so warm and cosy in there, all the curtains drawn and the heating on, and we all seem to sigh a small breath of relief at being back inside. The snow is falling again, in small, wild flurries, and it feels good to be safe and comfortable indoors.

Cal has come back with us, allegedly to get his Christmas gifts before going back to Saffron, and there is still an air of unfinished business between us. I don't know where any of it is heading, and feel edgy and nervous and excited. Also, a little tipsy.

I remind myself again of that part as I wander into the kitchen, and pour myself a glass of water. It's not a good combination – tipsy and nervous. It's making my tummy squish around and my brain fizz; I feel tired and wired at the same time, and even thinking about our Last Christmas kiss is enough to make me gaze off into space and sigh. Honestly, I don't think I've ever been kissed so bloody thoroughly – he wasn't lying that night he promised me godlike skills.

I'm standing there, leaning against the counter, sipping my water and wondering just how godlike it could get if we took things further, when Martha walks into the room. She has her boots dangling by their ribbons in one hand, and a packet of Cheezels in the other.

"I'm knackered," she says, brandishing the bag. "And I'm stealing these. Need to get in touch with my Aussie heritage. I'm off to bed. And ... well, happy Christmas and all that. I wasn't looking forward to it this year, for obvious reasons, but ... I suppose it wasn't as shit as I'd expected."

"Wow," I reply, grinning at her. "High praise indeed. Sleep well, small evil princess."

She grimaces at that, and flounces out of the kitchen. I hear her footsteps on the stairs, and a dull thud when she drops her boots to the floor, and the sound of her door closing firmly. That, I think, just leaves us – me and Cal. No audience. No teenager. No buffer zone. I wonder if I can make a break for it, and go and sleep in the motorhome...

Deciding that it's way too cold and way too late for escape plans, I walk through into the living room, pretending to yawn, holding a hand in front of my face. I'm reminding myself of Martha now, which can't be a good thing.

As soon as he sees this performance, Cal starts to laugh. He's sprawled on the sofa, a few buttons of his shirt undone, golden skin peeking out, blonde hair all mussed up and wild, looking like some kind of cowboy Adonis. An amused cowboy Adonis.

"Really?" he says, once he stops laughing at me. "You're going to pull the 'I'm-so-tired-I'm-going-straight-to-bed-to-avoid-you' routine? What are you so scared of?"

I make a small 'hmmph' noise – nobody likes being called out on their silly behaviour – and ignore the fact that he's patting the space next to him on the sofa. Instead, I sit on the arm chair, and try to look both prim and unafraid.

"I'm not scared of anything. Apart from wasps," I reply, narrowing my eyes at him.

"Yeah you are. You're scared of me. Of us. Of that kiss – that pretty damn phenomenal kiss. You're scared of what might happen if you kiss me again. You're a great big cowardly custard, Zoe – no getting away from it."

Against my better judgement, I have to grin at this. He is, of course, spot on in his assessment.

"You never told me," I say, ignoring that assessment, especially as it's correct, "how you got that scar. And you promised you would."

"I'll tell you," he responds, "if you move your arse from that chair and at least come and sit next to me. I promise I won't bite. Unless you want me to."

I weigh up my options, and without even knowing I've reached a decision, find myself settling down on the sofa. Crikey – it's like the man has mind-control powers on top of everything else. He immediately pulls me closer, and I end up nestled against his chest, my hand on the flat of his stomach, inches away from the belt buckle. Big gulps.

"Well, it happened when I was 12," he says, once we're still. "No sharks. No crocs. No Russell Crowe in a barfight. Basically, just me, a skateboard, and the back windshield of my dad's jeep. Went straight through it – dad was more concerned about the car, obviously, being a sensible bloke, but it was pretty nasty. Ended up with a few surgeries, and a lot of stitches in the face. Just like that, my future as a male model was gone."

"Is that it?" I say, looking up at him, tracing the pale line of the scar with my finger. "I feel strangely disappointed. I think I'm going to forget you told me any of that, and tell myself it was definitely a shark attack. While you were rescuing Nicole Kidman from cannibals."

"That works for me," he replies, laughing. He catches my hand in his, and kisses my palm gently. It's not much of a touch, but it's enough to make me breathe faster, and feel a delicious kind of panic wash over me. My fingers seem to have found their way beneath his shirt, and his skin is warm and smooth over the hard planes of his belly. They drift upwards slightly, meeting soft hair, firm muscle.

I hear him pull in a breath of his own, and he moves his lips from my hand to my mouth. It doesn't take much to ignite things all over again, and as he kisses me, he pulls me onto his lap, my legs straddling him, my hair covering both our faces. He holds me close, and kisses me hard, and wraps his fists into my curls, both of us lost in the moment.

His lips move to my neck, the sensitive skin of my throat, and I seem to be unbuttoning his shirt. He's a glorious creature, and my fingers fly to touch his flesh, skimming his shoulders, exploring his back, arching to meet his touch when his own hands start to explore my body.

I can feel him, hard beneath me, obviously as aroused as I am, and it makes me feel even more hungry for him. I writhe and wriggle, and groan when his fingers find my nipple, as his mouth lingers on my neck, as I hear him breathe out my name. Months of foreplay are suddenly exploding for both of us, and I badly want him naked. Naked, and inside me, and on top of me, and beneath me. I want him everywhere, and know that I've wanted him since I first met him – I was just too sensible to do anything about it.

Being sensible isn't really an option any more, as I find my hands reaching down, leaving his chest, heading for his waist. For the belt, with the big buckle, that I very much want to remove, along with the rest of his clothing.

He's grinning as I start to fumble with it, swearing as I struggle to get it undone, and it gives us just enough time to remember where we are, and what we're doing, and where we're doing it. And more importantly, who is upstairs.

I hear the sound of Martha moving around through the ceiling; a door opening, water running in her bathroom – and I can tell from his reaction that he's heard it too.

We both freeze like guilty teenagers, staring at each other in horror as we wait to hear her footsteps on the stairs...

I jump off him, just in case, and land in an undignified heap on the floor, hair all over the place, face bright red, bra unhooked and bunched beneath my T-shirt. He takes one look at me, and laughs.

"It's okay," he says, offering a hand to help me back up. "We're safe. Sounds like she's gone back to bed."

I stand up, feeling wobbly and unsteady on my feet, and back away from him as though he's radioactive.

"Yeah ... but ..." I mutter, still in fight-or-flight mode, trying to contort my arms backwards under my top to re-hook the naughty bra.

"I know. It doesn't feel right, does it?" he says, sighing and running his hands through his hair in frustration. "Not with her upstairs. If we're going to do this – and I very much want to do this – then we should do it right."

I feel my heart rate soar as I imagine that ... if we'd just been doing it wrong, then what would right feel like? I nod, and take a few more steps away. I need a bit of distance. I need to cool down. I need to not be looking at his bare chest, the fair hair snaking down his stomach. I need to not still be thinking about the way it felt to have those big hands touching my body.

"I'm going to bed," I say, quickly, turning to leave before I can change my mind. "Erm ... thank you?"

I'm not sure that's an appropriate thing to say, but feel that I have to say something.

"My pleasure. And Zoe?"

I pause as I reach the doorway, look back at him. Long and lean and still very clearly ready for action.

"Yes?"

"This is to be continued, all right? Don't go to bed regretting this, or conjuring up reasons to pretend it never happened. The lyrics to Last Christmas do not apply here, and this is not 1993. Your heart would be safe with me."

I nod, and scurry up the stairs on all fours, like a terrified monkey.

Chapter 37

I wake up the next morning with the strangest of feelings. It takes me a while to recognise it, as it's not a hangover, self-loathing, or the desire to go straight back to sleep.

No, I think, as I stretch out my legs and arms and luxuriate in the warmth of the duvet – it's actually happiness.

We had a great Christmas, against the odds. We did a good deed helping Peter. We had a civil conversation with Barbara and Ron. We exchanged amusing gifts. We had a barbecue in the snow, and a party with our friends. Martha kind of told me she loved me, even if she called me a tramp while she did it. We only cried about Kate a little bit. And, of course, I think – realising that along with the happiness there's a hefty dose of horny – things got a little bit scorching hot with Cal.

I allow myself to wallow in the memory of that for a few minutes, recalling the way he kissed me, the sensation of having his hands on my bare skin. His final comments ... to be continued...

I have no idea where it's heading, but I want more of it.

Even if it's only for a few days. All my previous caution seems to have evaporated; resistance seems futile when a man can kiss like he can. At the very least, it will be fun – and Lord knows I'm probably way overdue a bit of fun.

I know that beneath that, under the physical attraction and the curiosity and the basic lust, there is more to this. That my feelings for him are a lot more deep than fancying him. That he has carved out a place in my life that will entirely possibly feel unfillable once he's left – but for now, I concentrate on the good stuff. The fact that I'm warm, and headache-free, and actually looking forward to the day and what it might hold. Time with Martha, time with Cal, time to enjoy each other while we still can. This is time that Kate never got, and I plan to make the most of it.

Maybe I'm finally getting all mindful in my old age. Or maybe I'm so excited at the thought of some world-rocking sex that I'm managing to over-ride all my usual reservations. Who knows?

I drag myself out of bed, and don't immediately freeze – that means the heating is on, which means it might be later than I thought. I glance at my watch and see that it is, in fact, almost 11am, and I have had a humungous sleep-in. No wonder I feel good. So good, I half expect to see tiny bluebirds fluttering around my head when I look at myself in the mirror.

No such luck – just the usual halo of hair – but that's okay. The bluebirds must be the invisible kind. I get dressed in leggings and my David Bowie T-shirt, and make my way onto the landing in bare feet. I feel light and breezy and almost giddy, and do wonder if I'm not perhaps still a bit high from everything that happened the day before. From Martha's obvious contentment, from the cafe community, from finding myself sitting on top of a gorgeous and supremely gifted cowboy Adonis. A cowboy Adonis I feel I can trust – who told me my heart would be safe with him.

Whatever it is, I like it, and hope it sticks around.

Usually when I feel like this, I poke at it with a big stick made entirely of 'yes, but ...' You know the kind of thing – I'm sure all women do. The 'yes, but – what happens next?' The 'yes, but – this is too good to be true!' the 'yes, but – he's leaving in a few days and what if you have a messy melt-down?'

Today, I build a big, solid wall between me and Yes, But –my very own psychological Great Wall of Zoe.

Instead, I look forward to coffee, and possibly cake – it's still Christmas, so it's allowed – as I tiptoe down the stairs. I'm pretty sure Martha will be up by now, but creep down just in case. I'm almost at the bottom when I hear sounds from the living room, and know that she's not only up, she has company.

I can hear her and Cal chatting, and sit on the bottom step for a minute. The sound of his voice has sent me immediately into a world-class blush, and I need a moment to let it fade. He must have come over earlier – or maybe he never left, and crashed on the sofa, feeling as tortured with frustration as I'd been when I escaped to my room.

I hold my flaming cheeks in my hands, willing them to cool down, and listen to them talk. I'm not trying to eavesdrop – that's really not my style – but the door is partly open, and I can't help but over-hear.

"I know," says Martha, her voice low, obviously trying not to wake me up and not realising I'm already there. "I'm really excited about it. But I'm worried as well – about Zoe. She might go nuts."

"You can't assume that, love," replies Cal, his tone reassuring and calm. "But we do need to talk to her about it, don't we? Probably today."

I hear Martha making a kind of 'uggh' sound, and can picture the grimace that comes with it. I'm interested now, and feel a stirring of concern in my tummy, and know I should walk through that door, or shout good morning, or start singing – anything to let them know I'm here. But I don't. Because I'm a deeply flawed human being.

"Yeah, okay. We'll tell her today, and hope for the best. Are the flights all sorted?"

"Yes," he replies. "We leave on the third, as planned. Stopover in Singapore, and we'll be in Sydney after that. I can't wait for you to see the place, Martha. It's beautiful."

When she replies, her previous hesitancy seems to have faded, and instead she sounds excited.

"It'll be great. You can show me where you grew up, and

I can meet my grandparents – weird! – and see a koala or whatever. And then ... I suppose everything will be different, won't it? After that."

"It will be different – but hopefully even better. Is this still what you want, love? Because it's not too late to change your mind. I know it's a big change, and if you're not happy with that, I'll understand."

There's a pause here, while presumably Martha thinks about what he's saying. During that pause, I sit with my hands holding my tummy, on that bottom step, wondering if I might be sick at any moment. I've come into this conversation half-way through, uninvited – but it's hard not to pick up on what they're talking about.

They're talking about leaving, for Australia. Together. Both of them.

"No," says Martha, firmly. "It is what I want. I want to see Australia, and I want us to be together, Cal – but are *you* sure? I mean, I'm a pain in the arse – just ask Zoe. I'm a lot of responsibility, and not a lot of reward in return. Are you sure you're up to it?"

"Zoe does not see you like that, and you know it," replies Cal, sounding a bit annoyed with her. Defending me, even as he's planning to leave me. "And yeah, I'm more than up to it. Plus, Martha, if we're going to be living together from now on, maybe you could try on 'Dad' for size instead of 'Cal' ..."

He's clearly joking with that last one, and she laughs in

response. I, on the other hand, feel like I might never laugh again.

"Okay, *Dad* ... we'll tell Zoe today, then. I am not looking forward to it. Get ready with the fire extinguisher, 'cause she's going to go off big time ..."

At this point, I hear movement, and the sounds of them standing and up. They might be heading out for a walk, or into the kitchen, and I need to scarper. I don't want to be caught here like this, perched on a step, looking half-feral and fully loaded with confusion and pain. I don't want to be the person Martha thinks I am – about to 'go off big time.'

I scurry quietly but quickly back up the stairs, and into my room. I close the door behind me in case either of them comes up, and sit on the bed to try and get my shit together.

This, of course, is harder than it sounds. I huddle there, completely shell-shocked by what I've just heard.

I turn it around in my mind, trying to see it from different angles and perspectives, trying to convince myself that there's some way I've misunderstood. But whichever way I look at it, I can't – I've just heard Martha and Cal planning to leave together, planning to live together, and plotting how they're going to break the news to the nutter upstairs.

I'm trembling by this stage, adrenaline coursing through me as I process it all. And, I realise when droplets plop down into my lap, I'm curled into a ball and crying.

I'd woken up so happy. I'd decided I could trust Cal. I'd built my Great Wall of Zoe. I'd defeated the Yes, Buts ... and it turns out I shouldn't have bothered. Because now it just made it even harder to face up to the fact that all the Yes, Buts were in fact true.

I feel sad, and alone, and betrayed – and the worst thing is that none of these feelings are new to me. They're always there, lurking beneath the surface, waiting for a chance to escape and take over. Waiting for a chance to say 'I told you so.'

People lie. I know this. People lie for all kinds of reasons. They lie to help themselves; to protect themselves; to hide away from truths they don't like. Martha lies, I lie, we all do it. And men ... well, I think, bitterly, men lie as well. It's not exactly unheard of for a man to lie in order to get into someone's knickers, is it? I'd just expected better of Cal – and I suppose that's where I made my mistake.

I'd lied to myself as well, which is where the damage has really been done. I'd tried to imagine me and him as fun – tried to ignore what was really going on with my own emotions – and now I was paying the price. Because Cal wasn't just fun – I was in love with him. Completely, totally, and hopelessly. Or at least I was in love with my idealised version of him – the version where he didn't lie, and scheme, and secretly plan to take my fake-daughter thousands of miles away to live with him.

I try not to blame Martha. She's just a kid. A kid who's gone through too much – who can blame her for wanting to leave? For wanting to start afresh, with the only parent she has left? It's not like I've offered her a great alternative, is it? I'm not her dad, and I certainly can't offer her koalas. I try not to blame her ... but I can't deny it hurts. I suddenly feel that every step forward we've made, every hope of progress I had, has been an illusion – moving us here, leaving my job, it was all for nothing.

Or ... not nothing, I remind myself. Moving us here led to Cal coming into her life. And bitter as I might feel about my own pathetic role in all of this, maybe this will be the best thing for her – maybe she'll be happier there, with him, on the other side of the world. Maybe at least one of us will get a happy ending.

I wipe my face with the duvet, and take some deep breaths. I don't want to be the nutter upstairs – I don't want to ruin Martha's chance at that happy ending. I don't want to be a burden to her. But I can't do this right now – I can't go down those stairs and pretend everything is all right, and flirt with Cal, and eat cake, and wait for the hammer blow to come. I just can't. I need some time and space and solitude to sort it out in my head, and be the person I need to be.

I need to forget my own disappointments, my own dashed hopes and dreams, and come to terms with it – but to do that, I need to escape. I need to do something I've become extremely adept at over the years, and run away for a while. Not forever – I promised myself I would always stick around for Martha, and I will. For as long as she needs me. But for now, maybe for a day or so, I need to run.

I shove a few things in my backpack, pull on socks and Crocs, and tie my hair back into a bushy ponytail. I grab my phone and keys, and don't allow myself any more time to think about it. If I think about it, I'll start crying again, and if I start crying again, I might never stop – and then where would we all be? They can live without me for a night – in fact, it seems like they can live without me forever.

I glance around at my room – at my scattered books and make-up and ginger-filled hairbrush – and wonder if I'll ever feel quite so comfortable again. This has been a real rug-pulled-from-feet experience, and I feel like slapping myself for slipping into what I now realise was a false sense of security. It's as though I've learned nothing from life.

I tiptoe down the stairs once again, this time feeling very differently. No bluebirds now – just carrion crows circling what's left of my self-esteem. I quietly open the front door, and then I run – for my car, for the open road. For home.

PART FOUR

The Woman Who Fell to Earth

Chapter 38

I'm back in my flat, swamped with relief that I decided against letting it out after all. I'd have been left standing on the doorstep, looking through the window like a Dickensian urchin, watching as strangers lived out their lives in my home.

It smells musty and unlived in, but it's still home. I noted as I parked the car, after a stressful drive through snow and sleet, that Kate's house is looking in tip-top form. Barbara and Ron have obviously been doing their jobs well; the small forecourt is spotless, the paint on the front door has been topped up, and the brass knocker is shining. I have no doubt that if I let myself in, I would be able to use the world's cleanest toilets.

I don't, though. That would be too much for me right now – confronting Kate, and the ghosts that swirl around those rooms. Way too much.

I called at a service station on the way back, and have come equipped with milk and bread and a bag of Krispy Kreme doughnuts that I probably won't eat. I've made a mug of tea, and put the heating on, and closed all the curtains. It's evening, and already dark. The sounds of city life are intrusive and noticeable after so long in Dorset – cats yowling, car doors slamming, the occasional siren.

I welcome it all – it's different, and I need different. I need to stop thinking about green fields and coastline that stretches on forever and cafes full of comfort and people full of kindness. I need to stop imagining a future where I kept all of that, where Martha stayed, where Cal ... well. Where Cal existed at all.

If there's one thing I've learned how to do over the years, it's cope with disappointment. I have so many techniques for this I should probably write some kind of self-help guide: What To Do When Everything Turns To Shit – Again.

Some of it involves tea, which I have. Some of it involves music, which I also have – Bowie's *Diamond Dogs* is playing in the background. Some of it involves sheer bloody-mindedness and the will to survive at all costs.

Sadly, for the time being at least, I seem to be all out of that. It's not the kind of thing you can pick up at a service station, or download from iTunes. It comes from within – and at the moment, the well is dry.

This is also a familiar feeling, and one that I know will pass. I just need to regroup. To toughen up. To hide the tender spots away, and pretend I never had them in the first place – apply the emotional plasters that will give me the strength I need to go on.

Once I have that, I'll go back. I'll smile and react well when they tell me. I'll wish them all the best, and I'll drive them to the airport, and I'll wave them off as though I'm excited for them. I'll make promises about staying in touch or coming to visit, and Martha will be able to start her new life free of guilt or worry about poor old me. I'll do all of that, and then I'll collapse. But that's okay – she won't be there to see it, and neither will Cal.

I tell myself all of this as I sit there, alone, surrounded by the person I used to be. The person who went to festivals and stuck posters on her walls and wore tie-dye T-shirts. The person who made herself a tiny shelter in this flat, and lived a small, contented life. The person who never dreamed of meeting someone like Cal, or being a mother, or taking the risk of plunging herself into a community of friends. Maybe I can be that person again, one day.

One day – after they've gone.

They've noticed I'm gone, of course. I've had three missed calls from Cal, and several snarky texts from Martha. Even one from Laura, which tells me they've been over to Hyacinth looking for me.

I reply to them both in as reassuring way as I can. 'Needed a post-Christmas break,' I say to Martha. 'All that mushy stuff got on top of me. Be back tomorrow.'

She'll get that, being Martha – she's also a bit afraid of the mushy stuff. Cal, of course, has assumed that I've done a runner because of what happened between me and him the night before, and I go along with that. It's easier.

'Be back tomorrow,' I say to him. 'Thought we both needed some time to cool down.'

Now, excuses made and promises to keep, I allow myself the luxury of facing up to how I actually feel: absolutely bloody dreadful. I wish Kate was here, to give me a hug and tell me it'll all be okay in the end. Or that I had parents I could turn to. I even ponder visiting Barbara and Ron, but soon come to my senses.

By about eight o'clock that night, I'm on my fifteenth mug of tea, and have only managed to eat half a doughnut. I know this isn't good, that I need to look after myself, but my stomach isn't playing along and refuses to co-operate.

The snow has turned to grey, sleety rain, and I can hear it slapping away on the windows, as though it's a monster trying to batter its way in. I'm lying in bed, listening to it, trying to persuade myself to drift off to sleep, when someone thumps on the door. I ignore it – it's probably a drunk person, and I'm in no state to deal with a drunk person.

I clench my eyes shut, as though that will somehow stop me from hearing, as the thumping comes again. I continue to ignore it, and hear swearing as well. Then the sound of a car door opening and slamming again, and some commotion across the road. Drunk people, like I thought.

A few minutes later, the drunk person seems to have somehow found a key to my flat, and I sit up in alarm as I hear the door scraping open. I jump to my feet, ready to rock, and grab up a hefty hardback copy of the Oxford English

Dictionary to protect myself with – words can definitely be mightier than the sword.

I have it lifted in the air and ready to swing when the door opens, and Cal walks in. He takes one look at me – at the dictionary, at the aggressive stance, at the expression on my face – and immediately backs up, holding his hands in front of him in surrender.

"Hey! It's just me ... take it easy, Zoe ..."

I let out a big puff of air, and lower my arm. Part of me would still quite like to whack him across the head with a dictionary, but I don't. I put it down on the bed, and arrange my face into something more neutral. Something less damaged.

He's in the room now, making it feel small and crowded, which I don't like. He's forgotten his usual cowboy hat, and is soaking wet – presumably from traipsing around in the sleet outside. His hair is trailing rain down his neck, and his white T-shirt is moulded to his body in a way that very unfairly makes me feel vaguely lustful.

"What are you doing here?" I ask, stamping down on the vaguely lustful and performing that artfully British task of distracting myself by putting the kettle on. Again. "And where's Martha? Is she all right?"

He strides over, takes the kettle out of my hands, and places it out of reach. He turns me around so I'm forced to face him, and stares into my eyes as he talks.

"She's over at Kate's house. She gave me the spare key, and she's waiting there – she knew exactly where you'd be."

"Yeah. Well, I'm very predictable ... why *are* you here, though? I told you both I'd be back tomorrow. I told you both I was fine."

"You did. And we both knew that was bullshit. What's going on? Why did you run away? And how do you live in a place this small – it's like being in a hobbit hole!"

I feel strangely insulted at this comment, and snap back: "Well it's perfect for me! I never asked you to come here, being all tall and big and filling the place up – bugger off back to Budbury whenever you feel like it!"

"Not," he replies, taking hold of my hand and pulling me over to the bed, where he sits us both down, "until you tell me what's going on. You disappeared without a word of goodbye. You send us some nonsense texts about needing to cool down. And you look like shit. I don't believe for a minute that all of this is because of what happened with us last night ... so stop lying, and tell me what the problem is. We've both been worried sick about you."

He sounds angry now, but is still speaking quietly and slowly, as though he's trying to control himself and not go completely ballistic. He also sounds, truth be told, a bit hurt. Maybe he expected his godlike skills to have a different effect on me.

I stay quiet, chewing my lip, and wishing he'd just go away.

"Come on, Zo," he says, more gently, reaching out to hold one of my hands. "It's just me and you. No Martha. Be honest with me, for heaven's sake – what's wrong?"

He's right, I think, letting my fingers fall lifelessly in his. It is just me and him. No Martha. There's no reason I need to carry on faking it for now – and maybe he deserves a bit of honesty. Maybe he deserves to know how much he's hurt me, even if it does mean I sacrifice my dignity.

"I heard you," I say, staring straight ahead at the bookshelves. At the posters. At anything but him. This is hard enough without having to look at his face.

"I heard you, and Martha, this morning. Talking about your plans. Talking about leaving for Australia, and living together, all right? I heard it all. And it's fine … I get it. New start. Daddy and daughter. I understand. And as far as Martha's concerned, I'll appear one hundred per cent okay with it – for her sake. But I'm not. I'm not okay. I trusted you, Cal – I *trusted* you! And for me, that's a bloody big deal …"

I hear him sigh, and feel his fingers tighten around mine. He holds my face, and turns it towards his. I try and pull away, but he keeps me there – and I have no choice but to meet his eyes. Deep, dark, and sad.

"You," he says, shaking his head. "Are an absolute bloody idiot."

My eyes widen at this, and I wonder if I can grab hold of that dictionary again – I expected anger, or embarrassment, or regret. I expected him to apologise, or feel guilty, or explain. What I didn't expect was to be called a bloody idiot, and I don't like it. I open my mouth to snap something back at him, but before I can, he starts speaking again.

"No! Just be quiet, and listen, will you, woman? So, you heard us talking this morning, assumed the worst, and did a runner? Without giving either of us the chance to explain? Is that about the size of it?"

"What is there to explain?" I say, voice high and desperate. "You're both leaving on the third. She's going to Australia. You're going to be living together. You're both worried about breaking the news to me. And you want her to call you Dad ..."

He actually laughs out loud at this point, which again is unexpected. I'm now as confused as I am upset, and none of that is helped by the fact that he kisses me, quick and hard, a brief encounter that's over almost as soon as it's begun. He reaches out, tucks stray hair behind my ear, and trails his fingers over my face – he strokes them beneath my eyes, sore from crying, and sighs deeply.

"Like I said," he continues, "you're a complete bloody idiot. You only heard half the conversation, Zoe. Yes, Martha's coming back with me on the third. She's coming back with me for two weeks, while I sort my life out, and put my affairs in order. Say goodbye to my parents, pack up my stuff, and move back here. And yes, we're hoping to live together – in Budbury, with you, you daft cow. Frank's offered me a permanent job, managing the far, so he and Cherie can finally retire."

I blink at him, unsteadily, not quite able to compute what I'm hearing.

"What? Why didn't you tell me?" I splutter, frowning in confusion.

"Because I needed to talk to Martha first, see if she wanted her old dad to stick around or not. And then I needed to talk to you – which I was planning to do last night, but ... well, we kind of got distracted with other stuff instead, didn't we?"

Predictably enough, I go red at that comment – which is nice, as it means my skin is now colour coordinated to match my eyes. I nod. Yes. We did indeed get distracted.

"But why were you so worried about telling me? If she was just coming with you for a holiday?" I ask, still struggling to keep up.

"Because it'll be during term-time. She's due back in college on the fifth, and thought you'd go bananas about her missing school. That simple. I can't believe you thought we'd do that to you ... you really do have trust issues, don't you? So you've been here, all day, convinced that we were both dumping you?"

I nod, miserably, trembling with emotion. I just don't know how to react – I'd become so firmly rooted in my own sense of betrayal, so ready to think the worst, that I have nothing much left in the tank.

He puts his arm around my shoulder, and squeezes me into his chest. One hand strokes my hair, and he holds me steady and quiet for a few moments.

"Nothing to say?" he asks, eventually. "Run out of words? This is a first ..."

I clutch onto his T-shirt, and lay a single kiss on his chest, and raise my face to look at him. He's worth looking at, this man – but somehow, looking at him and knowing he's staying is even more scary than looking at him knowing he's leaving. Wow. I really am a mess.

"I'm ... sorry," I say, placing my hands on his shoulders. "I'm sorry I didn't give you the chance to explain. Force of habit. I suppose I was ... freaked out. By me and you being friends. By me and you being more than friends. By everything, really. I shouldn't have run. I was coming back, honestly – but I shouldn't have run."

"That's okay," he replies, looking at me searchingly. "I forgive you, and I think you've had a miserable enough day torturing yourself without me adding to it. But ... you still haven't said how you feel. What you think. About me staying. It's not just Martha's opinion that counts, and it's not just Martha I'm staying for ... it's you, Zoe.

"I told you your heart would be safe with me, and I meant it. I love Martha, and I love you. I think we've got something special here, but I need to know that you feel the same ... I need to know that I'm not the only one who thinks this is special."

I close my eyes, and breathe. Deeply. Cal has just told me he loves me. And I know I feel the same. The sudden switch from misery to elation has left me dizzy, and my heart is thumping so hard I can almost hear it. I've spent the whole day disgusted at myself for trusting this man – for allowing myself to hope – and that isn't so easy to set aside.

Not easy – but not impossible. I might have trust issues, but I'm not a complete loss. I look up at him, and smile. I let my fingers tangle up in his hair, and touch my lips briefly to his.

"I love you too," I finally say. "And I very much want you to stay. I'm terrified, but I really do want you to. More than anything. Now kiss me, properly, before we go and see Martha."

"Yes ma'am," he replies, grinning. And he does, in his very own godlike way.

Chapter 39

Cal uses his keys to let us back into Kate's house, and I falter slightly on the doorstep. I smell the pine-fresh aroma of cleaning products, and see the almost unnatural neatness and tidiness that Barbara's visits have left behind. But that's not all I see.

I see Kate cooking in the kitchen, me sipping wine as she stir-fries; I see me and Kate on the patio, laughing and putting the world to rights. I see us with Martha, sprawled on the sofas, watching TV and eating popcorn. I see her hanging her coat up, and I see her on the phone, and I see her having a sneaky post-work nap in the big armchair.

I see her everywhere – and I see her nowhere.

Cal sees my reaction, and takes me into his arms. He murmurs kind words, and holds me tight, and slowly the world sets itself straight again. I breathe in the smell of him, and let my fingers enjoy the feel of him, and I pull myself together. If coming back here has affected me so strongly, then it's probably even worse for Martha.

I slowly pull myself out of his embrace, and smile.

"I'm okay. Just ... well. Let's call it culture shock. I'll go and find her – give us a few minutes?"

He nods, and starts to prowl around the living room. This must be so strange for him – the first time he's ever been in Kate's home; the home that his daughter grew up in. Before I head up the stairs in search of the small evil princess, I make time to kiss him again.

"Thank you," I say, stroking his still-damp hair. "And I love you."

Those words have never come particularly easily from my lips, but I'd better get used to it – because it's so worth it to see the look on his face. I follow up with a wink, and then trot up the stairs.

I pause outside Martha's room, take a deep breath, and push it open, fully prepared to receive a pillow in the face or a screaming mouthful of abuse. I kind of deserve it, and am willing to accept my fate.

Huh, I think, as I edge nervously into the room – she's not actually there. Her bed is perfectly made, her duvet cover replaced with something insanely pink – thank you Barbara – and all of her left-behind possessions have been tidied, dusted and arranged on shelves.

I close the door behind me, and stand on the landing, gathering myself together. I know where she is – it's just going to be hard to deal with. Maybe Barbara's been in there as well, and sanitised it all. Maybe redecorated with Laura Ashley wallpaper, wound up the hair straightener cord, thrown all the old perfume bottles away...

I turn the handle, and force myself to go inside. As soon as I do, I know that even Barbara's brutal approach hasn't stretched this far. She's left it exactly as it was – only the fact that it's been dusted showing that she's been here at all. The curtains are open, and the streetlight shines through, streaks of sleet striping through it, casting dancing shadows on Martha's face.

She's lying on the bed curled up around her mum's old pillow, wearing the Glastonbury hoodie, black hair scattered on white linen. She barely moves as I come in, and certainly doesn't acknowledge me verbally.

I climb onto the bed, and wrap my arms around her. She stiffens slightly, but doesn't perform any karate chops or scream.

"I'm sorry, sweetie," I say, whispering into her ear. "Didn't mean to upset you. I was always coming back, you know that don't you? I was always coming back. I'd never leave you."

She sniffs a little, and uses my sleeve to wipe her nose. Nice.

"But you kind of did. Leave me. And I know I'm being a drama queen, but I wasn't sure what was going on. And neither was Cal. Has he told you? About me going to stay with him for a bit, then him coming back here to stay?"

I nod, and stroke her hair. Her eyeliner is smeared, unsurprisingly.

"He has. He says Frank's offered him a job. How do you feel, about him moving here permanently?"

"I was feeling great about it," she replies, then nudges me in the ribs. Medium strength. "Until you did a runner. Why did you go, without even telling us?"

I suck in some air as I ponder how to reply to that one. She doesn't know I overheard that whole conversation and jumped to the wrong conclusions. I could get away with blagging this one...

"I was a knob," I say, instead. The time for blagging has passed. We all need to start being more honest, no matter how hard it is. "I accidentally heard you two talking about flying away back to Australia, and thought you'd decided to go with him for good. It upset me, and I didn't want you to have to see me freaking out."

Her eyes widen in surprise, and she frowns as she obviously tries to recall the exact words that were spoken between them earlier in the day. As she replays the conversation, seeing it from my perspective, her confusion clears.

"Okay. Yeah. I can see how that could happen. Why you'd think that. So, basically, we've both been freaking out because we thought the other one was leaving us?"

"That's about the size of it," I say, sadly.

"What a pair of losers. I suppose it's natural enough, though ... we both feel like we got left behind, don't we? Even though mum didn't want to go, she did. So maybe we can forgive ourselves for being losers every now and then."

I squeeze her tight, and she pretends to gasp for air until I stop. Wise beyond her years right now, this girl – and so incredibly precious.

"I can if you can. And Martha? I'm not going anywhere. I promise."

She nods, and replies: "Me neither. Well ... not until uni. Then I'll be off like a shot. What about Cal? Are you okay with all that? I mean, you seemed pretty okay when you were under that mistletoe ..."

I laugh, and reassure her that I am one hundred per cent definitely okay with Cal and 'all that.' I tell her about Cherie's offer of a job at the Brilliant Book Café (which I've decided I will call my corner of the empire), and check she's okay with staying at college in Budbury, and she is. More than okay with it – and like she says, it's not that long until she'll be off studying anyway. Maybe, by that point, we'll both be a lot more cool with the idea of leaving each other.

There's a gentle knock on the door, and Cal pops his head around to check on us both. He sees us on the bed, and smiles.

"Room for a little one?" he asks, grinning at his own joke. He joins on the bed, scooting between us, grabbing me in one arm and Martha in the other. She splutters and pretends to object, but it's all a show – she's still a little girl, and has a lot of dad cuddles to catch up on.

We lie there, like that, all three of us on Kate's bed, for a while. We talk and we laugh and we hold each other tight, and we cling on to not only the past, but the future. For the first time, it feels like we have one – and I'm pretty sure that if Kate was here, she'd be saying 'go for it, girls.'

She'd smile her smile, that magical smile she had, and she'd be happy for us. For all of us.

"Let's spend the night here," says Martha, looking around at her mum's old room and maybe feeling the same about it all as I do right then.

"And tomorrow," she adds, "we can all go home. Together."